Lansdonne was watching me intently.

The moralist par excellence. He lectured interminably about the necessity not to despoil a good and innocent race. Well, the more I'd seen of the Oonaas, with their casual sex among themselves, and the ways they could look at us (especially the Oonaa women, with those olive green eyes!), the more I suspected that our belief in nonfraternization was based on outdated anthropology texts.

Then the Oonaa woman leaned toward me, put her mouth against my ear, darted a thin, snakelike tongue into the ear opening, seemed to explore much more deeply than was anatomically possible while her lips seemed to cause heat burns on my skin. . . .

Q COLONY

ROBERT THURSTON

ACE SCIENCE FICTION BOOKS
NEW YORK

Q COLONY

An Ace Science Fiction Book/published by arrangement with
the author

PRINTING HISTORY
Ace Original/February 1985

ISBN: 0-441-69660-0

Ace Science Fiction Books are published by
The Berkley Publishing Group,
200 Madison Avenue, New York, New York 10016.
PRINTED IN THE UNITED STATES OF AMERICA

To
Don and Ruth Thurston

ONE

THE OONAA WOMAN

I am coding the following document and transmitting it through the eighth-level secret channel, both for the protection of the document itself and to save my own neck from slitting by one of my overanxious and spiteful colleagues. The madness surrounding the unearthing of the Q Colony papers resembles nothing more than the kind of curse that has traditionally accrued around the opening of ancient tombs and the exploration of lost undersea continents. You would have thought that my appropriation of the Stoner Journal pages was some bizarre kind of coup, judging from the reactions of my colleagues— each of whom, incidentally, was furiously in the process of sorting out and claiming title to his or her own set of documents. I firmly believe they were jealous because they thought I had grabbed off the easy task. From their point of view, it is easier to deal with documents that are in one of our own languages, or at least an archaic form of a present tongue. They are piqued because the rest of the documents tend to be in native languages or

3

in the evolved form of the Kew dialect. They, poor suffering souls, have to translate, decode, make linguistic comparisons, actually work on their documents. They should know better. The task of assembling the Stoner Journal has been at least as tough as sorting out one morpheme from another.

When I found the Stoner material tucked behind a rock instead of in one of the hermetically sealed containers, it was immediately obvious to me that our mysterious keeper-of-the-records who had established the document chamber within the mountain had made one of those unpleasant historical preservation decisions, the kind which edits history so that subsequent readers can see it in its best light. In the case of the Stoner Journal, our mysterious keeper had clearly meant to expunge the acts and thoughts of the vile and opportunistic Henry Stoner entirely from Kew history. Destruction of documents has always been a prime technique in the rearranging of history by historians who, however erroneously, have a fixed idea about what the records of their culture should convey. Since such papers are usually burned, we should be grateful that our unknown keeper-of-the-records decided merely to throw them away, expecting undoubtedly that the material would decay in that damp chamber. I would not, however, discount the possibility that our mysterious record-keeper just might have wanted the Stoner Journal found after all, for whatever deep psychological reasons you might offer. Nevertheless, the paper of the journal had been manufactured from trees of the planet Ellda and it is not so easily destroyed. Dampness affects Ellda paper at a much slower rate than the product of any other planet's trees. Even at that, the leaves of the journal were quite delicate, fragile—each page had to be handled with extreme care. My colleagues chortled at my edginess in carrying out each page, dangling it delicately from my fingertips, threatening to murder anyone who so much as jostled my elbow.

When I had carried all of the papers to my quarters

and set the atmosphere content to a bearable dryness in which the material would be easier to handle, I set about the task of making sense out of my discovery. In spite of the little jokes my colleagues presented to me over the dinner table, I insisted on the arduousness of my project. The papers, after all, were in no particular order. It was as if someone had shuffled them randomly. Not only that, but many pages had disappeared or disintegrated. Some pages were only partial. My only method was to study them thoroughly and arrive at the present order through internal evidence. If only Stoner had had some consideration for the future and had numbered his damn pages!

I am sorry for the missing sections, if only because they leave such considerable gaps of time, especially in those events that apparently took place later. I decided not to guess at the beginnings and ends of sentences that came at those points preceding or following the sections that are missing. I hope the Committee can make use of the journal and perhaps correct any oversights I may have made in arranging the material. I will continue to seek new pages, plus any information that will provide answers to the questions caused by the missing sections. I am particularly concerned with some of the odd actions of Hannie during the later battle, especially the question of why she said she would not return to the camp, then suddenly turned up in the midst of the battle. Stoner's portrait of Dominique LaPointe, first leader of Q Colony, seems too much distorted by bias and by his own narrow perspective on human motivations. I firmly believe that the cynicism displayed by her after her leadership had been usurped is filtered through Stoner's own dark cynicism and does not at all represent what she really said or meant. However, that sort of interpretation is not my domain. I am merely the toiler in the fields who humbly hopes that this material, his own particular harvest so to speak, will result in much more refinement by the insights of members of the Study Committee. I would remind the head of the Committee, however, that my earlier dispatch registered all rights for publication in *its original state in my name. Any subsequent material relating specifically to the Stoner Journal which my colleagues will allow me to discover will be dispatched immediately.*

". . . getting the work level back to normal since the damn plague knocked us out," she said, rubbing an elegant, thin-fingered hand across the point of her long chin. Each of Dominique's gestures strengthened my opinion that she was a stolid, purposeful young woman. I was not surprised that the Q Colony Exploratory Team had chosen her leader. She exhibited the kind of toughness that made outposts like Q Colony working propositions. I say "outposts like" since the odds here seem to stack against a colony on a current run of bad luck.

"The plague must have been—must have been a horrible experience," I said, nauseated at my own continuing banality in what should have been a meaningful first encounter establishing the boundaries between our respective areas of authority. I was also unnerved by the gaze of the child-woman Hannie, who still languidly slouched in her chair, unmindful of the way her primitive garment had slid so far up her thigh, nearly exposing what I most wanted to observe. I could not be wrong about Hannie, I decided, she might be a little young for my tastes but the meaning behind those soulful childlike eyes was . . .

". . . me that the architecture of the abandoned village indicates a fairly advanced civilization, much more advanced than the primitive artifacts indicate."

"Yes," she said, "that has been duly noted."

Her tone was so crisp, so formal, that I felt I was being reprimanded for an offense of which I was unaware. Perhaps Dominique had noticed the glances that Hannie and I had exchanged earlier in the day and had correctly interpreted them (mine, at least). Her dismissal of Hannie had seemed to me rude and abrupt, although Hannie had certainly complied obediently enough. Was Dominique as sexless as she appeared, so that even a hint of lust among others disgusted her? Or was she in love with her scantily clad assistant? I did not think I could cope with jealousy from her, and it wouldn't do my investigation any good to have the colony's leader resentful of me, so I resolved to avoid Hannie for a while in order to keep Dominique pacified.

"Our whole team of archaeologists," Dominique continued, "was wiped out by the plague; so not much has been accomplished in that area. Some of us feel that clues to the odd mixture of primitive artifact and architectural sophistication will be found when we can resume the diggings."

"Some feel, you said, 'some feel.' Others have different opinions?"

"Well, the team has come up with a few theories so far. Not surprising when you consider all our differing backgrounds. There are some who feel that the builders of the city were, like us, alien visitors to the planet and that this village was no more than their settlement, intended to be temporary like our makeshift digs on the other side of the valley. Then, after the intruders had either died off or left, the primitive natives may have moved in and used the buildings for a time. Being less sophisticated, they left behind more of their own artifacts than the intruders did theirs."

"Interesting. Yes, very interesting. Some good thoughts there, don't you think?"

"Perhaps."

"You have another theory?"

"In a way. It's called 'wait and see.' I am not willing to conclude just yet."

"Well, of course, I think we should all reserve, ah, judgment, all I meant was that the, that the other theory was interesting and could be considered but of course I did not mean . . ."

"I am quite aware of what you meant, Stoner."

Her use of my name startled me. After our overly polite introductions on my arrival, she had not addressed me so directly since. I didn't care for the cold official sound of her voice either. Well okay, if she wanted bureaucratic distance, I'd give it to her. I decided to counterattack with my own brand of bureaucratic strength. It was important, I felt, to get the upper hand over the nominal leader of the group in order for me to perform my own duties with efficiency.

"Part of my mission here," I said, "is to evaluate whether to continue Q Colony or not."

"I've been informed of that. It was in your papers."

"Originally Q Colony settled here on . . . does the planet have a local name?"

For some reason she was disconcerted by the question and looked at me questioningly.

"Local name?"

"A name given it by its settlers. Some settlers choose historical names, others adopt names derived from the indigenous—"

"Oh, yes. No, that's odd, isn't it? We've never called ourselves anything. Ourselves—of course I mean the planet. Or our settlement. Or this village, for that matter. We have been very slow about the naming of things. No, we've come up with no local name. A few blunt descriptive reference words, but no local name. You'll note that in all our paperwork it's still referred to as Q111.4."

"I did notice that, thought it was habit. So, where was I?"

"You apparently were about to summarize for me the history of Q Colony."

She was of course being sarcastic since, as an original settler, she already knew the colony's history. Dominique was beginning to annoy me considerably.

"Q Colony," I said, "was settled on the most inhabitable of the first discovered planets in what has come to be known as the Trisystem, a name covering the three solar systems that were—"

"Yes, yes. I'm aware of that. Get to the point."

Well, we were officially at battle stations now. A bad mistake on her part. Some leaders were like that, thinking that a tough, bullying attitude would influence me. I either dealt with bullies or sycophants, it seemed.

"At the time of first settlement," I continued, "Q Colony found the conditions quite like Earth, quite suitable to further colonization. Not terrific, but the best we'd found thus—"

"Yes, yes. Substandard—point seventy-five—on the scale.

Nothing's been found to change that statistic."

"Substandard—point seventy-five—or three-quarters Earth. Q111.4 had been observed from the outside with much interest because its conditions were so close to that of Earth's. Especially interesting was the fact that the atmosphere was better than point ninety and—"

"God, man, I don't need this lesson. Are you at all capable of getting to the point, Stoner?"

"Some points must be prepared for, LaPointe."

A slight widening of her eyes noted that I had taken up the name-usage cudgel and was quite prepared to speak to her as bluntly as she addressed me.

"All right," she said, sighing. Was I mistaken or did I detect an aroused nipple against the thin material of her work shirt? Whatever, it was certainly an intriguing physical response to our little administrative combat. I decided the nipple must have been aroused by the fight itself. It seemed unlikely that Dominique LaPointe was capable of such obvious sexual arousal, at least not by a man like me whom she saw as her enemy, out to cancel the years of Q Colony work that had kept her going.

"Three-quarters similarity overall, when most colonies had to settle for little more than half. I came here, in fact, from a half-Earth that is functioning much better than your little—"

"And they didn't have a plague wiping out more than two thirds of their members, did they? That's more than point six-seven, that's—"

"I see, I shouldn't have said it that way. I'm sorry, I—"

"Get to the goddamned point, Stoner."

I cleared my throat, inhaled deeply. I was impressed by a slight sweetness in the air.

"Well, our explorations of the area beyond the Trisystem have borne further fruit. We have discovered planets that are statistically much closer to Earth than Q is—some planets that are, in fact, better. Many of the colonies in the Trisystem have already been abandoned. Financial, manpower, and logistic considerations demand the closing down of even more planetary projects. Those that now remain have certain purposes, certain goals yet to achieve, and they have been given limited permission to continue. The same kind of permission may be applied to Q if I can discover sufficient—"

"Yes, Stoner, I get you. You want to hold a sword over us, get us to justify ourselves or else, send us to Conventry in a wheelbarrow."

"My job is simply—"

"Okay, okay. Simply."

She looked like she wanted to square off and belt me one. I wondered if she could do it. She was, after all, big-boned and gave the appearance of a tightly wired muscular structure. Now she held her body tense, and it seemed to me that she would become enraged at any . . .

. . . through the meal I didn't even taste the food, assuming that most of it was colony ration anyway and not worth being conscious of. Also, I was so pissed off at LaPointe's anger at me, that stupid little scene she had concocted out of anger at Hannie's attentions to me. I was angry both because I was not guilty of the bureaucratic infraction and also not guilty of what Dominique suspected about me and Hannie. So I was halfway through eating the alien fruit before I noticed its musky and long-lasting flavor. I tried to comment on this to Swartmann, who was sitting next to me, but LaPointe butted in:

"We just call it fruit," she said. Her tone, though she was clearly trying to make it sound conversational, had the residue of her anger in its timbre. "Mainly because we haven't discovered any varieties of fruit. It's the only one, therefore, fruit. You like it then?"

"It's quite, quite delicious."

"Quite, quite. Yes, I think so too. Took us a long time before we ever tried it. Tested it forever it seemed. But it's nutritious. The Oonaas use it for everything, can do some extremely surprising things with it. Isn't that so, Ted?"

"True," Swartmann said. "They even make a kind of bread with it."

"They have hundreds of uses, some that've nothing to do with food. I think—"

She stopped speaking as she noticed me staring past her.

Hannie had come into the room. Her eyes were red-rimmed from crying—no doubt at Dominique's reprimand. I vowed I must find out just exactly what was the relationship between those two women. Dominique looked over her shoulder, saw Hannie. Hannie quickly backed out the door, into the darkness of the city's streets. Dominique looked back at me. I thought she was about to say something but then she just picked up . . .

Swartmann was lousy at pulling off a joke. The smirk on his face told me that his explanation of the Oonaas' language was a fake. Well, I know how to treat deadhead scientists who "like to have their little jokes," and I smiled and pretended that he had caught me with his absurd little story about nonstop lovemaking and unlikely grunts.

"Okay, the real story, Ted," I said after we had gone through the ritual.

"Nothing very complicated, I'm afraid, Henry," he said. "After they first let us get near them, and that took up some time incidentally, we had extreme difficulty separating their phonemes by ear and our linguistic devices could analyze only a bit of it, and then the data seemed somewhat incorrect, and so all we could distinguish with surety were the utterances that sounded merely like a series of repetitive oonaas. You know, oonaa, *oo*naa, oo*naa*, oo-oo, naa-naa, naa-oo, and so forth."

I could see that he was trying to impress me with his rendition of the natives' speech, the unsteady mimickry derived from his linguistic studies. But all I could really see was a fool trying to duplicate sounds that were quite difficult for human vocal equipment.

"Of course, Henry, we've isolated quite a bit of the phonemic material and have even made some headway morphemically. They have very subtle variations in their sound patterns, much more than the few at normal human command. It's a lovely language when your ear is attuned to it. Of course, such listening is beyond the abilities of many of us. Dominique, naturally, has the sounds down pat and has even managed simple communication with the Oonaas."

"She seems to have, well, special talents."

"That's not the half of it, brother. Dominique LaPointe is

special, more special than most of us get to see."

It occurred to me that perhaps Swartmann was in love with her, but I pushed that thought from my mind. Besides the fact that Dominique seemed impossible to love, even for a moronic type like Swartmann, he was at least eight inches shorter than she, and as a couple they would have looked eccentric. Still, stranger things had happened in the history of the universe, and I had to admit I derived an amount of simple lascivious pleasure from trying to picture Dominique in bed with *anybody*. I just could not see her admitting even a hint of orgasmic feeling with a moan or a grunt—or even admitting that her sexual equipment was operative. Well, I could go nuts trying to figure her out.

I got Swartmann off the topic of native phonemics and mentioned Lansdonne's odd, sly remark. Swartmann actually blushed. It took me at least five minutes to force an explanation out of him.

"It's the topic of some, well, bathroom humor around here, and I think it's ridiculous for grown men to—well, anyway, our scanners have come up with indications that the natives have a rather, well, better sex life than our species, say."

"I don't understand, Ted. I see that they're humanoid and do it about the same way we do—with perhaps a dollop more of innocence, maybe—and out in the open more often, but it doesn't appear better. Physically, they look passive and—"

"Don't let your observations lead you to grade-school anthropology conclusions—I mean, seeing Oonaas as analogous to the primitive island-types on Earth that were so dear to the early anthropologists. The Oonaas are an intelligent and sophisticated race. Their customs—well, some of them—are just different, that's all."

"Maybe, but what's the big deal about sex if they do it just like we do?"

"See, it's not *exactly* like we do. Okay, they do insert the whatjamacallit into the whozit, just like humans and humanoids and many others everywhere in our dear old universe, but once inside, well, the process is a little different. The female Oonaas, you see, have a, well, a kind of penile organ inside their vaginas. When aroused by the male arousal, the penile organ grows a bit, but doesn't harden like the male one. No, it becomes snakelike, and its actions are somewhat snakelike once the act has begun."

Swartmann's face was quite, quite red.

"See, this, this penile thing wraps itself around the male organ rather sinuously, if the scanner pictures can be believed, and, it seems, gently squeezes it during the act—which, you may imagine, must add to the male's pleasure. In turn, the male organ at certain times is capable of some, well, rather fantastic enlargement, often after it has disgorged its load and is, well, mainly concerned with the female's pleasure. At this time the female penile organ, while it becomes smaller, is still active—caressing, well, and other things—frequently making the male organ quite erect again and the penile organ more snakelike and—"

"I think I understand, Ted. Does this represent most of what you know about the Oonaas' interrelationships thus far?"

He realized I was probing for information to use in my report to the Commission. Since he did not want to incur Dominique's displeasure, he launched into further explanations with added fervor.

"Oh, no, Henry, there's lots more to be . . ."

. . . astounded by her vehemence on the subject. I was not one of her minions, not under her command. She had no right to speak to me that way. But speak that way she did.

"After the failures of so many projects, after the plague," she said, "there's no reason to stir them up. They work well without your interferences, no matter how much fun they may find you to be, Stoner. I don't want to influence them any—"

"Wait a minute, LaPointe. I'm not going to stand for this. You can't—"

"I am law here, if you'll allow me that sententious phrase. I can't have you performing the role of pimp and procurer for my men. Things were decent here until you came. Relatively decent. At least there wasn't any slimy undertone to the remarks, that willingness to do battle with anyone that makes the slightest disparaging statement, that licentiousness . . ."

I felt quite uncomfortable having this battle in Dominique's office. Her own domain—the neat and geometric arrangement of the room—gave her the advantage. I began to believe in her authority. I longed to return to the alien abandoned city where things seemed looser and where I felt I could answer back more freely.

"There is nothing wrong with what I've—" I started to say, but she interrupted.

"Nothing wrong! Look, they're all making plans about how they're going to seduce Oonaas left and right, and all because of your encouraging—"

"I did *not* encourage."

"Did you or did you not say you'd 'like to grab off a piece of one of those luscious Oonaa lovelies?' Well, am I misquoting, putting the incorrect emphasis on—"

"No, the quote's quite all right. And, believe or not, LaPointe, it is quite normal. Quite, quite normal. When a normal human sees something attractive in another human or humanoid, it is considered normal in many circles to express that attraction, and frequently such expression is done in crude terms. I regret the crudeness of my utterance but I did say it, and I see nothing wrong with it. It is—"

"And I suppose you see nothing wrong with the way your mates congregate around you for more of your encouragement and innuendo."

"Well, maybe from a certain point of view, that's crude too, but—"

"Get out of my sight, Stoner. If I catch you at anything more like this, I'll—"

She stood straight, seemed even thinner than usual, as if she had twisted her corporeality into a thin string. She looked ready to release her rage and tightness simultaneously.

"You'll what, LaPointe?"

"You have a good imagination. Imagine it. I have no more . . ."

"You've put on weight in the few days you've been here," he said, obviously referring to the midriff swelling that seemed squeezed over my beltline. I almost regretted my adoption of the native garb. Still, it was comfortable to wear no overshirt, and if my fat belly was exposed, well, so be it.

Swartmann put out a hand and stopped our movement. The alien encampment was just ahead, and no one in it had noticed our arrival. The Oonaas were gathered in groups, each group apparently intent on a speech from one of its members. I asked Swartmann what was going on.

"Far as we can figure, some variation of the oral tradition."

"They don't have written literature?"

"No, there seems to be plenty of that. But for some reason they enjoy passing on details of history, or perhaps legend, orally. If we had a better feeling for the language, we might be able to decipher some of it better."

"I see."

I watched the ceremony for a long time, then asked Swartmann what I could do.

"Not much. Dominique's orders were very explicit. She said *observe,* and if she hears we did anything but *observe,* there'll be a couple asses mounted on spears at the city gates. I don't know how you managed to get permission for a close observation, what with the way you two've been at each other's throats since you arrived here."

I tried to assume a superior expression, a hint of sneer in my easy smile, a confident raising of an eyebrow. I needed Dominique's associates to believe that I had powers, especially power over her—no matter what insults she might fling at me in meetings or at dinners.

"My mission's what's important, Ted. There's little she can do to prevent me doing anything I want to do. Anything in the name of the mission anyway. So, no matter how bitchy she gets or how much she tries to throw her weight around, she cannot refuse me anything that is within the domain of my orders. After all, Q Colony's existence depends on what I say about it in my report. Then all of you—"

"Look at that one," Swartmann said suddenly, pointing to his left. "Those're the eyes of passion if I ever saw them. You can't tell me the Oonaas don't harbor some desire for us."

"I never did tell you that, as I recall."

Swartmann smiled.

"Of course not. *You* wouldn't. I think you got a better understanding of the layout here than any of the rest of us, and you've only been here a couple of weeks. No, it's Dominique and her crowd; they're the ones who say don't misconstrue the looks of a civilization that's foreign to us. They think that none of the aliens have the hots for us. Never mind. Just look at that Oonaa! And I think, loath as I am to admit it, that her look's for you, Henry boy."

I was inclined to agree with Swartmann. The Oonaa woman's attention seemed definitely directed at me. While it occurred to me that I was the only new human around, and her looks my way might only be curiosity, I nevertheless felt a certain arousal inside me that no amount of logic ever could . . .

Something in the drink may have loosened her. Her shoulders, so much a part of her stiff-at-attention demeanor, seemed to sag. There was a gentleness in her eyes, a near smile on her lips that was so uncharacteristically Dominique that I thought of touching her to see if she might be some kind of fantasy that this ancient city had provided, a ghost from its unknown past.

"Strong stuff, that," she said, holding up the glassful of wine. "I must remember to credit Swartmann and his crew for their resourcefulness. When I first discovered the still, I reamed them out about it. Now . . . well, now I must say that they've certainly discovered another remarkable use for fruit."

"I'll second that."

She lowered her glass and glowered at me.

"You'll second that. God, Stoner, you're a walking cliché, a breathing bureaucratic pile of, pile of paperwork."

"You weren't going to say paperwork."

"You're so observant."

"My trade. To be an official observer."

"Yeah? Well, you know . . . never mind."

Her face was flushed. If I was any judge of womankind, she was giving off sexual waves and, since Hannie and the rest had left to return to base, I was the only one around to receive them. In one of those deceptive casual moves that are meant to imitate a person making himself comfortable, I moved a bit closer to Dominique. My next move would be to gently let our legs touch.

"Why never mind?" I asked.

"Forget it. I was just going to insult you, and I'm not in an insulting mood just now. I have had enough of attacking Henry Stoner for the time being. I think you've beaten me anyway. You and your damn report. Shit."

I might never get a better opening with any woman. The chance to sympathize and console was the best seduction technique known to civilized man. When I spoke next, it was in my gentlest voice:

"Maybe my report won't be as negative as you anticipate."

There was no way I could have anticipated her reaction to my declaration. I would have expected her to look at me with interest or perhaps cynicism. I would have expected one of her caustic remarks. I would have expected a businesslike interrogation exploring the implications of my declaration. But I did not expect her eyes lighting up and a look edging toward joy on her face. For a moment she looked like a little girl— she looked something like Hannie, with her wide eyes and hint of smile. I was so astonished that, if I had to speak again right away, I would have stammered just as she did.

"Do you—do you—I mean, is it true? You mean it? Will it be, are you planning to, to report favorably?"

I thought of the papers back in my cubicle, the balanced evaluation of the positive and negative factors of the work of Q Colony, the blankness of the page marked Concluding Remarks. I thought of the time I had spent staring at that blankness, wanting to say that my judgment was finally negative, that there was no further reason to continue Q Colony. I had not yet been able to write that paragraph. Q Colony had not really been given the proper chance; the plague had taken care of that. With a little more time, as Dominique argued so often, they might be able to reach the point where a decision to continue or abort could then be properly made. My mission, however, did not allow for such niggling reservations. They would be reversed, anyway, at higher levels, since no one at those elevations would be likely to approve a second time-consuming mission that would require the assignment of more personnel. Headquarters was very big on manpower control these days.

"I haven't quite decided, Dominique," I said. Sometimes

honesty was after all the best policy, and there might be something gained in using it on her.

Some of the light went out of her eyes. It was as if somebody
had pulled the dimmer switch of a spotlight.

"Haven't quite decided," she said, enunciating each word
carefully. A bit more emphasis on the quite—she turned it into
a two-syllable word.

"Well, there're a lot of factors," I said, "one—"

"Factors," she said. "Goddamned factors. You think like a
bureaucrat, you certainly do. Your brain is battered by typeface.
Factors! Jesus!"

"Dominique, we can talk about this rationally."

"Stop calling me Dominique as if this was some kind of
intimate discussion between friends. You have the gall of—"

She stopped quite suddenly, stared into my eyes. I was
disturbed at the feeling that she really saw something there.

"That's what this is all about, isn't it?" she said.

"What *what* is all about?"

"You're oiling me. The wine, the friendliness, that voice
that sounds like it's about to thin to tissue paper. 'I haven't
quite decided, Dominique.'" She did a quite good imitation of
my voice, its inflections anyway. "You want to fuck me, damn
it. That's what you're up to, you goddamned fool. All this,
this wine, the—you want to fuck me! You want to stick your
dinky lit—"

"Stop this! I'm not the sort who—"

She started to laugh. Heartily, like a man. The scorn in her
laughter was no less painful because it was based on an accurate
assessment of the situation.

"That's what you're up to. One good fuck, Dominique, dear
Dominique, and maybe, just maybe, I'll file a favorable report,
let Q Colony continue."

"I had no such—"

Her laughter stopped abruptly. I was more frightened by
the silence.

"Okay, Stoner. That's a deal I can respond to. You can
have your one good fuck. You can have two, three, unlimited
access. It's only my body, a body's as good a tool as any.
But—but I have to have your guarantee about the report. No

maybes. No maybe ifs. Before we climb into the sack, you write that report and file it, then it's Sodom and Gomorrah time for as long as you—"

I moved away from her. There was a beastlike sound to her voice, as if she had reverted to some original animal form. As her body tensed and she leaned in toward me, she seemed coiled like a snake, ready to take my throat for dinner. The effect was something less than sensuous. If anything, I was repelled.

"That's enough, Dominique!"

"Nothing's enough for a petty ass-grabber like you, Stoner. Rip off a piece. Just make that report."

She was breathing heavily. I could not help but note that the sounds were the sounds of passion, even if the body they emerged from was poised in a less than passionate way.

I tried to speak steadily, sanely.

"I understand what you think of me. I've seen that almost from the first minute I came here to Q. And I'll admit that I am somewhat—somewhat—that—I am sometimes a bit *manipulative.*"

She laughed sardonically.

"But I do my job. Not only that, I do it well. Whatever . . . weaknesses you may see in me, I'm not weak about my job. The report I make'll be a fair one."

"Then you weren't—ah, shit, let's forget it. Where the hell did you put the wine bottle? I saw it just about—"

She made an elaborate job of the search. I wondered for a moment whether I should tell the truth—tell her that, yes, I was trying to use the report to gain an inch or two with her, she had been accurate enough about that, but tell her the distinction I saw between such petty maneuverings and the accuracy I thought the job required. Hell, she'd probably make mincemeat out of that argument too. Better to let her off. Though, for some reason I couldn't define, I wanted her more now than I had when the thought of seduction had first crossed my mind only moments before. The movements of her long angular body as she thrashed about—searching for the wine bottle (which was propped up against my leg)—were downright . . .

• • •

...closest I could come to the color of her eyes was some variation of olive green. It was a quite attractive color which allowed her a distance that the odd dark blue had not. She no longer looked like the simple native female humanoid I would have originally taken her for. The color of her lips had changed a bit too. They were very pale, almost the color of her skin, that almost-white that didn't quite become white. If I hadn't been in the middle of a clearing, and if the rest of the team hadn't been performing their individual jobs around me, I might have grabbed her and taken her that moment. She was one of the most beautiful creatures I have ever seen. Maybe I could find a way to subtly lead her out of the clearing, I thought, take her to the adjoining clump of trees.

Lansdonne was watching me intently. The moralist par excellence. Oh, he could make dirty remarks with the rest of the men and was, in fact, one of the best of all the Q Colony staff at the sly Oonaa sex jokes. However, when he donned his serious cap, he lectured interminably about the necessity not to despoil a good and innocent race. Well, the more I'd seen of the Oonaas, with their casual sex among themselves, and the ways they could look at us (especially as the Oonaa woman had, with those olive green eyes!), the more I suspected that our belief in nonfraternization was based on outdated anthropology texts.

Then the Oonaa woman leaned toward me, put her mouth against my ear, darted what seemed like a thin, snakelike tongue into the ear opening, seemed to explore much more deeply than was anatomically possible while her lips seemed to cause heat burns on my skin. Then suddenly she was sitting back as before, looking at me innocently with those olive green eyes.

At first I didn't know what to think, except that I was so aware of my immediate sexual arousal that I knew I couldn't stand up for minutes. I looked toward Lansdonne. His face wore, I'm sure, a look as wide-eyed as mine. I looked back at the Oonaa. Her eyes had changed to a pale pinkish green. She almost seemed to be smiling. Coquettishly. Her lips were red, an almost human red. I glanced around the clearing. Nobody else besides Lansdonne seemed to have noticed her bizarre move. Or if they did, they were maintaining a discreet inattention.

I discovered I was breathing heavily. My hard-on refused to diminish no matter how hard I concentrated on the necessary shrinking, no matter how frantically my brain sent its physiological messages. My god, if an Oonaa could do this with a momentary act of sexual intimidation, perhaps they were capable of all that our scanner-study guesswork indicated. This was no race whose right to maintain their own culture needed to be supervised or protected. Q Colony's scientific tiptoeing around the Oonaas seemed hardly necessary. Christ, the Oonaas were positively decadent, or I missed my guess.

I suddenly became conscious of Lansdonne at my shoulder, whispering. While he talked to me, he too gazed into the hypnotic color-metamorphosizing eyes of the Oonaa female.

"I saw that."

"I am perfectly aware you saw that."

"What are you going to do?"

"I haven't the slightest notion why you are asking the question."

"I mean, are you going to follow it up?"

"Should I?"

I had to test him; he was too potential an enemy.

"I don't know what the hell you should do."

"Why do you bring up the subject then?"

"It's the first real overture any one of them has made. I mean, on occasion they've looked our way with what we interpreted as possible passion in their eyes, but we were too aware of the potential misinterpretation a human background might bring to such a—"

"Get to the point, Lansdonne."

I enjoyed adopting Dominique's style of prodding, especially on a pedantic weasel like Lansdonne.

"The point, Henry, is that this is the first overt sexual approach. The first interest of that sort. Damn it, it's communication. More progress than Dominique and Swartmann have made in their working with the language, more progress than our confused study of the Oonaas' habits, where the study changes conclusions as fast as the Oonaa tribe moves the location of its encampment. Communication, Henry. This may be an important—"

"Still, Lansdonne, I want to know what you expect me to do."

I knew what I wanted him to say, but instead he gave me the answer I could have expected from him.

"I wish I knew, Henry. I wish I knew."

No endorsement there. Like every other important option of my life, I'd have to make my own decision here too. Carefully interpret the data and act according to my best judgment. As I still felt the tingle in my ear where the native's tongue had explored and since my hard-on was only just beginning to soften, I was pretty damn sure at that moment what my decision was going to be.

"Let's keep this a secret for a while, Lansdonne, our discovery."

"If you say so, Henry, but the others need to know eventually."

"Oh, we'll tell them. Eventually."

"But first we should evaluate the data."

Did that mean he was joining me? Well, I could hardly discourage him if that *was* his intention.

"I think so, Lansdonne, a little evaluation, yes."

The Oonaa's eyes were changing color again, into a dark almost sensual...

. . . held her thin, elongated body at attention, livid. I felt as if she had seen right through me. As if I were guilty of an act that I had not yet accomplished, even though I fully intended to do it. I was just angry at Dominique for accusing me of accomplishing it before the fact.

"Honestly, LaPointe," I said, trying to sound as official as possible, "I have never molested one of the natives. I don't know what makes you believe—"

"What makes me believe it should be obvious," she said, her voice falling to a whisper. "Quite, quite obvious."

Imitating me, she made my voice sound weak and gratingly nasal.

"If you mean what happened back at the—"

"I was not referring to that. Not at all. But of course it pertains. You were willing to use me then, there's no reason why you wouldn't use one of the Oonaas for your lascivious—"

I tried to steady my voice. It seemed I was always trying to control my voice around Dominique LaPointe.

"Nothing has happened. Any more than anything happened between us back at—"

"Don't! Just don't! Nothing happened—oh, shit. Nothing happened. Of course nothing happened. But we came that close. I know your mind, Stoner. And I know whose report I can credit."

The problem was, whose report did she mean? Had Lansdonne had one of his fits of morality and turned us in merely for the thought? With him that was likely. In his own mind he had no doubt sinned sufficiently just by being merely tempted.

I'll take care of that bastard if it's him. But it's not him. I'm sure of that. He's just as hot for it as I am, I could see that in . . .

. . . looked as eager as a young boy drooling over his first prostitute. I was right about Lansdonne then. Underneath the pious lecturer was a man as lusty as I. I doubt if he was aware that the intensifying rhythm with which he pulled at his beard resembled sexual stroking. He wanted to speak first, but I was still too overwhelmed. I looked back at the Oonaa's eyes, which stared at me with their usual calmness. No trace of sexual aftermath there. One would not suspect that less than a minute ago she had been twisting and thrusting vigorously, placing me in anatomical configurations that I wouldn't have thought possible. With no knowledge of her language, I couldn't even ask if she'd enjoyed it or if it meant anything to her that she had been chosen as the first participant in Oonaa-human sexual interaction.

"Henry," Lansdonne whispered, and I looked back at him.

"Might as well be hanged for a whozit as a whatzit," I repeated. He looked at me strangely, as if he'd forgotten that was what I'd said as I'd entered the body of the Oonaa woman.

"I never saw anything like it, Henry."

"Don't know about the voyeur aspect, Lansdonne, but I can vouch for the feeling."

"It was good then?"

Oh, he was eager. He just wanted to get through this conversation and take his turn. I had really tapped the satanic in this man. The satanic and the satyric, I suspected.

"Good? God, it was good all right. You haven't felt anything until you've felt that—that thing inside her!"

I realized I too was sounding like a young boy. But I could not help it. Nothing in my life had prepared me for the experience.

"The thing," Lansdonne said. "That's the female penile-type organ that we've observed on the scanners."

"Exactly. And it's exactly like we've suspected. It wraps itself around your—your penile thing like a snake and gently squeezes. . . . Oh, friend, it's amazing! Not only does it intensify, but it prolongs. Not only intensify and prolong, but enlarge. My cock's never swelled to that size before, not in—"

"Jesus, Henry. It seems impossible."

I gestured toward the Oonaa, said: "Try it for yourself."

He hesitated for a moment. I rolled aside, giving him free access at her. I wanted him to discover the multiple orgasm part of it for himself. His eyes belonged on a preacher falling from grace. His fingers still fumbling at his clothing, he seemed to leap on the Oonaa. Her reaction was to scream in a way that I can describe as unearthly without meaning to be ironic about it. Lansdonne looked back at me, his eyes puzzled. His body had stiffened, but he still held the Oonaa woman tightly.

Her scream had been short, but she still groaned in obvious protest.

"What should I do?" Lansdonne pleaded.

"Go to it. It's just a sudden bout of shyness, man. Show her what you're made of. Unless you've already shown her of course."

He glared at me angrily, returned to the task. Sweat began to collect in his beard as he forced her further back and tried to pry open her legs. Just as he was making progress, she got a hand loose and made one swift pass at his throat. I didn't even see her do it, only knew from the aftermath as I heard that quick gurgle from Lansdonne's throat, a mixture of surprise and pain, and saw the first burst of blood fall on the Oonaa's garment. Lansdonne writhed briefly in pain, then his body went slack and he fell upon the Oonaa woman. She flung him away with more strength than I would have suspected possible from her, twisted her way out from under him, and ran into the bushes without looking once back at me.

I inspected his body, though I knew there was no point in it. I was only painfully verifying his death for myself. As I turned the body back I heard a rustle behind me. I turned, expecting to see that the Oonaa had come back, perhaps repentant. But I stared into darkness. Shadows. One of the bushes still vibrated from someone's touch. I rushed past it. Running ahead of me, between some trees, caught by the light from one of the planet's two moons, was the unmistakable form of Hannie, her long hair swaying from side to side with each running movement.

How much had she seen? How much did she know? How had she come to be there in the . . .

"So awful. I'm afraid to tell Dominique. It was so awful, the way the blood came out—"

"You don't have to tell her anything, Hannie. You weren't there, all right? Neither was I. Let them discover the body, draw their own conclusions. What difference does it—"

"What *difference?* But the man is dead. And the two of you, the two of you, the two of you—"

I felt like slapping some sense into her, but that didn't seem to be the proper strategy for the moment. It might only send her running to Dominique with the whole story. Somehow I had to find out just how much she'd seen. There was a chance she might not have seen everything.

"I couldn't stop him, Hannie. The man was like a maniac! I tried to talk him out of it. That's why I went out with him in the first place, to try to stop him in case he really meant to go through with his foolish plan."

Staring wide-eyed at me, Hannie looked like a child listening to the admonitions of a parent. I felt I was on the right track.

"Believe me, Hannie, I never thought it would come to this."

"Then you didn't—I mean it was just him—you didn't, it

wasn't even your intention to—"

"That's right. I tried to stop him but he pushed me aside. He was a maniac, a licentious demon, I—"

"I saw you on the ground. Where he must've pushed you. I thought—I thought that you had—you'd—you looked like you—I must not've seen right, I—"

"That must be it, Hannie. Don't know what you thought you saw, but it wasn't what you assumed. We had a struggle, Lansdonne and I. He was stronger than I thought. He pushed me away, pushed the Oonaa woman down, just literally jumped on her. I was going to pull him off when she killed him."

"It was awful, Henry. The blood, it just, it just—"

I could sense the need for a comforting moment, and I took her by the shoulders. All the tenseness went out of her body as she snuggled into my arms.

"Henry," she said, "I'm so glad it was him and not you."

I couldn't tell whether she meant that she was glad that it was Lansdonne that was dead or just Lansdonne that was merely guilty.

"Sshhh," I whispered. "Everything'll be all right. Let's just stay out of it, you and I, just—"

"Stay out of it? But we really have to tell Dominique, don't we?"

"Not at all. They'll find the body and make their own assumptions. Or mistakes. We don't have to tell them anything."

"But Dominique has to—"

"You know what she thinks of me. *You* had your doubts about what happened. What'll *she* think?"

She chuckled to herself for a minute.

"She'll think you're guilty, of course."

"So you see we shouldn't tell her."

"Okay."

Her agreement was so casual, so childlike. I gave her a little hug to acknowledge that I was pleased with her cooperation.

We enjoyed a moment of quiet that was shattered by Hannie's next utterance.

"I love you, Henry."

I don't think I had ever gagged at a female's expression of affection before. I had known, of course, of her attraction toward me, or at least that my inclinations toward her were reciprocated in my direction, but I was not ready for a statement on it at that moment. Days ago, during the time that Dominique seemed to spring up from nowhere each time I thought I had Hannie to myself, I would have thrilled at the idea of Hannie announcing her love. But now, in my already weakened condition, in the desperation of my dangerous situation, I didn't know what to think, what to reply to her. I'm sure she thought my confusion was that of a nervous lover and not of a desperate man, for she said again:

"I love you, Henry."

"Hannie dear, you're just reacting to the, to the, well, emotion of the moment."

Her laugh, with its edge of ridicule, was not unlike Dominique's. The ridicule itself was not so contemptuous, but the sound of it was at least similar.

"Emotion of the moment! You know, Henry, Dominique may be right about your ingrained pomposity."

"I never heard her mention anything about my being pompous."

"I have."

Coming from Hannie, the criticism bothered me more than it would had Dominique spoken it to me directly.

"Anyway, Henry, that's not the point. I'm not yielding to any emotion of the moment. I have been considering this for some time. I'm not as young and immature as you pretend. I know what goes on in your head. What's more, I like it!"

"Hannie, this isn't the time—"

"Course it is! I finally screwed up the courage to tell you. Whenever that happens, that's the time. Touch me, Henry, more. Caress me. Go on."

I *had* to do what she ordered. I had no choice. I couldn't afford to rile her, send her away angry, maybe to Dominique with her emotion-ridden account of the little that she'd seen from behind the bushes. I had to caress her. She took my hand and made my caresses more intimate. I had no choice. As Hannie drew me to her and made a crude inexperienced attempt to nuzzle her body against mine sensuously, I recalled my multiple orgasm with the Oonaa and thought that I could never manage another time. I felt weak, spent, exhausted, all the things you're supposed to feel after a transcendent sexual experience like that one. At the moment I had rolled off the Oonaa woman, I remember thinking that I might never be able to do it again, ever. Now here was Hannie, whom I'd wanted for so long, finally ready to, as they say, be mine. Why the hell was her timing so off? I tried to protest again that now was not the time, but she was determined, as resolute as I had been with the Oonaa woman. In the midst of my protests, I learned that Hannie's ability to caress was quite, quite learned. There were definitely some stirrings. For a moment I thought they might be ghost-arousals—but, no, they were real. Hannie gave the order to continue. I had no choice. I did not want this child to run the act this way, but I had no choice. I don't know by what miracle we proceeded all the way through the act itself, but it was accomplished.

As I pulled out of her, Hannie whispered that it was her first time—which I of course had realized. I was pleased that I had done so well with her. Days ago, I would have felt good for myself too. But no longer. My experience with the Oonaa woman, with all her special abilities, made my act with Hannie a mere expression of technique. I did not feel satisfied for myself. On the contrary—I felt empty, emotionless, saddened. It was as if I had used a dildo on her, as if my own sexual equipment had been replaced with a transistorized substitute. I felt like I wanted to cry.

"Thank you, Henry," Hannie said. "Oh, I know I love you. We can do so much together."

I almost blurted out, "Together?" with amazement, but I was shrewd enough (or too physically weak) to hold it back and merely stare down at Hannie's happy face. In her eyes I thought I could see the life she had planned for us. And I saw that, after all, she was as young as I'd always thought.

"Hold me," she said. "I want you. I want you in me again. I know you're . . ."

. . . had lost Swartmann as an ally. Somewhere along the way he had slipped back to Dominique's side; perhaps he was the one who serviced her on those rare times when she needed servicing. Somebody had to; after all, she was not as sexless as she pretended to be.

Anyway, most of the others were still with me, I could tell. They liked me for my easy affability, my humor, my whole project of organizing them into play, an area which had been sadly neglected under the leadership of Dominique LaPointe. Yes, I still had friends at Q Colony. They'd turn against me if they found out what had happened in the clearing, but Hannie had not told anyone and, since Lansdonne's body had so mysteriously disappeared, they had no suspicion he was any more than just a missing person. Some of them suspected he had been abducted by the Oonaas. It was possible that for some odd tribal reason they *had* returned to the clearing and taken away Lansdonne's body. If so, it worked to my advantage. There was nothing to connect me with his death, nothing to suggest our dark mission.

The Q Colony team trusted me. I could actually take over and run Q Colony, I suspected, and—in human terms—probably do better than Dominique did. But nobody could be more efficient than she, so it was better for me to bide my time.

What would I do with my report? It would make the most sense just to file it, whether my concluding remarks are positive or negative, then run, get the hell away from Q Colony as fast as I can. But, since yesterday, my thoughts have become more and more confused. Yesterday the Oonaa woman had appeared at the edge of the forest beyond our encampment and had stood there, unmoving, watching my every move. I know she wants me again. There is a strange monogamy among these creatures. If not a monogamy, a code. Yes, code makes better sense. I'm sure that the Oonaa woman has made love to a few of her own, but she chooses whom she is going to couple with. That's the point, and it's the explanation for what happened in the clearing. I am sure of it. She made love with me because she had chosen me. She came to that clearing because somehow I had communicated that I wanted her there. She had planned to receive me into her arms. But Lansdonne had not been part of the deal. (I wonder if she had even been aware of his presence before he sprang at her.) Perhaps in her culture an uninvited lover had to be responded to violently. Perhaps they could *always* kill the uninvited lover. Or perhaps the ordinary Oonaa assaulter could not be as easily killed as a more delicate human. Or perhaps Oonaas never made love unless invited. I am too confused. I do not like to dwell on the events of the clearing. Every time I think of it, I see that spurt of blood from Lansdonne's neck and his subsequent slumping into death.

Hannie just came in and grabbed me around the neck. She has got to stop being so open about...

. . . finally had to ask her about the scars. In the dim flickering candlelight, which bounced strange shadows off the ruined walls of the ancient city, the scars looked darker, looked like they made deep valleys into her body. I had been struck by their blotchy shape. Although yellowish in color, they looked like a burn scar would. I wondered if she had been trapped in some alien fire on this planet.

She looked down at the scars as if she was just noticing them herself for the first time. She touched them to verify that they were real. She ran her hand across them as if they had newly materialized because of the sexual act we had just completed.

"They're just plague scars," she said blandly.

"My God!" I said, studying them again. They covered so much of the middle of her body, with a few blotches on the thigh of her right leg, one large one on her left shoulder.

"I don't understand why you're so surprised, thought you knew, I guess."

"I didn't. My God! I didn't, didn't know you'd had the, that you were a survivor of—that you—"

She laughed.

"You know, I'm really amazed," she said, "didn't know you could be so frazzled by anything. They're just scars. I know I'm the only one who's got them but—"

"The only one?"

"Sure. Dominique never told you about that? Never briefed you about it?"

"No, afraid not."

"I'm surprised, you know, really surprised. Not like her to leave out information from any kind of report. Well, it's like this: I survived the plague."

"I didn't know anyone who contracted the plague had survived."

"Well, I'm your woman! The only survivor."

It seemed strange for Hannie to call herself a woman. I supposed that our activities together had given her the illusion that she had somehow passed from girlhood by the addition of an efficient (if a bit uninvolved) lover.

"Tell me about it, Hannie, about the plague."

She startled as if I'd hit her.

"Not on your life," she said. "I don't want to talk about it. I don't want to ever remember a minute of it."

"All right, I don't want to hear the painful details. I read the medical reports. I just want to know how you survived, that's all."

"If I could tell you, I would. It's all because of Dominique."

"Dominique?"

Hannie didn't realize how much that piece of information surprised me, I'm sure.

"Yeah. She'd always been sort of attached to me and, when my parents died of the plague, she took me into her quarters. When I actually got the bloody plague, she stayed by my side, didn't run away from the quarantine like some would. It's a wonder she didn't contract the disease herself."

"I wonder why she didn't."

"That healthy Dominique LaPointe constitution's my guess. She wouldn't allow a germ to get inside her, so the plague kept its distance. She nursed me through it. Everybody thinks it's some kind of miracle. When I was at my worst, just her touch'd bring me right back. It was like a cure. But it only worked for me. She couldn't cure the others, no matter how hard she worked at it. And she worked hard, believe me."

"Why are the scars so . . . so . . ."

I searched for a way of not saying "blotchy," but before I could find the words, Hannie said: "Blotchy?"

"Well, yes."

"Nobody knows. The remains of the rash that covers the entire body during the primary stage of the disease, perhaps. Unfortunately, we lost our epidemiologist very early in the plague. He was struck down while doing active research on it. I think they're just rash marks. God, the body's one whole rash mark during the middle feverish stage, and—Henry, let's not talk about this any more. Make love to me again."

That innocent-sounding request with the force of a command behind it. She was pushing me beyond my capabilities, but once more I rose to the task. She screamed with delight as we climaxed together. (I had never experienced simultaneous climax so often with the same female, and enjoyed it so little.)

"Oh, that was lovely, Henry. It was the time, I think. I'm sure of it."

"Sure? Sure of what?"

She laughed. Victory in the sound of it.

"You must know, too. You must get a sense of it. I can't believe all that shit about this sort of thing being women's domain, that went out with—"

"Hannie, what *are* you talking about?"

"I am saying, dearest heart, that this time we really made it. What I'm sure of is that this time will make me pregnant and I can't tell you how happy that makes me, dearest—"

"Hannie, how can you know about that?"

My question was desperate and deceptive, for I really believed her.

"I just know. It'll be a lovely baby. We'll bring it up as the strongest, proudest, most beautiful—"

I turned away, trying to hide my . . .

The Oonaa woman seemed more alien than ever as she stroked my face with her rough-textured hands. She was trying to tell me something, but damned if I knew what. I just wanted to make love to her again, discover anew her sexual artistry. I was obsessed by the thought of it. But when I made any move in that direction, she touched my shoulder and gently pushed me back. I remembered what she had done to Lansdonne and was willing to obey any touch-suggestion she made. I still had no idea how she had killed Lansdonne, although when I took her hand away from my face to hold it and saw how jagged her fingernails were, I began to suspect how she might have used them on him.

I listened to her softly uttered syllables and tried to discern her meaning in them. All I could observe was that Swartmann had been right. About all you could make out at first were the variations of the sounds *oo* and *naa*. (Swartmann, the bastard, is virtually Dominique's shadow these days; I don't know what the hell he's up to.)

I said to the Oonaa woman as gently as I could, while squeezing her thick fingers: "I'm sorry, love, but I don't understand any of this. I can tell it's important to you and may be important to me, but there's no way—"

The volume of her oonaa sounds rose. There was a sound of frustration in her voice. I looked at her eyes, tried to find the meaning there, but all I could tell was that they had taken on a new color, a kind of purple with shadows in it. Little blotches of deeper purple against an almost violet background. Her scars. But what did she mean? She looked quite, quite desperate about something. Should I take this as a warning and clear out? I didn't want to leave the Oonaa woman. Hell, it was not even a matter of choice, I knew inside I couldn't leave her. If I would ever have any notion of what love was, this was it. This was it, and not Hannie with her incessant brayings about her coming child, her harping on the idea of a life *together*.

I wished I could escape into the wilderness with the Oonaa woman. If I ran off with her, if she *let* me run off with her, the Q Colony would pursue me en masse. Dominique leading them with a raised saber, perhaps Hannie egging them on from the sidelines. Even if I could evade the Q Colony pursuers, I would probably not be acceptable to the other Oonaa natives. There seemed to be no useful solutions. How the hell could I know *what* to do if I could not find a way to communicate with my Oonaa lover?

Finally she stopped trying to tell me whatever she was trying to tell me and let me know, by darting her tongue in my ear, it was all right to make love now. I almost hollered for joy at the relief. I entered her with the intention of making love to her roughly, to show her the kind of mastery of technique that made Hannie scream with delight. But the movements of the Oonaa body slowed me down, the snake inside her began to wrap itself around me, slow me down further, curve itself around me as it guided each of my thrusts while squeezing me gently and then more firmly. When I thought I couldn't stand it any more, the penile organ pulled at me and brought me in even deeper as the orgasm started. I nearly fainted. After, she let me know she was ready for more.

. . . couldn't figure out why she pulled at my arm so, or seemed so intent on leading me to the abandoned city. After that last session of lovemaking I hadn't wanted even to move. But when I tried to say no, her eyes had changed to a deep fierce brown. The color struck me as warlike, though I had no idea why I saw it that way. As we reached the border of the abandoned city, she stopped pulling at me, held me back. Her gesture told me to stay where I was. It was satisfying to be able to interpret one of her communications soundly. She left me for a moment, disappeared into a shadow caused by an overhanging roof. I couldn't see where she went and was beginning to get nervous, afraid that one of the Q Colony people might be somewhere around, observing. I couldn't afford for one of them to discover my dangerous game just now.

I didn't know how long I could keep my clandestine meetings with my Oonaa woman secret. The Q Colonists were all bugging me now about when I was going to finally file my report, and I could not tell them, after all, that the delay was caused by my inordinate obsessive desire for one of the natives. Hannie thought that she was the reason I seemed to procrastinate. I had already fended off two urgent communications from headquarters about the delay in their hearing from me.

The Oonaa woman returned, took my arm again, led me into the shadows. I couldn't adjust my eyes at first, the usual response. Then I discerned a flickering light up ahead. I tried to hold back, tried to think of a way to tell the Oonaa woman that I couldn't go forward, couldn't risk the chance of one of the Q Colony people discovering me there with her. Her grip was too strong, and she continued to guide me forward. The flickering light was, as I suspected, one of the candles that Dominique insisted we use within the abandoned city in order to conserve our equipment. The candles were another product of the wondrous native fruit.

The Oonaa woman stopped me at a corner of a building.

All I could see was the candlelight and its flickering against an opposite wall. The shapes it created out of shadow would not resolve into the kind of recognizable configuration from which one could imagine seeing objects, lifelike forms, geometrism. I heard what I thought was the sound of a woman sighing with pleasure. The Oonaa woman edged me closer to the wall and guided my gaze so that I looked around it. I was not prepared for what I saw.

Dominique was sitting against a cushion which was propped up against the side of a doorway. She was humming to herself. I couldn't figure out what this could be all about. Did Dominique sneak away to the ruined city in order to enjoy solitary moments, times when she could relax her usual rigidity and play in her mind whatever fantasies could possibly be concocted in a mind that seemed so unimaginative? Then, from inside the darkness of the building, another figure emerged. A male Oonaa native. He was dressed in the usual Oonaa male garment, a kind of loose trouser that came midway down the lower leg and a strip of cloth like a sash that went over his right shoulder. However, an unOonaalike necklace hung around his neck. At first I didn't recognize it, then I realized it was the one that Dominique had worn when I had first arrived, the only piece of jewelry I'd ever seen on her.

So, I thought as I watched the Oonaa man lean down toward her and put his mouth against her ear, this was what Dominique was up to. That bitch! That bitch, she had probably been carrying on with this Oonaa male long before I had ever coupled with my own Oonaa. That bitch, she'd probably beaten me to the post in effecting this particular kind of human-Oonaa intercommunication. That bitch! That bitch! She allowed the Oonaa male to pull her to a standing position (she was about three inches taller than he) and lead her back into the darkness of the building. I was about to follow them in, shine a light on writhing bodies just to verify my beliefs, scream at Dominique about what a fraud she was. But my own Oonaa held me back, with a kind of desperation in her pullings at my arm. I decided it'd be more politic to hold my tongue, not let Dominique know what I'd observed. I might be able to use it on her later. I might be able . . .

• • •

Swartmann won't stop taunting me. He has noticed for some time the way the Oonaa woman watches me when we walk among the natives. Perhaps he's watched her come to the edge of the forest to observe me from her regular vantage point. He keeps talking about how she has the hots for me.

And now he's noticed how the both of them look at me, the Oonaa woman and the male I'd seen with Dominique in the ancient city.

"They just might be a bisexual society," Swartmann commented, "though I've seen no actual evidence to support that view. Still, that guy's keeping track of you pretty steadily. He's trying to appear casual, just like a spy. Why would he be watching *you*, Stoner?"

In recent days he had taken to addressing me as Stoner. To signal his allegiance with Dominique, I think.

"I'm sure I have no idea, Ted."

"Funny that the both of them stare at you so. Those two especially."

"Why do you say that?"

"Well, he's the one I've made the most progress with in my own study of the Oonaa language. He's not only been the most cooperative, but he seems the smartest of the Oonaas, the ones I've observed anyway. And I've worked with her some, though not with much success. She'll talk a little but tends to clam up suddenly, drift off into the distance sort of. Then she won't cooperate, just ignores completely what I've said. And, unlike the male, she shows no interest at all in learning any of *our* language."

I knew all about that, of course. I'd seen her mind drift off, and I'd realized her disinterest in using my language for communication purposes. But what was Swartmann up to in his casual and friendly discussion of them? He hadn't talked to me so much in two weeks.

"But you've been making good progress, Ted."

"Not by my standards. Or Dominique's. We've established a few nouns, a couple of verbs, not much more. That's why I'm so interested in the relationship between those two."

"They have a relationship? What do you mean?"

"I'm not sure. Haven't been able to figure it all out. They're allied in *some* way. Damned if I know. They might be man and wife, or brother and sister, or parent and offspring—or it might be a political or social relationship. They may be leaders of some sort, though God knows I've never seen any of these natives even seem to give another an order, nor have any of us been able to detect a social hierarchy of any sort, but I'm tantalized, have to admit that."

As I listened to Swartmann, I looked at the two Oonaas. Their eyes had the same peaceful shade of blue. And they stood close, like beings with some sort of attachment, as Swartmann implied. What were they up to? Was it some sort of plot on their society's part—him sent to service Dominique, her to seduce me? Were they using us while we thought we were using them? I longed to discuss this with Dominique. Could I dare? Perhaps if I filed the report now, and favorably? But what if the two Oonaas weren't all that calculating, what if they didn't have some mysterious purpose? What if they were merely the most sexually active among the...

"...Hannie, stop! Please stop!"

She breathed in great sucking gasps of air but could not get her crying under control. The gasps made me nervous, for they echoed all around us. If there were anybody else in the ancient city tonight—Dominique and her Oonaa perhaps—it seemed likely they might hear the sounds.

"It's all right, Hannie. I'm sorry I said it."

"You have no right—no right to complain—all I did—I did was try to make—make things better for—better for us. I thought Dominique might be—might be able to help us—she might—"

"I can't figure out how you got that idea into your head, but—"

"Oh, Henry—"

"No! Don't start the crying again. I can't help what I say."

She got herself under control. With a great deal of effort.

"I'm sorry, Henry. I'll be all right now. You're right about Dominique, I know. I knew it this afternoon when I saw the look on her face when I told her. She looked like she might kill me."

I was about to say that would not have surprised me, but for Hannie's sake decided against further commentary, especially anything that might start the tears rolling again.

"I don't know," she said. "I suppose that underneath it all I was just angry. Dominique acts so—so goddamned superior some times. With everybody, but especially with me. She thinks she's my goddamned mother or something. And she was insulting you, Henry. Said she wished you'd make up your mind, called it your 'feeble mind.' Said she wished you would just clear out. I said I thought you'd stay and before I knew it I was telling her how I loved you and how I knew there was a baby inside me and then she slapped me and I ran here and when you got angry I thought, well, I thought everything was falling apart around me and all I could think of was killing myself. If you hadn't—"

"All right, Hannie. Rest for a minute. I understand."

As I held her, the thought crossed my mind of how advantageous to me her suicide might have been. Maybe I should've let her run off, cut her wrists or shoot herself, whatever she had planned. But, however much I wanted to rid myself of her clinging self, I couldn't stomach the thought of her dead, especially if I were the cause. And there was the baby. No, Hannie could not die, I would not allow it—even if I had to keep up the pretense, had to pretend to live with her in whatever form matrimony took among the Q Colonists. Everything would now be out in the open, now that Dominique was aware of our liaison.

On the other hand, perhaps I could find a way to make Hannie hate me. Or just leave. Go my way just as I was supposed to after the completion of my assignment. Hannie couldn't expect me to stay, after all. I was not a part of Q Colony. Still, if I did stay, there'd always be the Oonaa woman, no matter what arrangement I had to make with Hannie. I couldn't get the Oonaa woman out of my . . .

. . . came with her to the usual place. I resented her giving away our secret to the Oonaa man. I didn't like the idea of them ganging up on me together, whatever their purpose. I certainly could not try to make love to her with him around. They both stared at me for a long time, their eyes an appealing pale orange. Then the male got down on his haunches, did a lot of strange things with sticks. They were trying to tell me something, I knew, and I did all I could to try to receive their message. But all I could see was that lot of strange things with sticks. The man seemed to get angry with me, but she stilled his impatience with a circular gesture of her hands. She turned to me, her eyes fading to yellow, she touched the point of my chin, she stared into my . . .

. . . keeps saying she doesn't believe I really love her. When I try to tell her that detachment is just my natural way and that she should learn that it doesn't mean I don't love her, she just pouts like the child she is, the child she keeps acting like more and more with each passing day, as if she'll become the baby and an adult will emerge from her womb. Dominique has not spoken to me since . . .

. . . a laugh so deep that it sounded masculine. I could easily believe that Dominique had been transformed in sex. She seemed stronger and tougher every day. She waved the copy of my report in front of my face as if to taunt me with it.

"And you've sent this off then?" she said.

"An hour ago," I replied, wondering why she was questioning me so closely.

"Just a minute, Stoner." She picked up the stone bell off her workdesk, went to her office doorway, and rang it with that hard down sweep that always looked as if she wanted to smash the bell against the frame of the doorway. The bell would summon everyone in the camp.

"Dominique," I said, "I—uh—wanted to talk to you alone about . . . ?"

"If it has anything to do with Hannie, I don't want to hear it."

"No, it's not Hannie, it's . . . something else."

"Look, I'm not keen on having any kind of private discussion with you, Stoner. Your mere presence gives me shooting pains. If there is something all that essential, we can accomplish it after the assembly."

"But, Dominique, we—"

Then Swartmann appeared in the doorway to let Dominique know that Q Colony was gathering outside. He had probably been crouching in wait nearby. Damn! I wanted to secure my position first, confront Dominique with what I had learned about her and the male Oonaa. Well, maybe she's right, I thought, I'll let them have their little victory party, and then get down to terms with her.

When I saw the whole research team together in the court-yard—all of them but the few still in the field, anyway—I realized again how pitiably small Dominique's group was. Even though I had read the figures on the plague, the losses they represented only came home to me when I observed how few people did remain. Some reinforcements were necessary, I had said in the report, knowing full well that headquarters' idea of manpower allocation is as stingy as their concept of financial endowments.

Dominique sent a sly glance my way before speaking. Swartmann took note of it and, I'm sure, filed his own private interpretation. He had mental files on all of us, perhaps physical files as well.

"Do you want to tell them, Henry, or shall I?" Dominique said, allowing a slight edge of pleasure into her voice.

"I think it more fitting for you to make the announcement, LaPointe."

"More fitting? Perhaps." Standing on a bench that Swartmann had thoughtfully, and obsequiously, provided, she addressed the colonists. "Mr. Stoner has made his report and it is on its way to headquarters even as we speak now."

A murmur went through the assemblage. Two simultaneous murmurs, actually. One hopeful, the other pessimistic.

Hannie appeared at the near edge of the crowd. She was pouting, no doubt the result of our earlier altercation.

"Mr. Stoner had decided that, 'in spite of our personnel difficulties and the threats of a planetary situation that could be defined as hostile—'" She was quoting the words of my report. "He recommends 'the continuation of the Q Colony project at this time. The several correspondences to Earth environmentally and the potential in the development of the planet's native population enhance the potentiality of the project.'"

She stopped and looked around at the Q Colony group. Those who had been optimistic now seemed smug. The naysayers looked shocked. Swartmann was the only colonist who appeared calm and not at all changed by the news. Then a wave of pleasure joined the team together for once, and they managed a kind of disorganized cheer.

Dominique smiled. That rare event pleased the group even more. After allowing the reaction to continue a while longer, she raised her voice and said: "That is not all of our business at this assembly."

I assumed she was going to go into detail about my report and I leaned against the doorway of her office, intending to rest while she discussed what would be for me tedious detail.

But Dominique's intention was not to discuss the details, she had only one detail in mind. I should have anticipated her, headed her off.

"It seems that Mr. Stoner," she said, glancing back at me mysteriously, "has appended an unusual request to his report. Here—" she held up the document—"in the Further Remarks section he has added what he may intend as the strings-attached portion of the report, although I doubt headquarters would see it that way."

I didn't like her tone and was tempted to interrupt.

"It seems that Mr. Stoner, whom we've all come to know and love in the past interminable weeks of his visit to us, has requested that he be assigned *permanently* to Q Colony—as, what did he call it in the report, oh yes, 'as a troubleshooting executive.' Whatever that is."

I moved forward ready to explain the term. I could understand her confusion since it was a job category I had made up. The troubleshooting executive idea had come to me in a moment of brooding over what it would be like to be under Dominique's command if I stayed at Q Colony. I knew that I could not stomach that. I couldn't remove her from power, so I made up the job. The "executive" gave me rank in the organizational structure of Q Colony; "troubleshooting" meant that in what work I chose to do, what research I wanted to perform, I was not answerable to the reigning leader.

Everyone was staring at me, and I got the impression that they were not especially enthusiastic about my staying with them. They had been *so* friendly before, I couldn't believe their looks at me now. Well, I thought, the hell with them. I was not staying for them anyway. Hannie was smiling, a pleasant counterpoint to the displeased looks of the other colonists. I appreciated that smile even while realizing how misguided it was.

"Mr. Stoner likes it here," Dominique continued, cutting off my chance at interrupting her. "The research here is so . . . *important."*

What did she mean by that dramatic pause and that stagey emphasis? I wondered.

"One might speculate about why Mr. Stoner is so keen on joining the Q Colony research group after being so critical in recent weeks. He has, of course, been quite affable and friendly with us at all times, even when voicing his more negative opinions. Quite, quite affable. Some of you responded warmly, joined in his somewhat less than intellectual adventures."

She glanced at Swartmann, who retained a calm appearance. Some of the other colonists, those who'd been quite friendly until Swartmann's defection from me, seemed embarrassed by Dominique's sarcasm. I knew of at least two who'd recently begged her forgiveness—for "swaying from the path," as it were.

"Of course it may be the work itself that attracts Mr. Stoner. He has been engaged in some research on his own, some troubleshooting stuff that may be a clue to his future plans, his—"

"LaPointe," I said, "this is neither the time nor the place for that sort of—"

"Quiet, Stoner! Let me get down to the essentials. Everyone here has a right to know."

Most of the colonists assumed a kind of look that clearly displayed they too felt they had a right to know. Hannie looked scared. A hint of confusion came to Swartmann's usually enigmatic face.

"Although research is involved, I suppose, the real reason

for Mr. Stoner's need to remain with us is an age-old one. Elemental, one might say. You see, dear friends, Mr. Stoner is in love."

Hannie ran forward, shouting: "No, Dominique! Not in front of them! I won't have you degrading—"

"Hush, Hannie. I was not referring to that little escapade of Mr. Stoner's versatile career. I suggest you keep out of the way for the moment."

Hannie backed away, bewildered. By this point I'd perceived what Dominique was up to, and my mind raced through possible counterstrategies.

"Mr. Stoner," Dominique said, returning her attention to the group, "has been, well, carrying on with one of the natives. He has fallen in love with an Oonaa woman."

She took a long pause, stared at me. So did everybody else. I decided to keep quiet for the moment.

Hannie broke the silence. "What—what did you say, Dominique?"

"I'm so sorry, Hannie. I should have considered your feelings. I forgot. Forgive me."

"What did you say, Dominique?"

Concern in Dominique's eyes. Then determination as she said, "I said that our Mr. Stoner has been carrying on—*fucking*—one of the female Oonaa natives for some time. That native is the reason for Mr. Stoner's noble desire to remain with us. It is both his research project and his romance."

"It's not true, Dominique, it's not—"

"I wish it weren't, Hannie, for your sake. We can talk about it alone later. But I don't think now is the time for us to—"

"Stop it, Dominique! Now! Stop! We've got to talk, you and Henry and me. Without them drooling over our shoulders."

"I can't do that, Hannie."

"Please!"

Dominique's voice regained its fierce sound of authority.

"I suggest you leave us, Hannie. I will deal with you later."

"God damn you, Dominique." Hannie looked over at me, including me in the curse too. I didn't know how to react. I couldn't admit guilt to Hannie. Not here, not now. I had no idea how to pacify her. I could only watch her start to cry pitiably and run out of the courtyard.

Dominique addressed the others again.

"You are to forget that." As if they could. "It is of a personal nature that has no business in this assembly, let it remain between me and Hannie. The kind of personal subject we can consider, however, is that of Mr. Stoner diddling the native woman against the express order of Q Colony bylaws, against the generally accepted policies of all exploratory projects everywhere."

I would have to speak, use my strategy any minute now, I knew. But I decided to give Dominique more rope, enough to tie knots in. Her pause was carefully dramatic, a chance for me to react, but I merely stared at her, hoping I was reinforcing that stare with an outraged look of self-righteousness.

"Okay then, Mr. Stoner," Dominique said. "I don't think we need to continue this. I've made the accusation. You may introduce any evidence to counter it that you will. But first I must explain the reason for this little unpleasantness. No matter how much power you may wield back at headquarters, and I suspect it's very little, there is no way you can be assigned to Q Colony without my approval. There is a clause that requires the endorsement of the project's commander for any personnel assignment. Well, Mr. Stoner, owing to your violation of our laws about the natives, I'm sure you can see why I cannot endorse your assignment here. Especially as a 'troubleshooting executive.' We are of course pleased that you recommend the continuation of our project but—"

I sensed this was the time for my interruption. Instead of shouting at her, as she must have expected me to do, I chose to counter her strained accusations with a whisper.

"You're a hypocrite, LaPointe. You have all the ethics and morality of a—"

"I don't think personal vilification is in order, Stoner! I understand its reasons but—"

"That's enough, LaPointe! All right, you said I could have my say. I'm going to. Right now. With no interruptions from you or anybody."

Dominique gestured eloquently.

"You have the floor," she said.

She backed away and leaned against the office hut. Knowing the importance of position, I slowly walked to the bench where she'd talked, stood on it, and addressed the Q Colony research team. I was very concise, deliberate. I struggled to use no emotionally loaded words. My voice was quiet but firm; I put the old ring of truth in it at every word. They listened quietly. Dominique tried to interrupt a couple of times, but for once I had the advantage.

I admitted my alliance with the Oonaa woman, and then told of how the woman had brought me to the alien abandoned city and shown me Dominique making love with her own Oonaa male. When I reached that part, the group gasped collectively. Except for Swartmann who simply looked at Dominique with hatred in his squinted eyes.

"So," I concluded, "our noble leader, the beautiful and ravishing Dominique LaPointe—" Dominique muttered something I couldn't discern as I carefully pronounced the adjectives—"has been doing exactly what she terms as a violation of law on my part. She's been fucking one of the natives, probably for longer and more often than I—"

"You bastard, Stoner!" she shouted. "It's not like that at all. It is not like that at all."

I was about to respond, nail her to the wall, but Swartmann stepped in front of me and took over.

"What was it like, Dominique?" he asked.

Her stare at him was filled with nearly as much loathing as the one she'd directed at me. She whirled on him, shouting, "Don't try that, Ted! I know a power move when I see one. You're not going to—"

"Dominique," Swartmann interrupted. His voice had taken on the tone of authority. The tone of *command.* "Dominique, I simply asked what it was like. You said it was not like that at all. That? What do you mean by *that?* What? Did you not perform sexual acts with the male native, as Stoner here has accused?"

"Perform sexual acts," Dominique said, her voice now lower. "You always resort to fancy phraseology when you believe you have the upper hand, Swartmann. Don't think that anybody here doesn't see what you are—"

"I don't think any of us feel you should avoid the answer, Dominique."

The group murmured again, this time a murmur of agreement. I sat down on the bench, my body relaxed. Muscles that I had held too tightly in tension began to hurt as the tension went out of them.

Dominique looked afraid. I think she'd just perceived Swartmann's strategy and knew that she would lose.

"All right," she said, a defeat in her voice. "What was it like? You really want to know? It was like fucking. It was fucking. And you're not going to understand even if each of you run out now and grab off your own native."

Many of the people in the courtyard looked as if they were ready to go out and grab a native right away.

"But the point is, the point is . . . not that I was weak. I was weak, but that isn't the point. It started when the plague was going on, when it was at its worst, when—but no, damn it, I'm not going to try to explain it. It happened, okay? I knew it was going to happen before it did. These natives, these Oonaas, are shrewd. They select *us*. This one had selected me from a long time before. Of course, I resisted him. I was strong, had no plague to—shit, I can't stop reaching for excuses. No, I did it. That what you want to hear, Ted? I did it. I fucked the native, just like this idiot Stoner here and his exotic Oonaa woman. But it's not the same and I don't know how to tell you the difference."

"Fortunately, Dominique," Swartmann said quietly, "I don't need to know the difference. Your guilt was all I wanted to establish. I've suspected it for a while. Your guilt and, as Mr. Stoner would have it, your hypocrisy."

"Shit, Ted," she said, "you could give us all lessons in hypocrisy."

"Have your say, Dominique. I haven't been sleeping with the natives like you and Stoner. Furthermore, I won't allow any of us to, from now on."

"*You* won't allow it! You!"

"I'm sure everybody here'll agree that you cannot continue in command, Dominique. It's only logical that I succeed you. You may, of course, continue in your research provided there are no more peccadilloes and that—"

"Peccadilloes! My God, peccadilloes!" Dominique threw her head back and laughed heartily. "You have the brains of a syphilitic toad, Swartmann." Then she saw that the others were now clearly allied with Swartmann, and she became frightened. "Wait a minute here. Okay, you have the right of judgment on me, all of you. I'll concede that. And I'll resign. But not as the result of a power play. Why not have an election? Then we—"

"Yes, why not?" Swartmann said amiably. "An election might be in order. Of course, I throw my hat in the ring and welcome opposition."

"What is this, the *reichstag?*" Dominique said. "Wait a minute. Now that we've got my guilt out of the way, let me tell you what I've achieved. I would've eventually. I just needed to get Stoner and his goddamned report out of the way first, I just—"

"This has the flavor of *ex post facto* reasoning, Dominique. You're struggling to rationalize your crime."

"Crime! Honest affection between two—"

"It was a crime when you accused Stoner, it's no less of one now."

Dominique sighed, slumped, seemed shorter.

"All right, Ted. I can't take any more of this. I've constructed my own petard, particle by particle. Just let me tell you the one thing. Yes, I did it and I'm going to remember feelings none of you can approach with your miserable limited brains. But I've also accomplished something. I have managed to break down the barriers to communication that've been the main obstacles to fulfilling the goals of our association with the natives ever since the beginning of Q Colony."

"Many of us have been working on that," Swartmann said.

"I know, I know. You've managed to break down a few oo and naa sounds into a few words that, on rare occasions, you can even accomplish communications with. That's not what I mean, though it would've been a few weeks ago. But in the time that I've been meeting with the native—he has a name, by the way, but I'm keeping that for myself—I've managed an elementary grip on the language of gesture and paralanguage that is at the heart of their communication. I can communicate with the Oonaas now. It's the most important breakthrough and, because—well, because of the nature of my research methods—" She smiled. A smile with sadness in it. "—because of them, I couldn't allow Stoner to find out, though he managed some of the basic research himself. A small part of it. They tell me they worked on him for hours, for—no matter, the point is there's so much to be learned, so much more. . . ."

"And we will learn, Dominique," Swartmann said. "Don't think we won't. Don't underestimate us. But we will accomplish the learning without demeaning ourselves, through logical and sound methods, through—"

"Hypocrite," Dominique whispered. She pulled herself up to full height and strode back into her office without looking back.

Swartmann was disturbed at being walked out on, especially in midsentence, but he was in command now and he could accept a dash of insubordination from the deposed commander. Swartmann was at heart a romantic, I always knew that. He asked if anybody objected to his assuming leadership, at least until the mess was straightened out. The sheep bleated approval. I wondered how many of them would be sneaking away from the herd with some Oonaa research on their minds—which led logically to the speculation of how many would turn up in the morning with throats raked to pieces by Oonaa hands?

"And now, Stoner," Swartmann said, turning to me. "About you . . ."

. . . pushed me hard against the wall. I was positive that something in my back had separated from something else.

"Where is she?" he said again through the clenched teeth he seems to have acquired recently—one of the burdens of leadership, I suppose.

"I don't know, Ted. How the hell should I know? She's as much my enemy as yours. She's hardly inclined to let me know where she's sneaking off to, she—"

"Okay, I believe you."

He released me, strutted back to his desk. He never does look right when he sits behind that desk, as if he shrinks whenever he takes his seat there. Swartmann was so much shorter than Dominique; the desk's height seemed designed for only her. I moved away from the wall, testing my shoulders to locate my phantom dislocation.

"Everybody's spooked about her disappearance," Swartmann said.

"Nobody's been, well, too organized emotionally since you
took command away from her."

As soon as I had said it, I wondered why. After being nearly
beaten up by the man, why should I blithely offer criticism of
his reign thus far? He displayed no reaction to it, so perhaps
he agreed.

"Frankly, Henry, I don't know what to do." He took a
leadership kind of pause, then looked up at me. "I need your
advice."

I had to sit down right away.

"You need *my* advice?"

He managed a hint of a chuckle, then the most amusement
I'd seen from him since my early days here when he'd shown
me the ropes.

"Yes, well," he said, "you're the only one with a mind for
strategy around here. Except for our missing Dominique, of
course."

"Strategy, huh? That's what you call treason when it's on
your side."

He scowled.

"You know, Henry, I've never cared much for your urge
toward the fallaciously epigrammatic."

"Epigrams are the abbreviated—"

"Stop it!" His leadership voice again, so I nodded. Another
kingly pause, then: "I have to do something about Dominique,
about her defection."

"Defection?"

"What else would you call it?"

"Escape."

"Let's not quibble about the words, please. I have to do
something. The others are beginning to wonder if her crime
warranted her removal from authority."

"You persist in calling it a crime."

"Isn't that what it is?"

"Technically maybe, but—"

"But, since you did it too, you see gradations of guilt."

"Okay, sure."

"I even understand, Henry. But that doesn't help. Do I send

out a team to get Dominique back, or do I leave her out there, or what?"

It was the "or what" part of his question that suggested to me that Swartmann wouldn't hold onto leadership for long. It occurred to me that I might manage some shrewd treason/ strategy simply by waiting, biding my time.

"If I do return her here, how should I punish her? I can't kill her, though that would be the easiest solution."

"You could send out an assassin."

For a moment he seriously considered the idea. I suspect it sounded like the best one yet.

"No," he said finally. "Too risky. With the possible exception of you, there's nobody who could accomplish the deed."

"Thanks for the vote of confidence, but I wouldn't do a killing for you."

"Perhaps. Makes a difference what you'd get for it, I think."

"There's no—"

"I need advice, Henry, not a petty argument."

I wondered briefly exactly what was so petty about this particular argument. The discussion of assassination seemed somewhat more than petty. But we were back to interpretation of words again, so I declined to comment. Anyway, Swartmann had restored that leadership tone. The more I heard it, the more leadership seemed an erroneous word for it. Even at its best, it was the sound of a district manager, not of a boss. He'd be okay at headquarters, but he seemed out of place behind the wrong desk at Q Colony. Working out my own strategic pause, I said:

"Best I can do for you is go out and look for her. I can move among the natives, maybe learn to communicate with them, better than any of—"

"You're just looking for a chance to bed down with that Oonaa woman again."

I could not help but smile at Ted's sneer.

"That too," I said. "But I might find Dominique, talk to her. It's worth a chance."

"If the others know you're out there grabbing off your piece of—"

"Okay, make you feel better, I'll make a vow of chastity."

"Forget it. Nobody'll believe a vow from you anyway."

"Well then, that's the best advice I can offer."

He remained quiet for quite a long time, lightly rubbing the ham of his fist along the surface edge of the desk.

"Okay, Henry," he finally said, "we'll chance it. You go out, find her, talk her into coming back and making peace with us. That's the important part. She must publicly announce her loyalty to the team. Not even to me, just to the team."

I tried to imagine that, but nodded agreement anyway.

"One thing, Ted."

"Name it."

"I want you to fill out the order that Dominique wouldn't, the order that'll allow me permanent assignment here."

He didn't want to agree, but he did.

. . . leaned over my bunk while I was getting my things together and whispered in that stagey way he always used.

"You were right, Stoner," he said. I had never seen Davis's eyes, usually dull with stolidity, so bright.

"Right? Right about what?"

"About those natives. The Oonaa women. They can really do it. To a turn. I never felt anything like it. It was like—"

"Spare me your descriptions, Davis."

"You've become an irritable son of a bitch, you know that?"

"Yes."

"What are you? Angry that I'm poaching on your territory? That I've got my own little Oonaa maiden to—"

"No, not angry about that."

"About what then?"

"About how much of myself I can see in your ugly, piggish face."

"Stoner, goddamn you, I'll . . ."

. . . was the first human to enter the native village openly since Swartmann had put the clamps on further field research among the aliens, for the time being. Of course, Davis and probably others had been managing secret alliances with the natives. And maybe Dominique, who I suspected had fled to the village. And maybe Hannie, whom nobody had seen for days. God, I hoped Hannie was nowhere in the village.

The Oonaa woman separated herself from the group that stood in front of me, their shoulder-to-shoulder stance appearing almost defiant. She walked to me. Her eyes were nearly violet, one of their colors that most pleased me. It felt good to see her again, after all the troubled dreams I'd had about her. She stopped in front of me, many questions in those near-violet eyes. I touched her arm. She allowed it, but didn't seem to desire it.

"Dominique," I said, pronouncing each syllable carefully. She looked toward the others. I said Dominique's name again. Some of the Oonaas in the defiant line took a few steps backward and I could see Dominique, leaning against the wall of a hut, looking for all the world like a . . .

. . . and the echo of her mocking laughter seemed to hold steady, remain inside the hut for a long time after she had stopped laughing.

"I take it then," I said, "your response should be phrased in the negative."

"Come on, Henry, did you expect otherwise?"

"Of course not. What I did not expect is the way you're calling me Henry."

"Logical. Somewhat anyway. For the moment, a brief moment maybe, we're allies, Henry. I think you had figured that out before you accepted your mission and came here."

"Not exactly. Not until I saw you again."

"Oh? I don't understand, I'm afraid."

"It came to me suddenly. You see, I made all these arrangements with Swartmann. If I make you decide to return, I get to stay at Q Colony. In fact, the stupid bastard already signed the paper, and I don't really have to bring you in. But, when I saw you, I knew that Swartmann's signature on a document wouldn't bring a single thing I'm angling for. The only way to get Q Colony back into operation is to get Swartmann. We have to attack him directly, if that's the only—"

"*We?* As I said, I recognize the fact we are allies for the moment, but I don't like the tone of that we."

"You're stuck with it."

"I don't see."

"I'll explain."

She was looking quite, quite happy. Her eyes were so bright in the light of the flickering alien-made candle that I was almost tempted to . . .

Even though I could not understand the Oonaa language, Dominique's struggling with it while she explained our plan to the Oonaa leaders made me tense. When she was really stuck for a word, she appealed to her own Oonaa male, her lover, to help her with the explanation. Usually his response to her harried pleadings was a blank look. She seemed antagonistic toward him. At one point she looked my way and said:

"He understands but won't help us. He doesn't agree with the plan, wants no part of communicating it to the others."

She returned to her desperate attacks on the Oonaa language. Finally her points began to get across. The Oonaa leaders started talking among themselves, with furious gestures of their hands and odd uncommunicative (to me, at least) jerks of their heads. One of them made a rhythmic hand wave that caused the group to disperse immediately.

Dominique returned to me, saying: "It's in the hands of fate now." She told me the Oonaa word for "fate." It sounded like all their other words. "They are not completely unwarlike, as it turns out. They just have to believe in the reasons for the battle, and since they question everything at length they rarely go to war."

"Sounds like we don't have much of a chance. So much for your optimism."

"Oh, I'm still optimistic. They've been assembling a few reasons of their own for hating the research team. Especially since Swartmann took over."

"Why especially since Swartmann?"

"I'm not sure. There are clues in what I understand of their language which indicate a solid dislike of the man. He seems to offend some standard connected to their beliefs of grace and decorum. You have to admit Ted Swartmann is singularly ungraceful. They like us, you and me, because of a certain grace they observe in our movements."

"I don't usually think of myself as graceful."

"Maybe not graceful exactly. But, kinetically, you communicate quite a lot it seems. Ask your precious Oonaa lady when you can condescend to learn some of their lingo."

I chose to ignore Dominique's precisely enunciated satiric thrust.

"And they'll go to war for us?" I asked.

"*Us* is the operative word. They wouldn't do it for me—or for you—but together we may be an irresistible combination. We complement each other, I was informed." She glanced angrily toward her Oonaa male. "They perceive us as well matched, at least in some backwater Oonaa way. The bastards. So they'll do what we say. And they understand we don't want a full-scale battle anyway. Just enough fuss and feathers to spook Swartmann and make him capitulate."

"What if he doesn't capitulate?"

"It's your plan, Stoner. You work it out. What would you do?"

"Get together a little more fuss and feathers, I guess."

Dominique stood up straighter, as she often does when she wants to make a point since it makes her a full inch taller than me.

"Look, Henry, I don't want killing. But I'm not sure whether you do or don't. Nevertheless, if we have to kill Swartmann, it's okay with me. I'd just rather lock him up and save him for something along the Torquemada line."

"I'm beginning to have my doubts that Swartmann will respond as expected, and I'm not sure we can trust the Oonaas. Our sense of them is only as strong as your command of the language."

"And that's not enough. Yes, I know. But I can't go native any more than you can. Or can you?"

"I'm not sure."

"No, we both need this. We've got to do it. It's for the good of Q Colony, after all."

"And for the good of us. *Us* in the Oonaa sense, of course."

"Power is its own corruptor, whatever I mean by that."

"I understand it."

"Yeah. Me, too. Well, we are about to be approached by the tribal elders or whoever this crew is. Look your best."

The Oonaas looked determined as they strode toward . . .

• • •

The city had been scouted but, just before we massed our troops there, I felt a need to double-check. Walking through the darkness I had an eerie feeling of being watched, which turned out to be true, as I found out when Hannie stepped out of an arched doorway into my path.

"What's going on?" she said without greeting me.

"Nothing you have to be concerned with."

"Tell me, Henry."

Dominique might not have approved, but I told her. She said she'd go warn Swartmann and the rest. I said it didn't matter. We didn't need the element of surprise.

Hannie stared at me a long time, then put her hand on her stomach, rubbed it in a circle.

"Your baby is growing," she said. "I wanted to abort it for a while. Now I don't want to anymore."

"If you had, I wouldn't have hated you for it. You're the one who has to decide such things."

She slapped my face. Not expecting it, I could not ride with the blow, and it stung considerably.

"I'll have it. That should be enough punishment."

"Come with me. Dominique is concerned about you. She wants to see you."

"No. I can't see her. I'm leaving."

"Where're you going?"

"There's another city, miles from here. Members of our team visited it in the time before the plague. It's different from this one, not abandoned. It's populated by Oonaa natives who are less nomadic than that tribe you deal with. They will kill your tribe if they come anywhere near the city. They don't want to have anything to do with them because they've had so much to do with us. But they're kind, charitable. They'll overcome their distaste and take me in."

"After this is over, I'll come see you there."

"No, stay with your Oonaa woman. She's beautiful, and kind, and she loves you."

"How can you judge whether or not an Oonaa loves any of us?"

"I know."

"I'll still come to see you."

"No."

"Why not?"

"They'll kill you. I'll see to that."

"Then I won't see you again?"

"Maybe, maybe not. Maybe I'll bring you your offspring so that you can judge its value. Maybe I'll sell it to you."

"Hannie, stop!"

"Good-bye, Henry."

She stepped back into the shadow of the doorway. When I stepped into the shadow, she seemed to be nowhere around. I searched the entire building. There was not even a . . .

. . . a convenient vantage point. I could see the whole camp. Swartmann came out of the office and stood outside, surveyed the terrain, stretched his arms. Other members of the team were assembling equipment. Others went to the work areas. A normal day in Q Colony. Everybody seemed to be in the encampment. Perhaps Swartmann's injunction against field study was still in effect. If he discovered that some of his people had already made clandestine alliances with the natives, the result might be a permanent claustrophobic quarantine, not the best atmosphere for a group of people whose main interest was research. Dominique was right then. The colony was paralyzed under Swartmann's command. It was right that he should be deposed by nightfall.

Suddenly the valley was filled with noise. Fuss and feathers, just as I'd planned. The battle had begun, or rather the mock foray designed to frighten Swartmann into a quick surrender. He had to be frightened, had to be. I kept my eye on him, watched him react immediately to the noise with a surprising alertness. He shouted orders to nearby people who carried his orders elsewhere. He did not look frightened enough.

. . . were wrong, so wrong. Both Dominique and I had been so sure that Swartmann would not immediately engage his firepower, the supplies were simply too low. Not only that, he had too much of a sense of responsibility, too much inhibiting cowardice. He had no ethical right to endanger the colonists by aggressive reaction. He would not do something so desperately foolish just because our side put up a smokescreen of activity. All the manuals said to exercise extreme caution before even firing a warning shot at intelligent aliens—much less the whole damn artillery!

I couldn't believe he would not have waited us out longer. Couldn't accept the fact that he had been spooked much too early. Not even when I looked all around me, on both sides and down in front, and saw the many Oonaa bodies. I could not stand the strange post-battle quiet. Swartmann and the Q Colony forces crouched behind their barriers and waited. Nothing for me to do but to return to Dominique and . . .

". . . should have figured it. Why didn't I figure it?"

"I don't see why you're so frustrated. Swartmann's only content when he's working out the fantasy of his role. It's always been *fantasy* with him, playing at being the leader. I knew enough about him to—oh, why didn't I see it? Of course he'd fight back. Meager supplies wouldn't worry him. It's all cowboys-and-Indians to him. Of course."

Dominique sat back, her body balanced precariously upon the narrow rock. Stretched out like that, she looked distorted, as if she'd changed into her own elongated shadow.

"What do we do now?" I said.

"Watch."

"Dominique, this is no joking matter, it's—"

"Look, Stoner, we have no supervisory rights here. We just set things in motion. We have just catalyzed and dissolved with no further power to set up reactions. Swartmann's killed Oonaas; the Oonaas know what to do now. Time for them to kill."

"But that's not what we—"

"I know, I know. Just shut up about it, will you? I have to think, to—"

. . . Hannie was there! Standing next to Swartmann. She was supposed to be miles away. That's what she'd said.

A noise to my left. I whirled around. It was just Dominique, come to my post to observe. Silently, I pointed to Hannie. Dominique went white.

"What the hell is she—"

"I was just asking myself that."

"The Oonaas'll be—"

"Any minute."

"We've got to get her out of there."

"We have to? Us again?"

"Yes. C'mon."

She started making her way down the hillside, sending a small avalanche of scree ahead of her. Reluctantly I followed her, with no idea of what to . . .

. . . startled back. Just before the alien would have raked my throat into a bloody mess, he recognized me. There was a strange repellent acknowledgment in his rust-colored eyes before he went off to find another human to kill.

Suddenly Dominique was at my side again, leading Hannie roughly by the arm.

"This way," Dominique said, and led us on an intricate trail across the battle. Hannie, reluctant, kept pulling at Dominique's arm. We passed the body of Swartmann, blood flowing from his throat and chest. I stopped to look more closely but Dominique . . .

The last I saw of Hannie, she was running to the west away from us. She had not spoken at all during our escape from the battle. When the Oonaas had gathered their captives, she had walked around the outside of the caged group, examining them as if she belonged to the natives and not to Q Colony. When some of them tried to speak to her, she appeared not to listen. Then, abruptly, she started running. She got such a jump on us that neither Dominique nor I had any chance to catch her.

I was surprised that so many of the Q Colony team had survived. And more surprised when Dominique told me that the Oonaas were inclined to be merciful. Winning the battle had been sufficient vengeance according to their code of warfare.

"We'll have Q Colony running efficiently again in no time, the two of us," Dominique said.

"Two of *us*."

"There're debts to be paid in unholy alliances."

"I want no part of leadership."

"Makes no difference what you want. In order to revive things around here, we need to present a solid front. Tough, Henry, but that's the way it is. Wear the mantle with grace."

"Dominique, I..."

As I watched Dominique maintain her vigil beside the dead body of the Oonaa man she had loved, I remembered one of the times I had been in the abandoned city with Hannie. I said that I didn't think that Dominique was capable of a really deep feeling of love. ("A love like ours," I had said to Hannie, and I felt coldness penetrate my spine as I recalled those words.) Hannie, in a good mood that day, just smiled at me and said of course she was capable. If I had seen the affection with which Dominique had nursed Hannie through the plague, I'd know that. I said that bedside affection had little to do with real love. Hannie had just giggled and speculated whether I knew much about either. She seemed disconcerted when I admitted that might be true. As I came out of my reverie, I realized that Dominique was staring at me. Then her eyes shifted to the left and she was staring at something else. I looked over my shoulder and saw what. The Oonaa woman stood a few yards away, a silent mourner. Dominique beckoned her over, and they both took up the vigil by the body of the dead warrior. I felt...

... embraced me and for a moment I thought that she wanted to make love to me. My heartbeat quickened and I tried to lead her away to a less conspicuous spot. But she pulled away from me, and her eyes had changed to an opaque gray. Then I realized what she meant. This was her manner of saying farewell. I nodded. She copied my nod, seeming to understand its meaning. She reached out a hand and briefly touched the side of my head, then turned and walked away from me. She kept on walking, past her people and toward the hillside. For a moment I was in panic, wondering if there was some kind of ritual involved here that I didn't understand. Was the Oonaa woman being punished, sent into exile? Dominique seemed to read the panic in my face, for she put a comforting arm on mine, and said:

"It's okay, Henry. She just needs to be by herself. She'll return."

I let out the breath I had not realized I was holding.

"That's good," I said. "I was worried she—"

"I understand. But you should know that, when she returns, she'll not approach you any more. That part of your life and hers is over."

"What do you mean? I can—"

"No, you can't. I'd order it, if it weren't already their custom."

"Dominique, you've forced this, just because you lost your own—"

"God, Henry, shut up. No, it's not that. This parting is her decision. Neither you nor I had any part in it. If you make any effort to try to renew your relationship, she'll rake her hand across your throat. They do that, you've seen it, and she will. That's it, Henry."

"But I love—"

"No, you don't. Don't pretend to. It's over."

"But, Dominique—"

"It's over. Now we can . . ."

. . . every night in my dreams. We make love over and over again. I seem to feel everything I felt when in the midst of the real act. And just as intensely. Then the scene changes, always changes, and she is back among the natives, never looking at me (just as she doesn't look at me now), ignoring me, no record of our past on her face. Just like the other times, I woke suddenly, feeling very alone—until Dominique shifted her body and sleepily flung one of her arms across my chest. Daintily I removed it. She stirred a bit, returned to her deep sleep. I tried to remember how we had gotten here, especially here in the abandoned city where . . .

Dominique laughed when she told me. I sat in a chair, unable to assimilate the information.

"Didn't you think it could happen?" she said.

"No, I thought it biologically unlikely, even considering the similarities between us and—"

"Well, be proud then. It will be the first baby ever conceived and born as the result of a human and Oonaa coupling. Pass out cigars or something."

"I—I want to go to her."

Dominique scowled.

"No, that is impossible. I know it's your usual custom to disregard the rules, but this time it's for your own good. She doesn't want you anywhere near her, and perhaps near the child. Possibly we can arrange something about the child."

"It's not fair, Dominique."

"No, it isn't. But it's the way we're doing things, especially now when Q Colony is really beginning to work again, some thanks to you and your diligence. We can't afford to—"

"Damn it, I want to see her!"

"Look all you like. Just stay your distance. Don't worry, you fertile bastard, I'll really work things out about the child."

I slouched in the chair, defeated.

Dominique chuckled again, said: "You fertile bastard. God! You fertile bastard. Jesus, I just thought. If we don't get supplies soon and I run out of my birth control caps, I'll have to—God, what a horrible thought. Henry, when I tell you to stay away from my bed, you goddamned better be sure you stay away. I may not be able to rake nails across the throat the way an Oonaa can, but what I can do is . . ."

Dominique, the rash color now gone from her face, blinked her eyes several times, looked up at me and said: "The last I remember I was walking and I—what happened?"

I explained it all to her. It started with how she had walked out of camp late in the afternoon a week ago, and nobody had noticed her absence at first. When her disappearance was acknowledged, I felt—I told her—that I was getting tired of the way fate was treating me, that I was getting damn tired of the women I knew always walking or running out of my life suddenly. But I knew that it was not Dominique's way to just walk off, and I set out to find her. When I did discover her at the bottom of a dry riverbed, I thought that the search had been in vain, I was too late. Then I saw she was still breathing, and I tried to care for her immediately in that riverbed. Others came and we set up a camp. When I could examine her more closely, I saw blotches of rash on her body, and then I was really fearful for her. I recalled what Hannie had told me about Dominique taking care of her during her sickness and I tried to administer to Dominique similarly. But instead of the rash getting worse, as it had for all the others, it faded. She had already been through the worst of it. The exhaustion on her face was just as much a mark as the plague scars. She had wandered across the land for days in the delirium of plague and had somehow survived.

"I don't know how," I said.

"You were brave," she muttered weakly.

"How so?"

"You weren't around during the original outbreak. Any immunity the survivors may've built up doesn't apply to you. Yet you cared for me in spite of all that."

I could not reveal to her the fright in my stomach and the congestion in my throat as she made me aware of that. Instead, I worked up a brave and comforting smile.

"A risk I had to take," I said. "I can't run this damn collection of misfits and duty-shirkers all by myself. Need you."

She smiled.

"I'm afraid I don't remember walking away from camp or anything that happened after. I don't even have the blur of delusion to go by."

"That's probably for the better."

"Ah, you're so pragmatic, Henry. Still, I guess I do owe you thanks—"

"You don't have to—"

"I won't. But I'll keep the debt in mind. I have to go back to sleep, just..."

Hannie stood at the edge of the clearing, the bundle in her arms. For a moment I didn't realize that the lumpy gathering of cloth contained a baby. I walked to her and smiled. She didn't return the smile.

"I thought you should see your son," she said, her voice businesslike.

"That wasn't what you believed the last time we talked."

"Maybe I've matured. Giving birth adds somehow to maturity. Look at him."

She held him out to me, said: "You may hold him. I trust you. You won't steal him."

Looking at the child, I was not so certain I might not be tempted to thievery. He was asleep, serene, his few strands of black hair brushed carefully, it seemed, toward the front. He had that kind of compact, squeezed-in face characteristic of infants. Hannie had wrapped him in so many blankets I could just barely feel his tiny body inside them. I thought of what she must have gone through in the last months, of how I would have liked to be present at the birth. Why had I let Hannie run away so easily? I thought. But I knew I was just being sentimental, fantasizing a life with her that would have been painful, even more painful for her than for me. Looking at this babe, I thought of the way the Oonaa woman's body now bulged out with her pregnancy, and I wondered if that baby would be as beautiful as this and if I would be allowed to hold it. Then I thought of Dominique and her hint that, if her birth control caps did run out, she might just change her mind and let me approach her after all, might just after all admit me to her bed and take her chances. I don't know if she meant it, but the thought of my seed bearing so much fruit frightened me, especially when my association with the offspring would be denied me—by Hannie in her exile, by the Oonaa woman through her incomprehensible custom, and, if Dominique should really decide to chance pregnancy, by Dominique through determination and will.

I had become a drone, at least for all intents and purposes. I was useful to Q Colony, but I no longer could be what I wanted to be or have what I wanted to have. I could die now and the deprivation of my offspring would be no worse than if I lived to their adulthood. Perhaps I should steal this baby now, run off to the hills, raise him as a wolf-child, teach him to rely only on instinct, stay quiet and deny him my language.

The child suddenly woke up and looked up at me in the

way he would have looked at any other new phenomenon in his life. His eyes were dark. He started to squirm in my arms and squeal in little spasmodic cries. Hannie reached out and suggested I return him to her arms. I did, meekly.

"What's his name?" I said.

"Colin," she said.

"I like that name. Hello, Colin."

Colin just went on screaming, until with soothing hums Hannie quieted him.

"May I see Colin again sometimes?" I said.

"Sometimes."

"You wouldn't come back here and—"

"No, I wouldn't. But I'll arrange for you to see him from time to time. Often."

I thought of how Dominique had said she would *arrange* for me to see my child by the Oonaa woman. There was the same kind of sound in Hannie's voice. She might for the moment intend to bring the child to me often, but I doubted that would happen. I wondered if I should be allowed to see either of my children.

Hannie turned and . . .

I handed the communiqué back to Dominique.

"The ship should be here in two days," she said. "Good, we were out of so many supplies."

"I've got all the further requisitions ready," I said.

"Fine. I'm happy with the way you've been handling that sort of thing."

"What sort of thing?"

"Paper sort of thing."

I guess my anger showed even though I tried to suppress it.

"Henry, you know you can leave with the ship if you want."

"No, I'll stay here."

"You should leave. There's no—"

"I'll stay. Drop the subject."

She nodded.

"Sure," she said. "Just wanted you to have the chance, that's all. I don't really mind your staying."

"I'm glad you don't really mind my staying."

"Don't be sarcastic. I can always work out a power play that'll fling you back through the ranks."

"Dominique, I..."

TWO

A SOLDIER NAMED SAILOR

As ordered, I am transmitting my document, known already as the Sailor Papers, even though I am certain there is more work to be done, more nuances for me to work out in order to obtain the best proper translation. It is not my fault that my colleagues, in their infinite infantile fussy wisdom, won't allow me sufficient time to finish my work. Excuse my bluntness. One tends to get testy when she realizes that she is not likely to receive the credit for work she's done, work which is not only significant but ground-breaking. I am not even allowed to register the discovery in my name, and only because it was not my original find. The young man who is trying to take the registration away from me never knew what to do with the Sailor Papers, and I should know that better than most, since I was married to the baboon for more than two years. Should he get the honors for lifting a few fragile papers out of an atmospherically controlled crypt, where they had been so neatly stored by our unknown keeper-of-the-records? Should the others who have worked some on the papers get more credit than they deserve for breaking only a bit of code here and there, and only because they like to throw their rank around like children's rubber balls?

I did the major work on the Sailor Papers, and I want that on the record. And I want it also on the record that I know fully the significance of my achievement. My work on these documents is like the ancient Rosetta stone breakthrough of centuries ago. I recognized the similarities between orthography and probable phonetics (the phonetic conclusions being based properly on what remains of the ancient language in the plethora of current dialects we were studying for long before the cave of documents was discovered and descended upon by the high vultures of archaeologists whose previous findings on Kew were a bunch of ambiguous-looking rocks). I'm sorry, my anger makes me lose my syntax as well as my temper. All I wish to inform the Committee is that I made this particular breakthrough, I showed the way, and further it was I who made the final translation of the entire document, the one you are receiving when I get through with my part of this transmission—that is, unless the vultures choose to add their own rancid little footnotes to my message. I know these transmissions are encoded, supposed to be secret, but I also know they can find out anything they want to, and all through proper channels, properly misused channels if you ask me. They would prefer that you not receive my translation. They wanted one of their own to do the official translation. And they would have succeeded in their devious hateful fussy strategy, they would have aced me out of all proper credit, if I had not stolen the Sailor Papers and rushed off to my own secret cave to accomplish the bulk of this translation.

I do not expect the Committee to give me any awards for that grand theft. I know I did wrong. But I hope you will see from the text that unusual action was necessary. Sailor needed a sympathetic translator, one attuned to the nuances of his tender side along with the playfulness of his more sardonic strains. I was just the person for that. The others would have missed the tenderness, would no doubt have distorted the sardonicism (simply by filtering it through their own nasty and cruel feelings— I'm sorry, I should hold in my feelings, not let them get to me, not let you of the Committee judge against me just because I am so damn mad I could set fire to wet matches). Perhaps I am protesting too much, but I have lived among my colleagues for long enough to know that they would have treated the Sailor Papers as just another document, another laundry list with some history in it, and that they would have reduced it to a dry, tasteful-but-without-taste kind of academic presentation that has been the specialty of all, or most, of them for their entire professional careers. I know some of them are able, and there are a few whom I might have trusted with these papers had they not so firmly allied themselves with those whom I could never trust. So I hope the Committee will make an effort to see that, from my viewpoint, I had to steal the Sailor Papers and that even now, facing judgment from my colleagues on the matter, and probable demotion in rank, I feel that, while my act was ethically wrong, it was definitely for the best. At least my colleagues were pragmatic enough, what with the broad range of their duties concerning the multitude of other discoveries in the documents cave and their own lazy reluctance to add time to the overall project, to accept my illegal translation of Sailor's document and allow it to be transmitted to the Committee. I am grateful for that. I worked hard on the translation, and know that I have much to offer the others that will help them work their ways through other documents, much that will help to make our work here much more swift and efficient. I will give them all the help I can in spite of my hostility (and yes, a plea-bargain has been made, my help for the lightest of legal admonishments). I am valuable here. I know it, they know it. They will not throw me away until they have used me up.

I have said enough about my colleagues and about

my theft of the Sailor Papers. What I wanted on the record is now on the record. Perhaps they will find a way to punish me for that, but I no longer care.

A few comments about the Sailor Papers themselves. As the text indicates, they were found in the Oonaa version of a notebook, not much different from our notebooks. Papers were tied together by a kind of wirelike string that proved to be quite resilient when removed from the manuscript, although it had proved exceptionally firm as a holder of the papers. The papers were in excellent physical condition and the writing on them quite neat and readable, except in the later pages where, because Sailor became afraid of running out of pages, his handwriting was cramped and small. Reading those pages I had to hold the paper close to my eyes, a neat trick with the kind of firelight I was able to manage in my stuffy dark cave. The last five pages were blank, indicating that, in spite of his willingness to write more as indicated in the last section of the papers, Sailor did not indeed write more than this notebook. At least no other writings by him have been discovered, unless of course my colleagues are keeping them from me, a possibility that had not occurred to me until now and a possibility that I vow will not go uninvestigated. I wish he had written more. This is all we have so far that tells anything of this period, the later Q Colony time. It might be useful to know more about Colin and the others. If Colin was such a hotshot ruler, why has nothing more about him survived, either in the discovered documents or in the oral history of the Kew people? I asked many of them about Colin and none had an inkling of whom he had been. Look on my works, ye mighty, and all that. Perhaps one of the books Sailor wrote about him in his lifetime will turn up.

I think the text itself needs no comment. It is a bit disorganized, true, but so was Sailor.

After so many years of hearing about it, I was disappointed to find that Q Colony, the original Q Colony, was just a group of small buildings with little geometrical distinction. They looked to be placed in their valley with no sense of planning. I remember thinking, as I stood on a hill overlooking Q Colony, that perhaps humans did things this way, just threw buildings, objects, people wherever they wanted to and then called it organization. Colin Hanneson did whatever he wanted to and called it logic. And I followed his lead.

As we approached the settlement, I began to think that it must be deserted. Then a short man came out of one of the ugliest buildings and limped toward us. He was old. He had a pinched face. Whiskers stuck out all over his chin. Some of them were white, some looked like little bent needles. We don't have whiskers. They do. I couldn't stand looking at the whiskers.

"I am Henry Stoner," he said. "Who are you?"

Colin, shocked, looked as if he had just swallowed poison and was about to spit out the emetic. He looked so unhappy that I wanted to embrace him, make him immediately forget this meeting he had looked forward to for so long.

"I am Colin," he said to Henry Stoner. "Your son."

Stoner showed no emotion. He nodded once, I think, at Colin's introduction of himself, then he raised a hand, turned, and started back toward the settlement.

"Come to my quarters," he said. "We'll have a drink." He walked a few steps, the two of us following silently. "To celebrate," he said, then started laughing in a way that, even now, years later, I could not possibly interpret.

Hannie, Colin's mother, had pale blue eyes. Very pale. They did not shift in color as ours do. But that didn't matter. I loved the serenity of her eyes. Their gentleness drew me to her, made me go to her at the time of my sexual indoctrination.

I had just turned fourteen, the age when our law allowed me to choose any lover who would accept me. Among our people the ritual of first love, though secular, is treated as sacred. Not only must the fourteen-year-old make a wise choice, the object of his selection must consider well any reason he or she might have to send the young one away without fulfillment. Since refusal may be made for a good reason, the ritual is always tense for us. (Just before the commencement of my adjudicated retirement here, I was approached by a tiny fourteen-year-old and she asked me to be her first love. Me. Ancient, bent, weak. Remembering my own first-love experience, I very much wanted to oblige her, even though I felt she had chosen me out of a kind of hero-worship. She had probably been reading a book or essay of mine. But I am too old. Recalling Hannie's example, I refused the youngster tenderly. Sad.) Most proposals of first love are accepted, almost all in fact. My elder brother chose an old hag for his indoctrination; she was delighted. My elder sister chose one of her peers who didn't even like her much, but nevertheless performed his part with what she described as a persuasively passionate willingness. I had known that Hannie would be my first-love choice almost from the first time I delivered a loaf of my father's special Nulqua bread to her household.

Hannie was small, smaller than our women. Until Colin grew as tall as me, I always thought humans were probably a smaller race. Hannie's face was thin. Her cheeks weren't hollowed, but there was a suggestion of shadow there. There was darkness around her eyes, a darkness ridged by the only age-lines in her face. (She was not old, except perhaps from a fourteen-year-old's perspective.) Her body was thin, too. Her shoulders bent slightly forward as if to emphasize her slimness, making her appear, in certain lights, emaciated. She was thinner now than when she first came to our city, I had been told. In the loose-fitting garments she chose to wear, in mild defiance of our city's dress codes, she seemed to have no hips, and her legs appeared from beneath the hem of her garment as two sticks.

I sought her out during her daily nap. She was lying on a mat which she had placed on a cushioned shelf she had built for herself. Since ground is good enough sleeping area for most of us, I always found the cushioned shelf curious, even amusing. She was lying on her back, her mouth slightly open, a somewhat bemused expression on her face. She'd explained dreaming to me, and said she'd at first been astonished to find that our people never dreamed. I could see she was dreaming.

She looked troubled by the images in her head. I thought it would be all right to shake her awake. (I'm normally courteous, very much so, but a youth planning his first-love encounter can be uncharacteristically rash.) Contrary to my expectations, she awoke more disturbed than she'd apparently been in the dream. She seemed afraid of me.

"Ah, it's only you, Sailor," she said, after a moment. "In the light I thought—well, no mind."

"You thought what?"

"You wouldn't understand."

"I am fourteen now."

I meant that to be my signal to her that I was here for the first-love rite, but she misunderstood me.

"Being fourteen won't help you to comprehend dreaming, but I'll tell you. I thought you were Colin's father standing over me."

"I look like him?"

"Not at all. But it's dark and I was dreaming about him. Dreaming about him and an old abandoned city. I couldn't get out of the dream at first, that's all. What do you want, Sailor?"

In the room's dimness, with light entering only from a pair of small windows on the opposite wall, Hannie's reddish brown hair seemed to shift its color with each move of her head. The changes in the red-brown tints were at least as fascinating as our own variations in eye color, although my love-stricken state may have brought on that thought. Her hair was long, falling over her shoulders and down her back. That alien quality of her hair made her seem more alluring to me than any of our own women. I knew even more that I couldn't choose any of our women, not now when I saw Hannie in this light, or lack of it.

"Sailor," she said, "you don't come into a person's room, wake them out of a sound sleep, and stand there, looking like you've added a couple of extra feet to shift around on, for no reason at all. Out with it."

"I am fourteen now."

"Yes, I know. You said that."

"At fourteen I must lose my chastity. That's the law."

"Ah, I see. So you need advice. I'm not sure I should be

the one to give it, not being born into your culture. All I can advise you, Sailor, is this, go out among your young ladies and find one. You deserve a good one, Sailor. A beautiful one. A—"

"I choose you, Hannie."

Something went wrong with her voice and she made an odd noise in her throat. Her eyes, previously heavy with sleep, threw off their weights. She stared wide-eyed at me. Her mouth seemed to be struggling with a smile. I did not like that. I did not want my offer of first-love to be mocked. Finally she was able to speak:

"Oh, my. Oh, my. How can I say it?"

"It is my privilege at fourteen to choose. I choose you."

"Sailor, I don't deny your right, your privilege, I just didn't expect this."

"I love you, Hannie."

"That's merely your ritual and you know it."

"Please, you mustn't say that."

"Sailor, I'm not one of you. I can't playact this game of—"

"Please, it isn't a game. Anyway, I really do love you. I've loved you since I first—"

I stopped talking when I saw the tears flood her eyes, begin to fall down her cheeks. A handkerchief lay beside the sleeping-shelf. Hannie had stitched its intricate flower pattern herself. I picked it up and started to dry her cheeks with it. She grabbed it from my hand, wiped her face in rough, almost violent strokes, and tried to stem the flow of tears.

"This is absurd," she said when she was finally able to speak again. I didn't know what to say. I was troubled by her criticism, direct and implied, of my declaration. I didn't want to become that rarity among our people, a youth turned down by his first-love choice. Silly in a way, since actually the condition bore no humiliation except to oneself. I remember thinking that Hannie better have a good reason to turn me down. At the same time my body was shaking with fear that she wouldn't accept me, trembling with desire for her to accept me. I hadn't been merely obeying the ritual when I said I loved her. I really did love her. No matter how ridiculous it may appear now, I really did.

"I love you and I am fourteen," I hollered, my voice squeaking a bit in the high range.

Hannie, calmer, talked to me gently.

"Pretend this didn't happen, Sailor. Pretend it was, oh, a practice run. A trying-out of the ritual on an old and dear friend. Here, give me your hands, let me hold them."

I did as she ordered.

"Sailor, in a way you can't understand now, a way that has nothing to do with your ritual, I love you too. Please no, don't respond right this minute. I can't be your first. You would receive no pleasure from it, and it's important that it be right. Your first time must be spectacular. And that's important to me as well. My first time with Colin's father was special to me, has always been special. Though I am sure it was not special for him. Sad thing, it's probably never been special for him. Well, no matter now. Sailor, your first time must be with one of your own people. I simply can't do as well. The act is, well, more complete with your own kind, as you'll discover. I'd just disappoint you."

"But I—"

"No, Sailor, this is a ritual, you have to remember it forever, judge by it later. I—I have not responded to your men when overtures were made, and I'd thought it was common knowledge among you that I wouldn't be available for sex here, even your sacred indoctrinary sex. I'm really sorry, but best to pretend—"

"I can't pretend. This is no pretense. My feelings aren't illusions."

She smiled. "Perhaps not. But, logical or not, I must refuse, and I'm so, so—"

She did not finish her sentence because I was crying. She took me into her arms and rocked me until I stopped. She said I was like a son to her, a second son, and that was another reason why she had to refuse me. I did not know then that sexual relations between mother and son were forbidden among humans, and so I tried to explain to her that a child's introduction to sex may be with his/her parent in our culture, but she lightly touched my lips with her hand to make me stop talking. I saw there was no way to convince her it would be all right for her to be my first-love choice. I could only let her rock me gently, and accept that. I did feel better when I left her, looking back once to see her hair reflecting even more variations on its reddish brown color.

I wandered the streets for a long time. Anyone with sense would, I suppose, have had a second choice at ready when the first refused him. I had never had another choice. Days passed before, in a moment of frivolous recklessness, not at all what the ritual called for, I selected one of our women. She had favored me, I could see that in her eyes. They virtually whirled through a sequence of colors that any idiot could interpret as sexual attraction. I pretended to her that she was my first and only choice, one arrived at after intense contemplation and consideration. She was pleased and no one was hurt but me, as I couldn't adjust to the fact that my chosen lover wasn't Hannie.

Later, much later, I discovered that some of Hannie's cautions to me dealt with simple differences in anatomy between ourselves and the humans. I was older by then and felt I was much more mature than she had been. It was true that our women did possess an inner sexual organ that human women did not have, the organ that nature gave them to allow control over when they wanted to conceive (not quite the pleasure device some humans thought it was, as I discovered when I roamed among more humans, or perhaps it was a pleasure device when seen from human perspective, since it did—well, no matter). It was also true that for us the enjoyment of the sexual act had less to do with such immediate physical sensations. Whom we did it with was much more important. I was in love with Hannie. Making love to her would have been a far greater, far more enjoyable experience than it was with my casually chosen substitute. With Hannie I'd have had the kind of memory she begged me to have with someone else. I could have had sex only with her for my entire life without ever once enjoying the supposed sexual benefits of my own people. I wish she were alive now so I could tell her that.

I have always been wishy-washy. Colin said to me:
"Sailor, you couldn't come to a decision quickly if your life depended upon it. Maybe if *my* life depended on it, but not yours."

He chided me often for it.

Now I am wishy-washy and my mind wanders, an awesome combination. Age. Everything happened so long ago it is not even real to me anymore.

What is not real to me is what I'm our world's foremost expert on, an irony Colin would not only have appreciated, but would have enjoyed considerably as well.

Everyone is dead except me. Not everyone in the world, of course. Only everyone who has ever been important to me. Hannie, Colin, Joline, Henry Stoner, Dominique. Well, possibly not Dominique. Her death has never been reported to me. But the rest of them, they're all dead, and the individuals around me now are all shadows, figures with no substance. It is a new time, a time of no substance. A time to die quietly in, or during, or of.

What was I planning to write about in this notebook which my caretaker insists I asked for only yesterday?

Many lies were spread about Colin. I spread many of them myself in books, articles, essays. It seemed politically feasible at the time. Now I'm not so sure. I'd like to record the truth about him in this notebook, but I'm not clear about my memories anymore. Which of them happened? Which of them did I create in my study? Certainly I can't deal with the adventures any more. I can't separate other people's embellishments, much less my own.

So whatever the purpose of this notebook, I will fail my reader. What do you think of that, reader? I can't even imagine whom you might be, since I plan to destroy the notebook as soon as it is used up. Of course if you are reading this, it means I failed in my resolve or died before I finished or simply, in my normal old man's mind-wandering way, forgot my resolve. Or I may have changed my mind.

Colin always said I could not make up my mind about anything, from a choice of two separate food dishes to deciding the destiny of my people.

I failed my people, and I go hungry often.

I can always burn this notebook.

I could also sneak it into the archive room of the city museum, let it lie there, perhaps until long after I am dead, maybe to be discovered by a scholar (you, perhaps) seeking some unusual tidbit not written about before, maybe even to publish a misinterpretation of this material. No, I don't like that prospect either. I don't know what I'll do with this notebook.

My caretaker is younger than I am, but looks older. Taking care of people does that to you. He's always taken care of people. He started out by taking care of his sick mother, then his sick wife, now in his own dotage he's been awarded a sick old man pensioned off by a supposedly grateful government. They used me well in these last three decades, those bureaucrats whose power Colin and I furnished. I was their advisor when their brains couldn't find a simple stupid way to dispel their customary clouds; their public figure when someone had to be put ceremoniously on display; their award recipient whenever a couple of medals or gold-plated gewgaws were lying around unawarded. All this time nobody asked my caretaker any advice, displayed him anywhere, gave him even a token. Apparently he never noticed any of this.

He fusses over me, my caretaker. He's always asking me questions, a dangerous practice with me since I'm incapable of a clear-cut answer to the simplest of questions.

"Would you like eggs or meat tonight, sir?"

"Oh, I don't know. You decide."

"But what would you like?"

"Well, maybe eggs then."

"Very good, I'll—"

"But meat would be nice."

"All right, I'll—"

"Eggs then."

"If you—"

"Meat."

"Would you like a bath drawn now or later, sir?"

"Well, I'm a bit clammy now so—"

"I'll do it now then."

"But, well, it's going to get hot later and I'll just be clammy all over again, so maybe it's better to stay clammy now and do it later."

"If you—"

"On the other hand, why suffer the discomfort that long?"

"Then—"

"Still, it's a lot of effort to climb into a tub."

"So—"

"Did I have a bath yesterday?"

"You never decided."

"Didn't I?"

"What time of day would you like to die, sir?"

"Afternoon, I think. In the quiet time when everyone's napping."

"A good choice. Shall—"

"But morning might be good, too. Go out when you're already feeling good and chipper and all that."

"I don't know if I'd choose morning, but—"

"You're right, morning's wrong. Evening, when the dusk is coming on. That's so appropriate, isn't it?"

"It does have a certain—"

"Or night. The dead of night. I like that. Finish a day, then pop off in darkness."

"That's what I'd—"

"Still, the quiet of the afternoon is nice. But no—"

I made up that last part. My caretaker and I never had that particular conversation. If we had it, however, it probably would go like that. I'm glad I don't have to decide when to die. If I did have to, I would probably live forever, not from a desire for eternity, but from indecision.

"You're fools, both of you."

That was the first thing Joline said to us, that day when we came to Q Colony for the first time. She had been in another room, eavesdropping, while Colin babbled on about his dreams and I interjected endorsements at appropriate moments. It was the first time, but not the only time, she said that to us.

She laughed at us and I thought I'd remember her face for all time. I thought I'd be able to call her to mind just from that one moment, not to mention several wondrous later moments. But now I can't recall her face. Age. I can remember her body clearly enough. She was not very tall, and her broad shoulders made her look chunky, and she always covered her upper legs even when fashion dictated otherwise. But I can't recall her face. It was beautiful, her face, I know. Everybody said it was. It must have been.

I was deeply, madly, illogically, irritatingly, banally, futilely in love with her. What color was her hair? A very light red or a very dark blond. Or was it? It was one of those shades that tricked you in different lights. Once I had all the perfect words for her hair, her eyes, her smile. I said some of them to her. Now, trying to concentrate on words, they fly out of my head. I can't think of words. I have to write down words, and my language is fleeing from me. Wandering with my mind.

Joline's eyes were not like ours. Of course not. She was human, and human eyes do not change color. Hers could be different degrees of her natural color, but they did not essentially change. Joline had lovely eyes. How banal to say it. But if I can't say the color, if I can't express in some delightful figure of speech how they looked when the spirit of mischief possessed them, if I can't recall in some dramatic fashion the difference between how they looked when she was angry at Colin and how they looked when she was angry at me, how can I say anything clear about her?

I think she had dull-looking teeth and that her hair was rarely arranged neatly. It would be like her, to denigrate her own beauty. Perhaps she succeeded, perhaps she wasn't beautiful. I am no longer concerned with such aesthetic distinctions. I'm no longer concerned with aesthetics at all. I have been exiled from aesthetics, as I have been exiled from my people. Aesthetics is the subject of critics. I am a historian and biographer, not a critic. I could be a critic now, though, in my old age. I have become almost unfeeling enough. That's not fair, of course. Still, only people who are criticized by them really understand critics, how they parade their own weak-limbed faults and stupidities in the form of high-stepping crusaders. I am wandering again. Sailor's disease, wandering. Colin used to say that, too. I must get to the matter at hand, start using this notebook the way I intended. How did I intend to use it? For Colin maybe? Did I request this notebook to set a few matters straight about Colin and myself? Likely, perhaps. I cannot let my caretaker know that I don't know why I asked him for the notebook. He's already too smug.

Colin then. Colin. What? I dreamed of him, didn't I, last night? He was coming at my head with a knife.

I remember Joline saying:

"Sailor, Colin loves you more than anyone else in this world. But I know that, if the political or personal situation dictated your death, he would jump at you with a knife without the slightest hesitation. On the other hand, if your political or personal plight dictated *his* death, you'd still be thinking about it years later. Of course no political or personal situation will ever dictate his death, but still . . ."

I can feel again the uneasy feeling in the pit of my stomach as Stoner led us into his hut. He barely walked, just shuffled along, hardly lifting his feet from the ground. I discovered later this was just an act. He could walk quite normally, even with a youthful stride, if he wanted to. Threatened, he could spring into action like some crouching animal aroused from sleep. He didn't even look back at us that day. What if we had come to kill him? How would he know that we had not? Those questions occurred to me at the time. Now I know that, if we had intended to kill him, bury a knife in his back, say, he would have whirled around and parried the thrust, probably with his bare hand.

Inside the hut, there was a clutter of furniture, documents and books. The latter were piled in uneven heaps. Behind a desk that sagged in the middle, a sag probably caused by the mountains of papers piled on it over the years, sat another human, a woman. She appeared to be tall and very thin, her small head lying back against the top of her chair, accentuating the thinness of her long neck. Her eyes were closed and she was very still.

"This is Dominique," Stoner said. "My wife. She's dead. Been dead for years. I had her stuffed and placed behind the desk."

I would have believed him. She looked preserved, pale white skin, leathered, under snow white hair; even the pose looked arranged. However, her eyes opened as soon as he'd finished speaking, and she looked at Stoner with such well-worn contempt that even I could see that she'd abandoned any severe emotional reaction to him, such as hatred, long ago. She did not say anything, just stared at Stoner while he laughed at her.

"Say hello to our visitors, Dominique," he said. "You do remember the classic forms of greeting, I presume."

She turned her stare toward us, but didn't speak. I think she would have greeted us with some warmth if Stoner had not just then ordered her to. Dominique, for all her aloof and distant qualities, never seemed cruel to me, even when she had reduced me to ashes with a perfectly aimed sardonic insult.

Stoner turned around and finally looked at Colin and me again. There was a kind of happiness in his eyes, a cautious happiness. They had a hint of radiance in them that reminded me of the way my own people expressed joy.

"You look well, Colin. Healthy. You take care of yourself, I see."

"I am well, healthy," Colin said. He was using his low voice, the one that came close to a growl. Oh my, I thought, he's going to be difficult. I had spent the last third of our trip to Q Colony counseling him to be cautious, wary, not to do anything that would offend anyone, at least for the first day or so. I knew he could not hold himself in for much longer than that, but I didn't want him to have a confrontation with his father until I had at least gotten some sleep in a comfortable place.

"And your mother, is she well?"

I gasped, but faintly so no one took notice. I had dispatched a message to Q Colony about Hannie's death the day it had happened.

"She's dead," Colin said, still in the dangerous low voice.

Stoner's eyes seemed to die for a moment.

"I'm sorry to hear that," he said. "She was young, still young. Did she, did she say anything about me as she, as she died?"

"Not a word."

"She left us suddenly," I said, hoping to deflect some of Colin's sullen anger, hoping to find some points of mediation. Hannie had talked of Colin's father often, frequently with affection, although obviously Colin would not want Stoner to know that.

"I see," Stoner said. "I am sorry."

I was terribly confused. Stoner's regret seemed so genuine, yet he should have already known of Hannie's death. Unless someone had kept the information from him. I glanced over at Dominique. Her face had relaxed and she looked pleased about something. I realized that, as the actual leader of Q Colony, she could easily have intercepted my message. But why, I wondered. I knew humans could be devious, I had spent enough time with Colin to know that, but I could never conceive of the petty reasons that led one human to toy with the emotions of another. In my time I have felt bitterness, anger, even a wish for revenge; all the motives, in short, that they use as excuses for their cruel and devious acts. Still, I cannot duplicate their reactions, their lashings out, their destructive urges. Others of my race took to such behavior rather well. I spent a long section of one of my books on just that subject. My caretaker said he had read it some time ago and thought it quite specious.

You're wandering again, Sailor.

I am sure Dominique intercepted the message, though I never had the courage to ask her and, although endowed with considerable nerve, she never had enough to tell me, even in our friendly near-intimate drinking sessions.

"Why are you here then?" Stoner asked abruptly after a long nervous silence.

"I came to look at you," Colin said. "To see what you looked like. To hear the cruel underside in your voice. To stand before you and let you know what you gave up so easily."

As usual, Colin was not obeying my counsel.

"Oh," Stoner said laconically. "A quest then. I am your quest. Are you a heroic sort, Colin? One who has to define the borders of your life, isolate your urges and desires, and act upon them with selfishness and disregard for others? Perhaps you inherited something from your old father, after all."

"Leave him alone, Henry," Dominique said. Her first remark. Her voice was soft, resigned. Her glance toward Colin was sympathetic. "This is your son. He doesn't have to hear your self-important ramblings, your insults. Embrace each other. Or don't. I don't care. Just cut the crap."

She shut her eyes again. Shutting us out, it was clear. She may have even slipped back into sleep.

"Well, Colin," Stoner said, glancing at Dominique with some affection in his eyes, "what do you say? Embrace? Or not?"

Colin, I could tell, wanted to embrace his father.

"Not," he said.

Dominique believed that Colin would eventually kill Henry Stoner. She told me this one night as we shared a bottle of my own blend of Nulqua wines, each of us sitting against the trunk of a massive tree in the middle of a mountainside forest.

"He'll kill him," she said, while swirling the liquid around in her glass and sniffing at it from time to time. "That's what he really wants to do. That's why he came here. Kill him, probably with his bare hands, that's the way he'd do it, bare hands, curled fingers."

"But he said—"

"Sailor, he would tell you anything. He can tell you anything. You're like a drain, sucking in any kind of slop he tosses at you. He might tell you he merely wanted to *see* his father, then, oh, rail at him a bit, curse him for abandoning the child Colin as an infant, let Stoner know the resentment the child feels about the dreary abandonment of the mother. Hannie was like a—but I'm not talking about Hannie, am I?"

"You never say anything about her."

She looked over at me, her eyebrows slightly raised, impressed by something I'd said for a change. Her long legs splayed outward from the tree, she seemed taller than ever.

"No, I don't talk about Hannie. Maybe I will. For you, Sailor, maybe I will. Another time, though. Right now I'd rather destroy your faith in Colin."

"You can't do that."

"I know I can't. I wish I could. You're going to end up a shell, Sailor. He'll take everything of value from you. He's what his father tried to be, and failed at. Henry Stoner tried to take my emotions and press them into pulp. He couldn't do it. If anything, I did it to him. We make a great team, Henry and I. We're good for each other."

"I don't understand."

"I suspect you understand more than you pretend. This wine is almost gone. It is good, but it's not done its job. Anyway, Colin will kill Stoner, I'm sure of it. I can read it in his eyes. You know he will. I can read that in your eyes, even though they've shifted to some kind of nauseating mauve shade. Your eyes are lovely, Sailor. Do you ever make love to old women?"

"Sometimes."

"Now?"

"I'll try. But the wine . . ."

"I'll accept whatever you can do."

I tried. But I was right about the wine.

Today my caretaker ushered in a deputation of scholars. They all sat around, pretending to be awed in my presence, and asked the same wordy inane questions scholars always ask me. One, a short pudgy woman with an incongruous thin long neck, noticed my notebook and couldn't keep her eyes off it. She never mentioned it, just stared at it as if it were an icon from a lost religion. I think she actually hoped to steal it, but could not figure out a way.

"Did you enjoy the visit?" my caretaker asked after they had left.

"No," I said. "Well, in a way . . ."

"What did they ask?"

"The same old bilge. About Colin's adventures. I tried to tell them that the adventures never happened, at least not as reported. Colin allowed the exaggerations because he always knew how to use them politically later. He had to look like a hero to get the power he wanted. That was how much our society had degenerated by that time. They asked for heroes, practically begged for them. Colin told me we had to be adventuresome. Since there were no wars going on anywhere, and few challenges, we had to take what came and concoct the imaginative versions of the events to satisfy our followers."

My caretaker nodded at all I said. He's used to hearing it and doesn't believe a word. He much prefers the accepted versions, especially the ones that I put into book form at Colin's behest. I once told him my complete works should be burned. He said that would be a tragedy. In a way, it would. Like most historians, I am proud of my imagination.

From time to time my caretaker eyes the notebook in much the same covetous way the thin-necked fat scholar did. I have no place to hide it. I can hardly wait to get to the last pages, so I can burn the book in front of him.

We were trapped in a cave, Joline and I. We didn't know it at first but Colin was outside the cave entrance, digging. We didn't hear his rapid-tempoed scrapings for some time. An earth tremor had caused the shifting of rocks that sealed us off. We had attempted to explore the cave, seeking another way out, but had found only wet slimy rock that felt like the inside of fruit, and a sly sort of insect that could walk on our skin without our feeling it. Air was seeping in from somewhere, and we had a sackful of food, so we had not had sense enough to become too frightened. By that time we had already been in a flood and a fire together, and had too often dodged all manner of falling things. Such adventures seemed a mundane part of our lives.

I loved Joline by then. I was even aware that I started loving her simply because she was Colin's sister, half sister by human reckoning of relationships. Even though I could see genetic traces of their father in both of them, they were the only people I ever wanted to be with. I never settled down after Joline, and later Colin, passed out of my life. I never liked being with anybody, my people or the humans. Until my caretaker insinuated himself into my life, I could not sit still with anybody, talk with anyone for more than a short time. My caretaker is an idiot. I like that in him. He tells me that—but I drift away from my subject again.

Joline held my hand up to our torchlight and compared my fingers with hers.

"Your fingers are long. All you Oonaas have long narrow fingers. Few humans do. I'm jealous. Mine are so stubby. They look like poorly rolled cigars."

"What are cigars?"

"Those foul-smelling tubes my father sometimes smokes. And your nails. They're not like mine. They're sharp, like miniature knives. Weapons. You could kill with them."

"We can. We have."

"Have you, Sailor?"

"Never."

"What a pity. I'd like to find some trace of mystery in you, my pet."

I often wondered whether she called me things like "my pet" and "darling" just to frustrate me, or whether in some peculiar way she meant them. She and Colin were always saying things to me that I didn't understand. I grew tired of questioning them, since their answers tended to make the subject more obscure.

"I'm surprised we have the same number of fingers, not to mention that one of them is a thumb placed approximately in the right area. Yours *is* a bit closer to the wrist than mine, see?"

"Why are you surprised?"

"I don't know. I think it's that such nearly similar humanoid species could develop on two planets so far apart, at opposite ends of the universe almost."

"You exaggerate. And anyway, I'm told we aren't the only humanoid species that your humanoid species has discovered."

"I know. But isn't it amazing that *any* similar species was ever found? Makes me want to believe in some kind of divine force."

"Sentimental of you."

"Yes. Do Oonaas have any gods?"

"I'm told they do."

"But you don't have any yourself. Personally, I mean."

"My father forbade it."

A small lie, but it satisfied her. I don't know why I couldn't tell her that we cannot talk of, write of, or in any way describe our god to outsiders.

I kissed Joline. In a way, to get her off theological topics. She always let me kiss her and often kissed back with a kind of pressure that at least resembled passion. I didn't know then whether her toying with me was caused by youthful innocence or whether it originated genetically, a Stoner-inherited need for Colin and Joline to tinker with the lives of any of us puppets who draped our strings eagerly around their ready fingers. She drew her head back from mine in the middle of this kiss abruptly and, in awkward childlike gropings, crawled toward the sealed mine entrance.

"I hear something," she said.

"What?"

"Scraping. Very faint. I think somebody's working at the rocks." Then she shouted, "Who's out there?"

There was some noise vaguely resembling a voice on the other side of the entrance.

"Somebody's there," Joline said. "Working on the rockfall. Trying to get us out."

My heart started beating fast.

"Maybe you shouldn't have shouted."

"Why not? Seems only logical, let them know their rescue attempt will bear fruit. God's sake, I don't want them giving up! Hey out there! We're in here!"

"Joline, stop! It could be them, the ones that tried to ambush us at the old city."

At first what I said frightened her, but then she started to laugh. A sardonic merry laugh. I can still hear it.

"Sailor, we're already trapped in here. If they wanted to kill us, they could just leave us here. What kind of monsters could they be? Could they dig us out to kill us? I don't think so."

"But still . . ."

"No, Sailor, don't! I don't want to hear any of your worries. They're like side roads to the main highway, you don't have to take them, they go nowhere, and they're never kept up well anyway. So just relax, and we'll be out of here soon. Hey out there!"

The voice came back clearer this time.

"I'll have you out of there soon."

We recognized Colin's voice. Joline looked over at me. Even in the dimness of the cave, lighted only by our waning improvised torches, I could feel her look, could sense it separating me into little pieces.

Gradually the sound of Colin's patient chipping away at the rockfall grew louder. Joline remained by the entrance, waiting, silent. I tried to talk, but all my sentences ended in the middle, and my voice choked on words of more than two syllables.

Finally Joline spoke: "Sailor?"

"Yes."

"I do like kissing you."

"Why do you say that right now?"

"I might not be alone with you in the dark again like this. And I wanted you to know it."

"Why?"

She sighed. It was a sad sound, a giving-up sound. I hated it.

"No reason. A passing romantic wave. You know, with rescue imminent and us alone here and the deep sensuality of the damp walls. I don't know. I just wanted to say it. When I want to say something, I say it."

"I noticed."

"Oh, Sailor, shut up."

A moment later, a pinpoint of bright light appeared on our side of the rockfall. Joline laughed triumphantly, then started coughing violently on dust. I crawled to her.

"What can I do?"

"Hold me till it stops."

As her coughing subsided, the pinpoint hole grew larger. Colin's hand, shadowed so that it appeared more massive than usual, came through the hole, then withdrew. The cave grew dark again as he placed his face against the hole and shouted: "Can I come in or do you want to be left alone?"

"Come in," Joline said at the exact same time I said, "Left alone."

Joline kissed me on the cheek as Colin finished widening the hole.

I looked up suddenly from my notebook and saw my caretaker standing in front of me, his dried-up old face composed into smugness so overpowering that I considered setting fire to the overabundance of stiff sky-gray hair that he combs every day in such meticulous wrist-twisting strokes. He doesn't know that I've spied on him standing before the hallway mirror combing his hair. He does it with an almost athletic energy, strange in a man who has been so depleted by age otherwise. Not as depleted as I, perhaps, but he is younger. By a little, anyway. He stands differently when he combs. He stands straight, a bit proudly, nothing like the hunched poses he assumes around me. I think he's faking the hunch, maybe even the age. He wants to look like a servant around me, therefore the slight stoop, and the feet that lift above the ground so microscopically.

"What are you doing here when I didn't ring for you or otherwise request your presence?"

I tried to sound growly, to make my voice resonate with genuine old-age irritability. I suspect it came out as whine or, worse, uninterpretable monotone.

"Would you like your massage now, sir?" he asked.

"Yes. Well, no, I don't think so. I have this pain in my back, all up and down my back, I don't think a massage would help. On the other hand, maybe a massage would be just the thing. In a little while. An hour. Or two."

"As you wish."

"Why were you smiling just then?"

He smiled the same annoying smile again. I could have strangled him with the massage towel he was holding draped over his right arm.

"When I came out here, you didn't hear me. I even coughed to get your attention."

Coughed perhaps when I was writing about Joline's coughing fit.

"But you were writing so furiously, sir, you evidently didn't hear me."

"All right, but why the smile?"

"I was pleased. This notebook was a good idea, it seems."

"Your idea, was it your idea?"

"No, yours. I'm happy to see it working out so well."

"Yes? Oh. You're probably lying. It was probably your idea and you're trying to convince me it was mine. Well, you're wrong. It isn't working out well. I turn a page and immediately forget what I wrote on it. If I look back, my eyes won't focus properly. What words I make out do not make sense any longer."

"Life is never easy, is it, sir?"

"Oh, my. Oh my! I can't stand it. I can't stand you. 'Life

is never easy, is it, sir?' You exasperate me."

"At least once a day, it seems. Nevertheless, this job is mine for life."

"Your life or mine?"

"Let's leave that to speculation. And idle hopes."

I slammed the notebook shut.

"You shouldn't have interrupted me. I was in the middle of a section." That wasn't true, of course. I just wanted to get back at him for the idle-hopes remark. "And, now you've interrupted me, I've forgotten what I was going to say. And I'll never be able to get it back again. It was no doubt an important thought."

"No doubt."

"Perhaps the most important thought in the entire notebook."

"I can readily believe that, sir. Shall I return in an hour for your massage?"

"I don't want the massage, damn it."

"As you wish."

He turned to go.

"In an hour then," I said.

"Yes, sir."

"Or maybe not."

"Yes, sir."

He walked out slowly, the sunlight creating bright dots on his light summer clothing that looked very much like the flickers on the stones of the veranda. His back was still stooped, his posture obedient. Still, I felt he'd won this time. When he won, it was never in a clearcut fashion, never some points to him, more points to me. He was too careful, too meticulous for that. He treated me the same way he treated his hair. And I was just as much combed into place.

Colin Hanneson always seemed defined by *us*. We were the standard, he was the exception. Since he was an alien, with human ancestors who had come to our planet a generation before, his differences seemed more pronounced. He was fascinated with sexual differences, liked to joke about them over campfires.

"Surely you Oonaas . . ." (By then he'd adopted the repellent name for us, the one coined by the Q Colony team.) "... are blessed. So much you fellows can do that I can't even fantasize about. Other hand, you guys don't seem to get much of a thrill out of your abilities. Too normal for you, I suppose. Other hand, for me, it's ecstasy. You don't know what you're missing even though you're getting it."

He looked like us. That made everything more difficult. It was easy to forget he was alien, easy for him to forget we were alien to him. He had more skill with our language than with his own. Even if he'd resembled us on each and every biological, psychological, and anatomical point, Colin Hanneson would have been different. I don't know if I can explain what I mean by that. Perhaps it's better to shift the context and say that he would have been different even among his own people. No, that doesn't do it. It is as if he'd been inhabited by some universe-traveling monster or demon, one who leaped from culture to culture looking for a suitable being to possess. It had come to our planet perhaps and found Colin, then guided him through his life, made him go on inflated quests that had more meaning to his people than to ours, although he managed to convince us well enough of their import. No, that doesn't do it either. It makes Colin himself sound like the monster. He wasn't. How could I have been his friend? How could I have loved him? How indeed.

Perhaps it doesn't matter what he was, what he felt. He was different. He would have been different even if you had duplicated him and surrounded him with copies of himself. They would have then set the standard and he would have stubbornly found ways to defy them. He could not settle, maybe that was it. Whatever the set of standards around him might be, whatever the ways of life, he had to be different from them.

Is that it?

Not likely.

I keep feeling my caretaker is going to look over my shoulder when I'm unaware of his presence and begin clucking his tongue at what I write. Even when I published writings, I never got over the strange feeling that people elsewhere, strangers, actually read them. I could not talk easily to people; I certainly couldn't easily write to strangers.

I'm off my subject again. Typical. Maybe I shouldn't try to record anything about Colin in this notebook. I'm uncomfortable thinking about him again. I thought I was his closest friend. As far as I can tell, I was. Still, it's possible that no one was ever really Colin's friend.

That first day Colin and Stoner had at each other without either of them raising his voice. Even when Colin asked rather formally about Q Colony, his questions suggested that the place was too ramshackle, ill-run, and decrepit. Dominique opened her eyes from time to time but seemed more amused than angered. Colin told his father that he wanted to visit regions of the planet that had been neglected for centuries; wanted to discover new regions, meet the forgotten peoples, find some way to bring our people out of their lethargy, their decadence. Stoner was unimpressed. He said he'd explored enough of the planet, seen it from above in a flying craft. He said he had seen little to interest him before the ship broke down, as all Q Colony ships eventually did.

Suddenly Stoner turned to me and said: "And you, you want what Colin wants?"

Even though his tone was polite enough, I felt attacked.

"Yes," I said, "I do. My people have hidden behind thick city walls and their own thick lethargy for some time. We have legends, myths, historical adventures, none of them investigated for centuries. There's much I can do, learn."

"You are fools, both of you."

Joline had entered without us noticing her. She stood near a doorway, her chunky legs set fairly far apart, her hands on her hips. Smile on her face, mischief in her eyes. I liked both. I was immediately intrigued by her, an omen of feelings to come.

"Children, playing out dreams," she said. Each word was a challenge. She looked at me as she said them. I felt hurt.

"Idiots," she said, then her smile broadened. "Wherever you go, I want to go with you."

"Joline," Stoner said, "I should have left you on a hillside for shepherds to raise. Gentlemen, my daughter Joline." Then, as an afterthought, glancing her way: "Dominique's too."

Dominique opened her eyes, nodded curtly toward Joline, smiled.

"Joline, this is your half brother, Colin, and his friend . . . uh—"

"We call him Sailor," Colin said.

Joline laughed. Another challenge.

"A soldier named Sailor," she said.

"Yes," I said and struggled to think of something more to say.

"Sailor's afraid of the water," Colin said, and I hated him for saying it, even though it was true.

"He'll be a good soldier," Joline said. "I can recognize that in him. He's got the right obedient look."

I felt miserable. Here I was, a friend accompanying a friend on his first visit to the far side of his family, and there they were, all of them, putting *me* under attack.

I can remember the early days with Colin better than the later ones. My caretaker says that it is because I am old, and old people always remember the old days better. That's not precisely true. I remember the early days with Colin because he was forever reminding me of them. Remember this, Sailor? And what about the time you—? You must remember the way I—?

When he had flung the rock that had by accident killed one of our people, he became officially ostracized. Our custom. Colin's victim was another child, one about our age. If that victim had lived, he would by now be a doddering old fool like me. I'd like to chat with him, in whatever afterlife he's reclining, ask him what it's like to be a vague minor figure in a famous person's history. Someone whose name was not preserved, cannot even now be found in any record anywhere. I've looked.

"It's all right, Sailor. At least I know that I'm a part of history. I can sit here in the hereafter content to know that I figured so prominently in his life. And yours. What would I have been otherwise? Just a worker, a nullity, perhaps a dull official. At best one of Colin's followers. My life might have made no mark anywhere."

"But you are dead. You did not get old. You did not have

a life to speak of at all."

"Worse things can happen."

"What worse things?"

"Look around you, Sailor."

Ostracism wasn't a particularly difficult or distasteful punishment for Colin. Our people thought it severe, but he rather liked it. One of us would have been shamed by a period of ostracism. If I'd been ostracized then, the shame of it would have stayed with me for years, for the rest of my life. Now I wouldn't mind it so much. It would at least get my caretaker out of the way. Colin enjoyed not having any of us talk to him. He especially liked to taunt us and know he would not, could not under law, receive a reply. I'm afraid justice isn't practiced very successfully among us. That may have something to do with our cultural degeneration. Perhaps it's why we regressed so easily from a fairly advanced and even technological culture to the rather primitive state we have now endured so comfortably for centuries. The humans, especially the Q Colony experts in their various studies and treatises on us, have been rather contemptuous of our slide from greatness. They place a high value on progress, on social, scientific, and cultural advancement. Education and production. Useful activity and meaningful leisure. They claim life has no value without all of this. I'm not always sure what they mean. I can't see where their incessant activity has produced so much of value, and am not certain they have enjoyed or gained much from all their progress. I'm not even sure they've progressed all that significantly. A few boats that travel across galaxies, a few devices that help them achieve a few sedentary ideals, a lot of knowledge that isn't especially useful here on Kew. They have named our planet Kew for no good reason I can see. It's derived from Q Colony, I can see that, but I don't care for it. Somehow it makes it their planet when they are merely visitors here. Nevertheless, we've picked up the name Kew from them. We had neglected to give the planet a name. Odd custom, that. Colin always said I should try harder to understand human ideas, values, customs. I don't know about that. I've already been corrupted by the humans sufficiently to question what should not seem questionable. That's enough for me.

I'd only been vaguely aware of Colin's ostracism. Even

though he was one of our city's two humans, we tried not to separate them from us, isolate them, make them different. Our paths, Colin's and mine, crossed rarely and we'd never spoken, even before the ostracism. I delivered baked goods to Hannie and sometimes Colin would scowl at me.

One day I was returning from a delivery elsewhere, and I turned down a sidestreet that was a shortcut to my father's bakery. Colin stood in my way, in the middle of the street, his long toes (he always went barefoot in defiance of the clothing ordinance) curling around pebbles, lifting them a few inches, then flinging them toward a nearby wall, where he seemed to be imagining a target. He was really quite good at flinging pebbles with his foot, I noticed. I made ready to slip by him without speaking, in accordance with the regulations about ostracism.

When I was almost past him, he grabbed the collar of my coat and pulled on it. I felt the cold air of the day rush down my back. He caught me off balance. Even though I was taller and broader than he, he managed to hurl me against the same wall he'd been flinging stones against. He tried to hold me there though his leverage wasn't good. I've always been difficult to stir to a fight, was even more difficult then, so I merely stared into his clouded blue eyes. I was simply not a fighter. I liked to cook; cooking doesn't usually generate violent impulses. Even though I could feel sharp stones pricking my back, feeling like they'd break my skin if I moved, I relaxed in Colin's grip. For a while he put on pressure, trying to make me fight back. But he wasn't strong enough to hurt me enough. I continued unresponsive. Finally, with a scornful sweep of his arm, he let go. I felt many scrape marks on my back as I edged away from the wall. Something had ripped my coat, but no matter, I thought. I was as good with a needle and thread as a set of pots and pans.

"I've watched you a great deal," Colin muttered and looked to me for a response. I merely stared at him.

"You're quite a coward," he said.

I didn't react, and he seemed terribly disappointed.

"I always thought you had a yellow streak, from the first time I saw you."

I remained silent. He was getting furious.

"A bright yellow streak running from head to toe."

I shrugged. Then laughed. For some reason, suddenly, I wanted to speak to him. I no longer minded the regulations, my own breaking of the law. I felt I needed to speak to him, he needed to hear my voice.

"I'm glad the yellow streak's still bright. Afraid it had faded."

"You've spoken to me. Against the law."

"So it is. Will you turn me in?"

He almost smiled.

"Spineless, all you Oonaas."

I felt angry but was determined not to show it.

"I must go. I have deliveries."

"By all means, go your way. Deliver."

I started to walk away.

"We'll talk again," he said after me. I turned. "I'm even thinking of making you my second-in-command."

"In command of what?"

"I'm not sure yet, but you'll see when I am."

"I don't intend ever to leave the city. I will settle here and take over my father's bakery. Couldn't leave even if I wanted to, which I don't."

"You will. For me."

He was right, of course, but, in all the times I've thought of that moment, all the times I've considered what a hardship it was for me to leave the city and the bakery, all the times when I've felt pain in my chest thinking of the foolish things I've done in life because of Colin, I've never figured out how he knew. Or really regretted that I threw in with him.

We were friends soon enough. A lot of sneaky chatter during the period of ostracism, remarks muttered as we passed each other, quick looks to see if anyone had noticed. After the ostracism was lifted, we openly became friends, the kind of friends who frighten off other potential friends. There *were* other friends. They came and went. Some went with scars. Colin couldn't stop taunting, pushing, throwing painless challenging blows our way. He was lucky we were so trained in the restraint of violent impulses. Many of those he defeated so showily could have laid him out with a single blow or killed him with their hands. We Oonaas may be weak-willed, but we can kill with our fingers, with our knifelike nails. History has perhaps made cowardice a virtue among us so that we will not kill unless necessary. Even when one of us fought back a bit, even hurting him, Colin was adept at coming out of it looking better. By the time he had become an adult, he had collected a few scars. A knife wound in his left leg which at the time seemed to bleed forever left a deep and jagged scar from the front of his knee to the side of his ankle. He made me describe that scar with heroic metaphor in my book of his adventures, made me imply that it had come from a courageous but secret adventure. Once he broke a bone in his arm and it didn't heal quite right. At that time I was on the other side of the city in a park on an herb-collecting expedition, and so wasn't there to heal him properly. You could hardly notice the deformity the broken bone had left unless you saw that he held his left arm at a slight angle, pointing inward toward his body when he was standing at rest. He always said he needed the scars.

With his dark black hair and even features, not to mention the dazzling peculiarity of his eyes that didn't even change color, he considered himself handsome. Even though he had no other humans around with which to compare himself. Our people had paler skin and lighter hair, so at first I had difficulty seeing him the way he saw himself. I had a much easier time seeing Joline as beautiful, or Hannie. Our skin was also tougher in texture, not as porous-appearing as a human's. That was difficult to get used to also. But I had the greatest difficulty with his eyes. I was unnerved by the relatively unchanging hue. I thought then I could never be fascinated in the limitations of blueness.

When he was ready to launch his life-schedule, one that he'd planned since the age of twelve, Colin quickly got the attention of important people in our city. He always said ambition did it, my people weren't used to ambition. We were tough enough, he said, but too often single-minded, too often sedate. We stayed in the family profession, or waited for mysterious calls to duty. I claimed our way was better, although of course I backed down from the argument when he challenged it. Our society was serene, yes, I said, but it was also free. We did not have to make many choices, were under no pressure to decide any issue. We could change any aspect of our lives at any time and always were fairly certain of every opportunity available to us. We didn't need to waste energy with ambition. Colin said that, if that were true, he wouldn't need to be so forcefully ambitious himself. Well, I said, after all, you're unique, a different species, allowed to be ambitious. It was perhaps in his blood. He never did like my reasoning on the matter.

He was especially angry that my people tended to stay in the city, with only occasional forays into the nearby countryside and infrequent trips to other cities. His mother, after all, had lectured him about the human urge to explore. Hannie could weave magical tales about the exploration of space. If humans could wander around space, he said, at least Oonaas could take a few peeks at their own planet. I told him our history, of how we'd defined our world long ago, had kept sentinels high in the mountains and aloft in orbiting satellites, sacrificers who maintained vigilance on our world and transcribed even the minutest changes in order to keep our knowledge consistent. But in time the mountain sentinels had descended from their aeries, and the satellite sentinels had been brought home, their jobs accomplished. We had discovered one thing, that we felt better off remaining in our cities, living our small but happy lives, performing our minor but significant activities, enjoying a serene but content existence.

Colin, of course, railed at this. There was no wonder, no adventure, in that kind of life, he said. He wanted wonder in his life, adventure. You want to live out Hannie's tales to us, I said. He said, yes he did.

One day he told me we were going to leave the city. We were old enough now. Hannie was dead, so there was nothing holding him back. I learned later he had tried to get others, form an army of sorts, but everyone had refused him. He asked me last because he was so sure I'd go with him.

We sat on a high pedestal that supported a statue to a forgotten city hero, a veteran of an unknown battle in a war our historians no longer acknowledged. We drank great amounts of my Nulqua wine, brewed from a recipe invented by my great-grandfather, his greatest invention, a wine that was a pleasure and not the necessity its sour-tasting predecessors had been.

"I'm so happy you'll be with me in this, Sailor," he shouted.

For perhaps the twentieth time that day, each time Colin mentioned our adventuresome future, my mouth went dry and my blood stopped running. I looked up at the underside of the hero, a view grotesquely distorted by my perspective. I felt as if I was violating the statue's sense of modesty.

Could I say to Colin what I'd been thinking, I wondered. I started to say it, then said something else, something quite inconsequential, then I started to say it again, and managed to find a reason to take a long gulp of wine, streams of which I could feel running out of both corners of my mouth, making me think, well, I certainly can't say something momentous with wine dripping off my lips, and I resolved to say it on another day altogether.

"What's bothering you?" Colin asked, uncannily able to see my discomfort, as usual.

"Nothing," I said.

"You know you can't get away with that."

"I know."

"So say."

"All right."

I took a sip of wine and stared at him. His return gaze was so intense I had to look away.

"Sailor? Say it."

"In a moment."

"In a moment. Always in a moment with you. *Now*, Sailor."

I returned to my immodest viewing of the underside of the hero.

"Sailor!"

"I, uh, I don't think I can go with you. My business, that is, my father's business, well, it needs me, and he's planning on me to take over, and I don't see how I can set off on any—"

His reaction to my protests, which I'd expected to be angry and scornful, surprised me. He threw back his head and laughed, then he hugged me. An odd murky odor seemed to rise like mist from his dark hair.

"One foot over the city barrier, Sailor, and you'll be ready to make proper claim to your name. Sailor, voyager, adventurer, expeditionary. It's your fate. I chose it for you. So just forget all this talk of businesses and inability to go adventuring."

"You don't understand, Colin. My inventions are in demand. I've created ten new pastries this year alone. My pastries may be more important than—"

He hugged me again, fiercely, taking words and breath clean out of me.

"I have to have you with me on this. There are no other possibilities. Your people can get slim from the lack of your culinary wonders. What do *we* care? Your life is meaningless if it's just helping people to gain weight. No, no, don't argue for the taste of your inventions. They are marvelous. I plan to go home and eat several Nulqua pastries as soon as you admit I'm right. You're going. Now, do we need to hear any more futile protests from you, or can we go home?"

"I don't know if I want to go home right now. Maybe I'll—"

Another hug.

"Sailor, you must learn to be decisive. What kind of second-in-command will you make if you can't—"

"I'm only second-in-command because there're only two of us going."

"You'd be second-in-command if we were a thousand strong."

"I'm not sure I want to be second-in-command. Couldn't I just be a sergeant or something?"

"Sergeants need to make their decisions immediately. I would really worry about you as a sergeant. As second-in-command, at least we'll have the value of your carefully reasoned thoughts. Let's go."

I found his language unsettling. He seemed to assume we were going out to conquer rather just take a look around. He knew he had to be a hero, he had decided that long ago. Oh my, when I think of all the exaggerations, all the outright lies we had to concoct in order to make him one publicly, I wonder if I should have lived at all. I can blame the lies on Colin, I suppose, say his need to fulfill his ambitions led to the lies, and anyway they were done at his order. But I did make them up, I have to take the blame for that. I've been the fake just as much as he, perhaps more so. If I hadn't lived, or if during his ostracism I'd successfully resisted him, never spoken to him, he would in all likelihood not have found someone as imaginative as I to create his legends for him. After all, I was unusual, too. I, too, was a tiny bit larger than life. In his mind he was a hero. In mine I became a scribe with dreams. I enjoyed building up the stories, enjoyed finding the stuff of epic and legend within me since it was not otherwise evident in my character. Colin got his power; I got my comfortable position, an equitable trade. Now he's dead and I might as well be. In a way I'm barely alive, I'm just being maintained. My caretaker stands at the living graveside and waits with the first fistful of dirt oozing from between his clenched fingers.

I began to learn the meaning of chaos when we left the city. I'd never seen the barrier work before, never realized all the shoving of switches, punching of buttons, wrenching of levers that were necessary to make a door-size exit for us to go through single file. Once outside, the door closing behind us with what I thought was an ominous thud, Colin began leaping about, trying to take the longest jumps his long legs could achieve, waving his arms so wildly it looked as if he were trying to force them to separate from his shoulders. I edged back toward the door, afraid of the unexpected chaos around me. This chaos was not what I wanted from chaos. It was space everywhere I could see, very little of it broken up by trees and rocks. Our city was on a plain that stretched to mountains we couldn't even see clearly in the mist of that morning. Chaos was the feeling of absolute freedom that I didn't want at all. Chaos was the sensation of not being inside the city. My legs almost collapsed from fright.

Colin's glance at me was carefully arranged disappointment. It seemed to say he was chagrined that I was doing nothing to mark our achievement, so I did an awkward little dance, some skips and hops, trying to project an impression of joy and happiness, waving my arms like a wounded bird who was deliriously happy about being shot down. Colin's sour face vanished and he copied my moves, improvised on them. Later he codified them, wrote them down, termed the result Sailor's Dance, and I always felt pain in my stomach when I watched others doing it.

"Settlement's rather rundown I'm afraid these days," Stoner said just before he took us on a tour of Q Colony. He held onto Colin's left arm rigidly, like a tool he was about to use, and never noticed that the arm was slightly deformed from Colin's boyhood accident. I don't think he ever asked Colin about the arm.

Joline trailed Stoner and Colin, walking a little to the right of Colin. Dominique accompanied me, appearing hardly more awake than she had been inside the main building.

"We're no longer officially in operation," Stoner continued. "Closed down our mission some time ago, they did. Many in the colony departed on the last supply ship, but a surprisingly large number of us elected to stay. I simply didn't want to start out again someplace else after so many years here. Guess others felt the same way."

Dominique laughed abruptly, cruelly.

"He's going to pretend loyalty or some such thing," she muttered to me. "He wants to hide the fact he doesn't have any ambition left. That went out with—never mind what it went out with. And he's horny as a slithy tove, you should see him when he gets within smelling distance of one of your women, Sailor. You know, most of the men in the colony like to screw your women, Sailor, that keeps them here more than anything. Stupid bastards! You don't like me being, well, intimate with you, do you, Sailor?"

"Well, I guess, I mean, we just met."

She laughed harder than before.

"Right, Sailor. I like you. Glad you showed up. Hope you stay."

I was having a lot of trouble understanding Dominique, being understood by her. She seemed to be floating through our world without making much real contact with it. I wondered if she drank to excess or used narcotic substances. Among our people, the rumors concerning human habits were used to keep children awake at nights. What Dominique said disturbed me, in ways I would not have anticipated. There wasn't any reason why I should object that Stoner and the other colonists had been with any of my people. Nothing in *our* moral laws condemned that. Our people always made their own choices when it came to lovemaking with anyone or anything, even humans. Still, the part of me that was rapidly becoming human very much resented Stoner's sex with our females. Oddly, at that time he was no longer interested in such sex and didn't do much more than formulate sly leering insults.

"What do you think, Colin?" Stoner asked about halfway into the tour.

"I am surprised," Colin said, and I could hear the danger in his apparently calm voice.

"What surprises you?"

"The ugliness. I thought at least Q Colony would be presentable."

"Well, I guess we have let things go to seed a bit. . . ."

"Henry," Dominique said, "it never looked any better than it does now."

Stoner glanced backward and said emotionlessly, "Neither do you, my dear."

Dominique smiled.

"Good shot, Henry. Go on, Colin. I'd like to hear more of your impressions."

Colin was somewhat flustered by Dominique's question, especially since it had apparently been delivered as a challenge. He always was a bit put off by her, never seemed to know how to respond to her, or even talk to her normally.

"Yes," Stoner said, "I'd like to hear your thoughts, your observations about our ways of life, my son."

Colin rankled at Stoner calling him son, I could tell that by the way he hunched his shoulders. At that moment I didn't really understand. He *was* Stoner's son, after all. More acquaintance with Stoner made me comprehend Colin's reactions to the man better.

"Tell us, Colin, what are Q Colony's disagreeable characteristics?"

At first Colin could not speak. Joline moved toward him, apparently ready to say something in his defense. Or maybe against him, you could never tell with Joline.

"Well," Colin finally said, "for one thing, the Oonaas would not allow their buildings, their walls, their interiors, to become so rundown. There wouldn't be splinters, stains, age."

"So," Stoner said, "you're going to judge us by the Oonaas. Natural, I suppose, since you've been brought up among them. You know, you're like the legendary wolf-child. That's a human brought up among beasts of the—"

"We know what it is," Colin said. "My mother told us many Earth tales, stories from your past."

"*Our* past," Stoner said. "It's your past, too, my son, in spite of—"

"Father," Joline interrupted, "don't taunt. It's not right. Colin can—"

"Goodness," Stoner said, "maybe we are fated to repeat our legends, our myths. Joline can be the protector of the wolf-child, his interpreter."

Dominique started to laugh.

"You're such an ass, Henry," she said to him. "He's such an ass," she muttered to me. "You know what an ass is, Sailor?"

"In a way. Hannie told us a story of a human transformed into an ass. I can't quite picture the animal in question though."

"No need to picture. Just gaze at Henry."

"Dominique, please," Joline said.

"I know, I know. I hate it when I sink that low. Habit. Go on, Colin."

"I don't suppose there's any reason to—"

"No, you don't get off that easy. I'm eager to hear more of your impressions."

"Yes, Colin," Stoner said. "Go on, please."

Colin was clearly not convinced by their eagerness to hear him, but then he was not inclined to be silent either.

"The rooms, they're gloomy and they're furnished, well, like nobody cares what goes where or what it looks like. And all the tiny decorations. Oonaas wouldn't let the decorations interrupt the natural flow of the walls. And there's all the right angles, the way walls join each other, the way ceilings and

floors break up the walls. I don't know, everything's too rec-
tangular, too square, too alike, too formal. Oonaas' architecture
is smooth, flowing, all curves and slants. Walls flow into another without a seam, without straight lines dividing them.
Ceilings are domed or rippled. Their floors and walking areas
vary in angles of slant, degrees of texture. Do you understand
me?"

Dominique nodded. Stoner's smile was smug. Joline looked
at both of them, then at Colin with confusion.

"We understand," Stoner said, and I was already beginning
to feel threatened each time he opened his mouth. "You've
grown up in their environment, Colin, you've become one of
them, at least as far as your tastes were formed. And in cultural
beliefs, too, I assume. You're an *Oonaa*, Colin, you've *become*
an Oonaa. You're an Oonaa, my son, just the way a wolf-child
becomes a wolf. Your howls are Oonaa howls, you crave the
meat that Oonaas eat. We have to tame you."

"I doubt that you can," Colin said, then added with a derisive
inflection that rivaled Stoner's use of 'my son,' "father."

Stoner smiled broadly. I could see that he was not insulted
by Colin's response. When I think back on that scene now, I
believe Stoner felt that he had taken the first step in training
the wolf-child in human ways.

I fell asleep just now, right after writing something,
something about Colin. I can look back a page or so, see what
it was, but it doesn't matter. The important thing is that I dozed
with the notebook on my lap. I think I had a dream. I know
we aren't supposed to have dreames like the humans do, but
I've had several recently. I don't remember this dream, except
for one part. Hannie was telling me a tale and resting my head
in her arms. I was not young, I was old, as I am now. I felt
wonderful. Perhaps dreams are for that. To make one feel
wonderful when there is no chance of it in his waking time.
But the dream is not the important thing. What is the important
thing? I am drifting. I can't seem to concentrate. Yes, the
notebook. That was it. It was resting on my lap. Even in my
sleep I was sensitive to its gentle pressure on my legs. Suddenly
it was gone and, just as suddenly, I was awake. I stared into

the eyes of my caretaker. Glancing down, I saw that his palsied hands held the notebook. His eyes at first were scared, then he composed himself. I'm sure of that. I'm sure I caught him with a definite color of guilt in his eyes, even though he was able to shade the color in such a way that I couldn't be sure of it.

"What do you want with that?" I said, pointing to the notebook. His hands shook more, creating quite a breeze as the pages of the notebook rippled.

"It dropped from your lap, sir. You must have been asleep."

"I was asleep, that's true. But I don't believe it dropped. You took it. You want a look at it, don't you? Maybe you figure I'll die, then you'll pilfer that, make your fortune from it."

He managed a look of genuine shock. I almost regretted what I'd said, until it occurred to me that the shock was just another ruse on his part.

"I just now picked it up, sir. From the ground. Where it dropped. I would not intrude on—"

"Never mind. Just give it back to me. I'll forget your little attempt at larceny. I won't ask the committee to replace you."

An empty threat. The committee wouldn't listen to my wishes. I suspect my caretaker knows that, too, but he is sufficiently trained in service not to respond to my threat with a threat of his own.

"As you wish, sir."

"The notebook."

"Of course. Wait."

He rubbed a corner of the notebook.

"What are you doing?" I said.

"A bit of dirt from the ground. I was just wiping it off."

"Let me see it."

He handed it to me. There did seem to be a faint smudge in the corner, but he could have created that himself. A little dirt on his thumb rubbed in, to make it look like the book had indeed been on the ground. That would be easy for such a devious sort as he is.

"Do you wish some tea, sir?"

"It's too early for tea. Isn't it?"

"You often have tea at this time, after working on your writing."

"Do I?"

"Yes, sir."

"Well, perhaps I should have some then. I'd like some, yes."

"Yes, sir."

He looked much too triumphant.

"No, I don't believe I'll have any tea now, thank you."

"As you wish."

He turned to leave.

"Bring me the tea. Quickly."

"Yes, sir."

Somehow I can never quite emerge the victor with him.

I've recorded nothing in this notebook about Hannie's death. No surprise, I don't much like to think about it, to visualize it anew. I was twenty when it happened, ready to follow her son anywhere he led. One day she was alive and cautioning Colin not to take his ideas too far, to be more careful, to be sure he wore his boots into battle. Next day she was dead. I discovered her body. I had gone to her quarters because I wanted her to taste a pastry I'd just created. I always presented my inventions to her first. She was lying on her strange bed. I tried for a long time to awaken her. Her right hand was at rest on her forehead. I thought the color of her hair had faded. It was a long time before I could accept the fact that she had died. I sat there, waiting for her to open her eyes. Judging from the look on her face, I surmised that she had simply not awakened from one of her dreams. There was a slight bemused scowl on her face, a suggestion of scowl. I almost touched her eyes, to raise their lids. I just wanted to see her eyes once more.

Colin, summoned by a message I had sent, strode in and quickly performed the ritual prayer, made the death announcement, posted it in the right places, and had her body carried away and burned almost before I'd really realized she was dead after all.

In the days after her death I was obsessed with the worry that my own indecisiveness, my own willingness to obey what

I was told, had denied me Hannie when I had really needed her. If I had been decisive, I might have stood up to her, reasoned with her, made her agree to my wishes. But no, I had to be as gentle with her as she was with me; I had to perceive the fine gradations in her emotions as she tried to explain her refusal of first-love to me; I had to love her so much I could not hurt her. If I could only have been like Colin, taken what I wanted, been fierce, seen only the logic of whatever cause drove me. Seeing the other side was perhaps my downfall in life, as too many people have told me too often. Hannie was the first to tell me.

I've been sitting here, sipping at a cup of cold tea, flat-tasting tea, trying to remember what Stoner said to Colin that provoked the son to slam the father against a wall of the abandoned city. My concentration had not been on Stoner and his dull talk, his disconnected anecdotes about the Q Colony research on the city and all the conclusions they had come to, most of which I knew or suspected to be wrong. But it has become a custom among our people to allow the humans to settle easily and comfortably into their mistakes. As researchers, the Q Colony scientists reminded me of farmers, growing luscious crops from the tiniest of seeds, the only drawback being that they harvest little more than food for cattle, food with perhaps some nutrient value but not much useful substance.

Why did I slide into that digression? What am I writing about now? My eyes can't quite focus on my scrawls, so I can't make out much of what I was writing. My eyes seem to be going bad. Can't let my caretaker know that. He keeps asking me if my eyes are all right. I see I was writing about Colin hitting his father. I wonder why. I can barely recall that incident.

I was delicately scraping away at some lettering that my fingers revealed had once been inscribed on the side of the very building that Colin would in a moment push his father against. The lettering had become so worn away I could not touch-read it, I could just discern a few symbols. I had brought no paper with which to do a rubbing. My curiosity aroused, I was trying to find out as much as I could since I didn't know when I would be able to return with paper. I don't think I ever did return. That corner of a wall may still await decoding. I imagine it has more layers of dust and dirt on it now, to replace what I laboriously scraped away.

Colin and Stoner had talked quietly near me. By that time I had learned to ignore their conversations. I would only hear something I had already heard anyway, more sarcasms, innuendos, strategically phrased points of information and opinion. Then Stoner raised his voice and said that insult that I cannot remember. I know that, whatever it was, it made me feel as if my chest was a resounding chamber for the remark. I looked up. Stoner was angry, his normally placid eyes suddenly irate. Colin said, "I reject you as my father," and took Stoner by the shoulders and shoved him. Stoner's back met the wall with what I thought was a crunching sound. His head reared backward, hitting stone hard, too hard. His shoulders sagged and he began to slide downward. Colin grabbed him under the arms and held him up. He pulled Stoner away from the wall and for a moment I feared he was going to shove him against it again even harder. I believe even now that the thought did cross his mind, and that he had to gather strength to resist the temptation. Instead, he gently propped his father against the lower part of the wall. Frightened, I ran to them.

There were blood streaks on the wall by Stoner's head, a strange twisting to his left arm that indicated a bone there was probably broken or at least bent out of shape.

"Sailor," Colin said, "your job."

"Clean up your mess, huh?" I muttered, one of the few times I ever spoke back to Colin, at least one of the few times I spoke back when there was a danger of reprisal from him. I did not usually lose my head around him, but the fury of this particular assault had angered me. Stoner was not admirable, but I didn't think he deserved to die either.

"Sailor, I can feel death in him," Colin shouted. His voice was panicked. I can recall only a few times when Colin clearly displayed panic. Even now I'm not sure what scared him. I can't convince myself that the prospect of Stoner's death would so frighten him. Such a tenderhearted action on his part would have been unusual. Or perhaps I am misjudging him. I, who knew him better than anyone.

"Do something, Sailor! You can cure him."

"It may be too late. I can't fight off death, you know that."

"Try, damn it, try!"

I started to rub my forehead with all my fingers, working the healing power into them. At first I thought that the instinctual part of my brain had stopped functioning, perhaps shut off by some protective mechanism. Healing can kill the healer, I've heard, though I've yet to see it happen or even know of it outside of ancient legend. I wondered if I really wanted to save Stoner. What good would I be doing for anybody by giving him a few years more of crotchety ill temper? I wouldn't be doing any of *us* good, I felt that. I shut my eyes and concentrated harder. Gradually I felt the warmth enter my fingers, felt the rush of healing power go through my blood vessels, felt my hands swell to a third more than their normal size. Opening my eyes, I took my hands away from my forehead and stared at them. My stretched skin was almost transparent. I could almost see my vein pulsing, my bones softening. Telling Colin to get out of the way, I stepped in between the two of them and stood over Stoner. He certainly did not look alive, I thought. Yet I sensed the life remaining in him. I almost sprang back. It was stronger than I'd suspected, the life in him. I wondered if Stoner was faking, if he had perhaps seen Colin's act as a fortuitous opportunity for a sham, to scare us for some reason known only to Stoner, or perhaps for no reason. Stoner rather easily performed vile acts or said vile things with few reasons. Even then, I was not prepared for his strength, his massive reserves of emotion.

I rubbed my thumb along the tips of my fingers, studied my nails for the change in color from gray to silver that always came when the healing energies surged into me. They were shining. I touched Stoner's head, concentrated on the healing as I slowly moved my hands back from the crown to the wound, felt the skin beneath me tingle as the healing warmth closed the wound slowly. Then I moved my hands down to the affected arm, and healed it, an easier task, the bone obeying my summons and mending itself readily. Pain left Stoner's face and he looked quite asleep, just dozing against a wall.

"He's all right?" Colin asked.

"Yes," I said. "You're all right, aren't you, Stoner?"

"You knew I was conscious?" Stoner said without opening his eyes.

"I'm good at that sort of thing," I said.

"What a pity," Stoner said, finally opening his eyes, "I was hoping to eavesdrop on something momentous."

Colin appeared to want to hit his father again.

If Hannie hadn't told Colin and me stories—at night, beside fires, just at the edge of sleep—I would not have become the kind of historian I am. I might have been a dreary fact-collector.

I had not been used to stories. My father, intent on the creation and development of pastries, used up all his imagination in baking. My mother was merely used up much earlier. But Hannie! She could weave tales with such skill. She could take a line on a subject and develop it with vividness and appropriate imagery. I've tried to be like that, but I always digress too easily. Sailor's disease.

I remember after her death, just a few days later, Colin saying to me: "I miss the tales Mother used to tell us each night."

"Her stories, yes."

"Not *stories*, Sailor, not stories. They were history. Didn't you understand that? She was not making up what she told us. They were episodes from the history of her people. My people."

"Well, I knew they were about humans often, but—"

"But nothing. They were history. They really happened. They are about greatness, power, achievement. Subjects your world has filed away in an unused container. Considering your history, I can see where they might seem to be *stories*—to the unimaginative listener."

I brooded over that last jibe for some time. I didn't like being thought of as unimaginative, even more I hated being linked to the stolidity of my people. Even after Colin had corrected me, it took awhile for me to accept that what I had thought of as legend, as light fictions made up by a loving mother to entertain her son and his friend, were, in fact, true stories. Then I grew to treasure the tales even more. I think it was my love of Hannie's stories that made me so eager to embellish Colin's drab escapades into historical reports of wonder and heroism. A love of high adventure and chicanery impelled me more than my love for, or loyalty toward, Colin—or even more than any kind of love for history itself. It seems odd to me that Hannie, with her idealism and love of truth, should have told her stories so well that they turned me into a cynical liar in the name of idealism and truth.

I know my caretaker has been reading this notebook, sneaking peeks at my tiny handwriting, made tiny in case somebody tries to read it. I would have chosen to write in code but I am too old for code. Colin and I sent each other messages in code when we were children. I'd forgotten that. I've never written it down anywhere until here. What an historical find for anyone lucky enough to steal this notebook. I should burn it now.

I didn't think there was anything I could forget. I didn't think I would ever be an old man worried in any way about memory. My memory is like a waterfall, water against rocks, sprays dissipating into the air, droplets of water landing on dry pebbles. I didn't intend to be old, I always thought I could find a clever way of avoiding it, perhaps by becoming one of those vigorous persons of advanced age who walk along paths straightly in long strides, have clear eyes and rosy complexions, who smile just to show their teeth, who speak to display the clarity of tone in their voices. Instead I became *old*. Feeble. Continually sleepy. Often sleeping. Skin like sun-faded cloth. Pains in all parts of my body, especially in the fingers holding the Earth-made pen I write with, intense pain running up and down my index finger and thumb like a dancer practicing bigger and bigger leaps. I am getting carried away again. And of course I've lost my subject. This notebook will have to be burned not only to destroy the information I am recording, but to protect myself from shame at my misshapen ramblings.

Yes, the dough-lump of a caretaker has been reading these pages. Will read this section. What kind of insult can I lay before your eyes? Nothing I can say, no ugly image, no scathing metaphor, no stream of vituperation can do that particular job appropriately or effectively. To say you are no more than a speck of dirt falling on this page is to evaluate your worth too highly. I never can win over you and that's what I hate the most about my life just now.

I will not address you. I will not address him in these pages. He does not exist. He is a fictional character that I have invented in order to display graphically the sorry state that I, the great chronicler, have reached in my dotage. I am not cared for. I am alone. On an island. An old man, a notebook, and miles of crystalline red sand. No caretaker, no subtle exile on a country estate, none of the finer things to ease the pain of a dying man's last days. Just an actual unsubtle exile of a dangerous old man on a desolate isle with a smuggled notebook and barest subsistence. My tiny handwriting is not a defense against prying eyes but a desperate attempt to preserve the open space on pages that will eventually run out.

Colin is alive and in the capital, no longer thinking of his old friend whom he has ordered to a barren isle. Joline is by his side, sister-consort. Sailor became too dangerous. He had to be disposed of. But old friendships could not be denied. He could not be killed. Colin had lost too much of his Earth roots to assassinate a friend. Exile was the only solution. Colin is, of course, an old man, too. He ignores the foodstains on his chin. We could have grown old together, couldn't we? We did both grow old together. Joline doesn't let a day go by without laughing at Sailor, even Sailor in exile, Sailor dipping his toes in seawater that never before had welcomed him in spite of his name. Colin's greatness is all around him, in buildings, temples, great squares, great works dedicated to his name. He is a proper Earth-style hero. But Sailor is the one who'll be remembered when the great buildings and great works crumble and decay. Sailor who'll be seen as the prime mover and kingmaker. Sailor whose words will be remembered when the history behind them has crumbled and decayed. Sailor who'll—

I can see my caretaker shaking his head. The old man's really dotty now. How can you tell, you who do not exist except as a character on these pages?

My mind wanders. As Hannie might say to me in her curious way, what else is new? What else is new, Sailor?

Even though my body is now ruined with age and neglect, I can still summon up quite a clear memory of the pain caused by sharp rocks digging into my stomach, of the helplessness of my legs hanging over a cliff with my feet entangled in some kind of foliage I never did get a good look at. I can still remember the congestion in my chest as my torso pressed against what was left of the destroyed road, still feel Joline's hands tightly gripping each of my wrists as she tried futilely to pull me to her.

We had been walking along the road, a mountain path really, when we felt the first tremors. We hollered and shrieked like fools, but could not figure which way to run, whether to go uphill or downhill to safety. Up, Joline decided. Of course Joline decided. How could I have decided? We had only run two or three steps when a fiercer tremor came and the road fell out from under me. I can still feel the rush in my stomach as the ground instantly disappeared. Oddly, my fall was gentle, a mere sliding away downward, away from Joline. In an instant I was at her feet, looking up at her. Her face appeared calm. Later she told me she was numb, unable to believe what was happening. At first she didn't see that the path was half gone, it looked more to her like I had stumbled. I would have fallen to my death if my descent had not been blocked by a thick outgrowth, it may have been a roadside tree or bush that had slid down a little ways. Or perhaps it was merely an obstruction put there by a benevolent god who knew that I should be saved to fulfill my greater destiny. Look what destiny has been, a lifetime of lies leading to a privileged position as an old man drooling into his exquisite teacups.

Or perhaps the god's purpose was to prevent me from begging Joline to do deliciously carnal acts with me. Because carnality was the purpose of our trip up that mountain path. Of course I had told her we were merely taking one of our nature walks, to appreciate the grandeur of one of the rare lovely natural sites my planet had to offer. Later, when I told her the truth, when carnality was no longer possible for us, she told me she had known quite well the reason we had headed up that particular slope, the one with the plateau and many cozy resting nooks in its heights. The way of my life: my devious goals were blocked only by major obstacles, by earthquakes, floods, and the failure of my nerve.

We remained locked in position for a long while without further movement, myself half over a cliff, Joline holding on, the two of us hoping that another ground tremor would not come.

"I'm getting weak," Joline finally said.

"I feel numb," I said. "But I hurt, too."

"We've got to do something."

"What?"

"Can you hold onto that rock there instead of me?"

"I don't think I can reach—"

"Stretch."

I stretched, slowly and laboriously, with Joline holding tight to my wrists and trying to guide me toward the rock with what strength she had left. My arm muscles felt as if they were being torn to shreds. I finally managed to grab the rock and hold on, although it was slippery. I felt my hands might slip off at any moment. Joline gently let go my wrists and, before I could advise her against the wisdom of the move, wriggled down beside me, her head toward my feet.

"Keep your legs still," she ordered.

"It's hard."

"I think I can get your feet unhooked. There's really only one vine or something wrapped around the both of your ankles."

"Joline—"

"Keep quiet. I have to concentrate, damn it."

I could feel her hands on my ankles as she worked them underneath the vine. I could also feel her body against my side and I could not stop thinking erotic thoughts in spite of my potentially fatal predicament. Her bare leg was next to my head and I think I would have stretched my neck toward it, to kiss her there, except the action would have required an anatomical accomplishment I couldn't possibly manage without my hands slipping off the rock.

"I've got it, Sailor. Work your feet upward. Easy now. There."

"Now what?"

"Crawl. Make believe this is only a small hill. It's the only way."

Working slowly and pulling at the rock, I crawled. Joline, who had worked her body backward and upward more swiftly, helped me the last part of the way. Standing up, I saw that the road ahead was in even worse shape than the stretch we were on. There was no longer a route to the plateau.

"Sailor, look!"

There was a fire in the center of the camp below. People were scurrying about. Joline was already several steps ahead of me down the path. I followed. By the time we reached camp the flames were under control. Joline and I cared for two men and a woman who had been slightly burned by the fire. It was lucky their injuries were minor, for I had little energy left in me for the healing. When we were done, Joline hugged me and I settled for that, quite happily, forgetting momentarily my schemes for the plateau. At that time there always seemed to be other opportunities. We fail often merely by expecting further opportunities.

I awoke feeling good today. Light streamed in through my row of bedroom windows, early morning odors brightened my mood. I decided to take a walk on my own. An actual walk without consulting my caretaker, without asking him if he thought it would be all right, without, I hoped, even seeing him for most of the morning.

I went to my favorite area of the garden. The garden is designed according to Earth customs, arranged from stories Hannie told and some very practical information provided me by Dominique, who had considerable talent with flowers and plants.

My favorite area is a square of Nulqua-tulip hybrids I created from my own native fruit plant and flowers I grew from some forgotten seeds I found in a closet at Q Colony. I managed to devise a flower that had the beautiful spiked leaves of the Nulqua plant (along with a vestigial stub of vermilion fruit hidden delicately at the center of the leaves) and the lovely petals of tulips, standing straight above the Nulqua leaves. The effect is quite impressive.

I had a bench installed where I could observe my creation in all its various stages, during all seasons. I was quite disheartened when I discovered that my caretaker sat on this bench, his body turned away from me. He had not heard me approach and he started when I spoke: "What are you doing here?"

His face white, he stood up quickly, mumbled he was sorry. There were tears in his eyes. In his hand he clutched a picture, a photo taken by an Earth camera, I believe. I pointed to the picture, asked what was it. He said it was a photo of his dead wife, and quickly put it in his jacket pocket. I wanted very much to get a look at it, but it was clear he didn't want me to, so I remained silent. After a moment of embarrassment on both sides, I said: "I'm sorry to interrupt you."

"It's all right. I shouldn't be here. You told me. I just felt... it is no matter what I felt."

"Tell me."

"No."

He walked away without asking my permission to leave. I almost hollered to him to return and endure the proper rituals. After he left I tried to sit down and enjoy my flowers, but I could not. I couldn't concentrate on their colors and form. All I saw was an arrangement of flowers, any flowers might have done. The air was still fresh, the morning still bright, the garden still beautiful, but I no longer could enjoy any of that.

I think my caretaker has run away, or simply disappeared. I haven't seen him all day, not since our awkward encounter in the garden. There has been no sign of him. No tea, no massage, no veiled insults in the form of polite requests. He has not been where he has usually been every other day at the same times in the same places. Our people have a very intricate sense of shame, but I can't see where I violated that sense in any way. Yes, he was crying when I came into the garden. I cry sometimes. He, I know, has seen that, so why should it be different for him?

I've spent most of the day watching for him, waiting for

him to sneak up on me. I haven't written a thing in the notebook until now. There aren't many pages left. I'll have to write even smaller. Scholars will have to use lenses to read it, if it survives me. It won't survive me. Perhaps I'll destroy it now. There, I've torn it up. Now I'll burn it. It makes a lovely flame. I can see words wrinkle up, leap upward, then grow black and burn away.

Where is he?

Where is Dominique now? I keep thinking of her, writing of her, as if she were dead. But I don't know that she is dead. I only know that, after Stoner's death, she said there was no more reason for her to remain at Q Colony. She said she didn't know what had kept her and Stoner there anyway, especially after the mission itself had been canceled.

If she is alive now anywhere, and it doesn't seem likely she would be, I wonder if she knows what happened to Colin. I'd like to talk to her, find out how the intervening years have treated her. Did she just age, settle into comfort, opt for an ascetic life in a cave? How could she have disappeared so thoroughly? Colin had people looking for her, I know that. But some time had passed by then, and it is not surprising they found no trace of her.

I recall Dominique complimenting me on my linguistic skills.

"You speak our language very well," she said.

I told her she spoke the language of my people quite well, too, although she had a certain difficulty with certain nasal sounds. She smiled rather strangely and said:

"I had a good teacher. But your language is very difficult for us, Sailor. There is so much similarity in its sounds. For a while we could only distinguish two clear phonemes. That's how you got your name, your people, that is."

I nodded, not wanting to discuss the hateful sound of the name, especially when it was spoken by a human.

"You cringed a little bit just then," she said. "It's the name, Oonaa, isn't it?"

"Yes, afraid so."

She smiled.

"Our people have always been very adept at naming things,

at naming peoples. We like to have convenient names for people, and we don't seem to mind whether or not they are insulting. Well, Sailor, there's a long history to it, that's all I can tell you."

Then, without pausing for the change of subject, she said, "You are in love with Joline, aren't you?"

I didn't know how to respond. Dominique was Joline's mother, after all. There are customs. I didn't know the custom with humans. With my own people, I would have just said, "yes, I love Joline," but then my people rarely talked openly of love. I suppose we loved so clearly, so openly, that certain questions didn't have to be asked. I have also found out since that humans place strange emphases on their own rituals of love. Many things have to be said and done, often in a particular order. Declarations have to be made, ritual utterances spoken. I had to talk with a mother who showed no actual interest in her daughter in order to prove that I was a worthy match to her, even though she didn't really care about that. I discovered this later.

"Yes, I do love her," I said finally to Dominique.

"How much?"

I laughed.

"Is there a scale to judge such things?"

"Not really, I suppose. I care about you, Sailor. I'm trying to find out how painful your love might turn out to be."

"Is there a way of predicting that?"

"With Joline, I think maybe. I'm sorry, I know I'm being cryptic. You have to understand that I see just how much of her father is in her, and there is rather more than I've ever been comfortable with. Not as much of Henry as in Colin, but enough. Henry uses people, always has. So does Colin, as you know only too well. Joline *tries* to use them. She doesn't do so well because she's so young, but I very much fear she's learning. I've watched her with you. Right now you're her toy."

Suddenly she hugged me. Tightly, hurting my shoulders. She had never done that before. She had hardly ever touched me before, except for the one time we were drunk in the abandoned city.

"I changed my mind, Dominique. I will go. Leave Q Colony. We'll leave together."

She didn't respond, merely hugged me all the harder. We never talked about leaving again.

My caretaker's back. He looks terrible. The outside corners of his eyes seem to have dropped, as if responding to a special pull of gravity. His mouth looks dehydrated and brittle. His body has become smaller, thinner. All in the space of a day.

For a long time now he's stood in the doorway of the house, looking out at me. I have directed a few comments toward him, talked to him the way I always do, but he is mostly unresponsive. He offered to bring me tea, then moved away quite slowly when I said I wanted some. When the tea finally came, it was cold. I told him that, complained at length in my most grating voice. He merely nodded, took the cup back from me, and returned to the darkness of the house.

He's left the doorway. I don't know where he's gone to. He ignored all my attempts to find out where he's been, too. I don't want to see him again for a while. I hope he grooms himself before he reemerges. His hair has been uncombed. I didn't notice that until I thought of it now. It's unlike him to appear anywhere with disheveled hair.

I clutch this notebook like a lifeline. No, that's too stale a way of putting it. I am afraid even to put it down anywhere. Some part of me must always be in contact with it, I can't allow it to be stolen from me now. Not by him or anyone. It's what I have left. After Colin, after Joline, after Stoner, after Dominique, it's what I have left. Even though I've lost control over my memories, it's what I have left. I have tried to see again those parts of my life that have been destroyed by subsequent lies or hidden away because they didn't fit our historical goals. I'll never know which of my memories are true anymore. They could all be lies. I'll never write everything down in this notebook that I intended to. I can't possibly complete all of it. It's my way. Wishy-washy. The sailor without navigational instruments. I may die before I can even fill every page of the notebook. I don't like that thought. I don't like leaving blank pages as a legacy. All pages must be filled. Or I could simply forget about the blank pages, destroy the notebook before I have finished. Could I do that? I could. No, I couldn't.

After I healed his minor wounds, Stoner became friendly with me. He could be quite affable. I began to believe he genuinely liked me. I suppose he didn't really, you could never tell with him, but my antipathy toward him did diminish under his determined onslaught of back patting and good cheer.

"I'd like to adopt you," he said to me one night. He was very drunk. I had invented this little wine that improved on the previous Q Colony liquid stock, and he had misjudged his ability to consume it.

"I have parents," I said.

"But they're Oonaas."

Stoner never perceived the insult in the term.

"I am one of those, too," I said, realizing that my attempt not to say the word itself was awkward and foolish.

"Maybe. But most of the time, Sailor, you're so human you frighten me."

"Why's that?"

"Ignore it. I was just being flippant. I don't even want to adopt you. I was just making conversation."

Afraid of his drunkenness, I decided not to ask for explanations from him. Now I wish that I had.

"I almost killed him," Colin screamed at me the night after his struggle with his father. We were in the Q Colony shack assigned to us as sleeping quarters. Joline stood next to the doorway, a bottle of my wine clutched in one hand. Once in a while, she took a swig from it. She licked the rim of the bottle after each swig. Colin had already polished off the wine I'd given him, had started on another bottle. His eyes were still clear, but his speech was a little thick.

"If you hadn't healed him, Sailor, he'd be dead now. I'd've killed him"

"That's not true," I said. "He wasn't even hurt that badly. You cut off some air for a short period perhaps. Whatever, he passed out. He was nowhere near death."

"Dad has steel inside his neck," Joline said. "If you try to kill him, you only cut up your hands."

"I felt the life go out of him," Colin muttered.

"How do you know?" I asked. "Have you killed anyone yet?"

"Yes, I have. That boy back in our city."

"I'd forgotten that. What I get for trying to give smug comfort, I guess. But that was with a rock. You didn't choke him. You didn't *feel* life going out of him. And you didn't really feel it going out of Stoner either."

"He was going to die, I know it."

Colin was on the verge of tears. I realized that, if he cried, it would be drunken sorrow, but I wanted to encourage it anyway. Anything to diminish his complicated hatreds.

"Next time you'll do a better job of it," Joline said. Colin glanced at her, narrowed his eyes.

"A better job? You want me to kill him, Joline?"

She looked toward the doorway, as if there might be a spy listening just outside.

"Do what you want," she said laconically. "Whatever you do to him or he does to you, I'll be cheering the winner along. Makes no difference to me who it is."

I tried to see her eyes in the dimness. I didn't like her talking like that. It made me examine my feelings about her, and I didn't want to do that.

"I don't want to kill him," Colin said. "I want to understand him, want to know what he's thinking. But I don't want to kill him."

She shrugged, took a couple steps into the light. Her eyes seemed blank, emotionless.

"Fools, both of you," she said. I remembered her saying that the first time we saw her.

"Joline—" Colin said.

"Fools," she said. She turned around and, staggering just a bit, the wine bottle held against her hip like a sidearm, walked out of the shack.

Before Colin and I arrived at Q Colony, there was an adventure. I chose never to write about it, although Colin wanted me to. At least he asked me to often enough, usually after a drinking session or an act of exceptional cruelty. I could have turned the escapade into quite a set of delicate lies—or, as he might have called it, legend. However, my participation in the adventure was too strong, I didn't want to turn my own life into lies. I could do it for him, but not for myself. You will note that, in my histories, I rarely appear. I gave Colin the focus, implied that I was there from time to time to give my lies the ring of an eyewitness's historical truth. But everything I say I did in my histories I actually did, even when the event occurs in the midst of a lie.

Even though I never wrote of this adventure, Colin used to tell his version of it, sometimes when he had had too much to drink, sometimes as a whimsical device to influence some fool by including him or her in on a secret. His listeners looked upon the tale as a gift, a piece of unwritten history that they themselves could tell about in similar manipulative moments. I hated hearing Colin's version. It was not as imaginative as mine would have been. Besides, he lied about my participation, ignored my cowardice, made something of a secondary hero out of me, a role I never could have actually played. Because he told it so often in so many drunken moods, the story finally did get circulated and has been included in other historians' works and interpretations, usually to help support a fallacy of their own devising.

To give Colin's version credit, I have to say that the creature was enormous, the largest living being I had seen up to that time. It was covered with gray scales, had a beak like a bird and gills like a fish. It came out of a murky gray pond almost the color of its scales, and it looked at Colin with indifference. Colin's face broke into a wide smile, and he whooped with delight.

We had found the nameless creature and the out-of-the-way pond due to Colin's incessant questioning of the roadside nomads we encountered during our trek along a few of our world's rare paved highways. Several nomads had been on the way to some kind of annual market in some city I had never visited and have, in fact, still never visited. It was a city that executed criminals immediately after a verdict, a verdict that could sometimes come from a stupid judge. They never seemed to employ the kind of emotionless objective judge which so many of our tribes and communities have. I never understood such objectivity, such cold disposition of judgment and counsel, and often have believed judges were frauds. But our people set great store in the wisdom of these freaks who, by a quirk of nature, are able to view any situation objectively.

Colin often talked of going to war against this city of quick punishment. I always advised him against it, not because there were any overwhelming political reasons, but because I was terrified of being captured by such a vengeful people.

The way to the pond was treacherous. Colin always described it as a route filled with poisonous reptiles and growling beasts. It was not that. But there were many rocks that seemed as sharply faceted as jewels, and I could feel their points cutting my feet and legs through my shoes and clothing. Later in the day, after the adventure, I inspected my legs and feet and found tiny punctures and scratches all over them.

After the creature made its appearance, which occurred after Colin ran several times around the pond, hollering and beating the surface of the water with a large stick, it glanced around and, curving its neck, put its head back into the water, then settled its whole body back from whence it came. It had clearly not been impressed. Colin cursed it for a brainless creature, said it was probably no more than an overgrown cell whose cilia passed for limbs.

Colin, of course, always portrayed this moment as a confrontation, a meeting of man and monster, with man showing his mettle by staring down the awesome monster. Sometimes the monster spat fire and emitted smoke from its nostrils. When Colin used this detail, I always had a sharp memory of Hannie telling us some Earthly legend in which just such phenomena occurred. I often wondered, after Colin told me her tales were actual history, whether Earth was really such a wondrous place. But the stories helped me to understand the urges of a people who would leave their home and seek their fortunes on barren worlds like mine.

When it appeared that the creature was not going to resurface, Colin and I sat on the bank of the pond for a long while.

I didn't know what to do. I did not particularly want to join battle with this monster, it might forever end our grandiose plans for Colin's rise in the world. I felt nervous, afraid of what Colin was going to do, with of course a very clear inkling of what he was going to do. I was lucky, in a way. There were just the two of us, no army surrounding us as there would be later. That army, or rather its officers, distrusted me so violently that I always felt their threatening presence at my back, even when I was miles from them. Our army always was a mangy bunch, opportunists out to steal whatever glory they could, believing what Colin told them, willing to kill each other if it would help them achieve a higher rank, always ready to replace me at Colin's car. I often wondered what drove them. I think they were gamblers, speculating on our success, playing the odds against the dismal lives they would have otherwise led. You could see in their eyes that, if we brought back riches, they'd know immediately how to bank, invest, and enlarge them. I was not able to associate with them on any but the most necessary levels. I felt especially isolated then. I always felt isolated among Colin's followers, the warriors, sycophants, and politicians alike. I suppose that, besides Joline and at rare intervals Dominique, Colin was my only connection with emotion, friendship, knowledge, and intelligence. Others just did not care for me. Not because of any particular flaw in my character, or I suppose not, but simply because I was different. I thought differently, acted differently, even moved a bit differently. They hated my hesitations, all of them, whether they were hesitations of speech, action, or decision. Those who fell in battle, I regret their passing. Those who survived, I regret their continued existence.

And Sailor is wandering again.

"I have a plan," Colin said abruptly and stood up.

"I've been waiting for that," I said, while remaining seated on the pond bank. "Why do we need a plan? Couldn't we just say we've seen a quite impressive creature, and then leave?"

Colin smiled.

"Wait a while to start your wavering, Sailor. Right now we're going to build a boat."

"A boat? I don't know how to build a boat. Neither one of

us has ever gone on water in any kind of craft. What do you know about building a boat?"

He shrugged.

"Authenticate your name. Build me a boat. A raft, that's all I ask."

"I don't know how to—"

"Sailor, it doesn't have to be a good boat, we needn't have a decorated prow or a working rudder. Just a raft. We're only going to sail it here, on this pond."

"And then perhaps we can disturb the—"

"Exactly."

"I see."

"We're going to, as you say, disturb it. Churn its waters, get it to raise its ugly head again."

"Well, I wouldn't call it ugly exactly."

"Please, Sailor, none of your hemming and hawing over words. It's ugly because I call it ugly. That's how words come to mean something. You start taking a stand at the level of the word."

"But—"

"Sailor. We'll also need weapons. Oil them or whatever's necessary."

"Then you're planning to kill—"

"What did you think? We were going to make a treaty with it?"

"But it's just a dumb creature, a rare one as far as I know. I've never heard of any monstrous pond-dwellers before. It didn't attack us. It's more worthy of study than—"

"Are you going to argue technicalities for the entire rest of your life?"

"Probably."

"Do the job, Sailor."

I set to work on building the boat and fashioning the weapons. The boat. My, my. I have been glorified in Colin's drunken fabrications and, in historians' interpretations, I have been almost deified for the construction of that puny raft. Sometimes I craft the vessel after a vision. Sometimes I merely set myself the task and finish it with quiet and determined efficiency. Actually I hacked and tied, cursed and spat, putting together a grotesque flat boat, a raft, from memories of pictures I'd seen of the real thing. I almost chopped off a finger with my axe. Done, I didn't expect the raft to float for more than a minute. When we tentatively placed it onto the pond's surface, I expected to see water seep between and through every piece of wood, I expected to watch it sink like a stale Nulqua biscuit. Amazingly, it stayed afloat, drifting lazily from side to side. The pieces of wood in our various museums that are claimed to be parts of the raft are not authentic, none of them. We left the raft behind us afterward, at the edge of the pond, never looked back at it. I suspect it rotted away soon enough.

When, after hours of toil (while Colin paced around the pond looking quite ferocious), I had completed the raft, Colin told me he was pleased with my work. I felt pleased by his approval. Actually, I was very impressed with myself.

Colin strode purposely and fiercely into the water and firmly placed his right foot upon the raft. The boat slid away beneath his foot and he nearly stumbled. Pulling it back to him, he looked as if he were going to punish the raft before using it again. However, with his next try he managed to get onto the raft, somewhat awkwardly, his body swaying and his legs nearly buckling. Turning very carefully, the raft's erratic shiftings making him nearly lose balance, he looked back at me and shouted:

"Coming, Sailor?"

"I'd like to think that over."

He clearly resented my joke.

"Get out here!" he hollered.

As I crawled onto the raft (hands first instead of feet first, an unheroic though easier way to board a raft), I gasped: "I thought you might confront your 'enemy' alone."

Colin ignored my verbal insubordination and checked out his weapon, a crossbow I had devised from Hannie's description of just such a weapon. I had made a few adaptations along artillery lines. It was a long-barreled weapon with a pressure chamber in its barrel. When the pressure chamber was set and released, an arrow emerged from the arrow repository and settled onto the bow. At the pulling of the trigger, the arrow was sent flying with such force behind it that anything that got in its way was usually completely pierced. Since the arrow shaft was as sharp as a thin knife blade, the target was often sliced or partially severed by the missile. If the weapon was in proper condition, there was generally no more then a ten-second pause before the pressure in the chamber was restored and another arrow could be released from the repository. We used it occasionally in our clumsy battles, but it was never a really efficient war weapon. Hannie thought it clumsily de-signed but felt there was something quite graceful about its firing action. It never felt comfortable in my hands. That par-ticular crossbow met a similar fate as that of the raft, in spite of the many relic-pieces of it you see everywhere. The arrow displayed at Council Hall is, however, authentic. I brought it back to the city with me years later and donated it to the hall's small museum.

"I might be of more use to you staying on land," I said to Colin as soon as I could manage to stand up on the raft. "In case anything happens to the raft or—"

A hint of scorn in his look.

"Sometimes, Sailor, I think your cowardly protests are gen-uine."

What could I say to him then? If I told the truth, said that of course my cowardice was real, it might have annoyed him, hurt in some way our friendship. If I said I was just joking, I would have felt the pains in my stomach that always came when I lied. I said nothing, got the pains anyway.

Awkwardly I put one foot back into the water, found the stony bed of the pond and gave us a weak push, enough to set us toward the placid center of that unformidable body of water. The pond surface had odd slimy-looking items floating upon it, several small scummy algae islands.

Colin's version of our escapade always had the two of us standing tall and straight so that we seemed to skim raftless across the water. Of course the pond was a massive lake, sometimes even a churning vast sea.

Soon we were drifting around the center of the pond, in still waters. In spite of our motionlessness I began to feel sick. However, I could think of no way to hide any regurgitated material from Colin's scornful eyes. I carefully sat down and tried to clear my head by concentrating on eye-focus. Colin produced a handful of small rocks from the pocket of his tunic. I remembered him collecting them during his frantic pacing and at the time wondering why. Tossing them two or three at a time, he began to throw them into the water.

"Why're you throwing the rocks away?" I asked, in the midst of gasps caused by my swallowing to keep from throwing up.

"Not throwing them away, just want to get the monster's attention, force him to the surface again."

Even at that time, before coaxing the creature surfaceward, he was ready to embellish the adventure.

"Why do you persist in calling it a monster?"

"Isn't he?"

"He's just an animal, a pond-creature, a bit oversized perhaps, maybe even an ocean creature trapped here by some long ago geological shift, but just an animal who'd no doubt prefer quiet naps in his habitat. He's hardly a monster."

"If I say he is, he is."

"Suit yourself."

"If your face gets any grayer, I may mistake you for the monster and deal with you accordingly."

"I might prefer that, believe me."

"Sailor, this is just a pond, wait'll you get out on an—"

The waters around us started churning. Just a few waves at first, ripples. Colin motioned for me to stand and make ready. In pace and tempo the churning in my stomach was well ahead of the pond's churning. I brought up my crossbow, set its pressure chamber. Colin, without looking at his weapon, did the same. He continued to stare at the murky surface of the water, ready for the second appearance of our monster. A small whirlpool formed and the action of the water increased, sending our raft skimming back toward shore.

"Get me a paddle!" Colin shouted.

"What's a paddle?"

If he intended to respond to me, the answer was lost forever in the further disruption of the water. Sending high curled waves of water away from him, the top of the creature's head broke surface. And that, for the moment, was it. All we could see was the top of its head, what looked like a soft short-furred epidermal layer, its smooth surface disfigured in many places by wartlike gray bumps. The wavelike aspect of these bumps seemed to imitate the gentle waves which were then waning in a circle around the cranial hill. As our boat gentled down and assumed a calm floating state, Colin and I stared at what little our creature had chosen to reveal of itself. Both thinking, I suppose, of the gray monster beneath the gray iceberg. We were waiting, I guess, for it to do something. It perhaps was not waiting for anything special at all.

Slowly Colin raised his crossbow and took steady aim at the center of the head.

I touched his arm, whispered, "What're you doing?"

"I left the city, came to this pond, constructed a raft, and floated out here on this foul-smelling water, with you beside me on the verge of throwing up, for the sole purpose of bagging this monster. That's what I'm doing now."

"No!"

"What's the matter now, Sailor?"

"You can't kill the creature this way. I would argue against the logic of that."

"You would argue against—are we to debate on the rules of killing a slimy pond-dweller who hasn't any more awareness than one of those rocks?"

"How can you be sure it has no awareness, how can you know that?"

"I saw it. It saw me. I recognized in its eyes an intelligence somewhat less than the average fish. Is that a sufficient explanation? May I make the kill now?"

"You should think it over first."

"Think it over? Sailor, as a man of action you need further instruction." He lowered the weapon, stared at me. "All right, what would you have me do?"

"If you must kill the creature, at least make some sport out of it. You can't send a missile into its brain while it's peacefully resting in its home waters."

"What should I do then? It shows no signs of moving for the next day or so."

"Provoke it, I guess."

"Provoke it? How?"

"I don't know, but what kind of exploit would it be to tell around campfires if you bag it by sneaking up on it and killing it unawares?"

"I see. All right, we'll provoke it then."

Suddenly I realized what I had just said, the cause I had just argued and its ramifications to me. I could have had Colin shoot the damned creature, and we could both of us have slipped back to shore in a healthy condition. Why did I have to argue the ethics of the matter? Why not just let the huntsman perform the kind of cowardly act that distinguishes huntsmen throughout the universe? Suddenly I just wanted to get back to shore, get behind a tree and let my digestive system finish what it had started. This was only the first time I was trapped in this particular ethical dilemma. I was forever cautioning Colin to act fairly, in the name of logic, and then putting my own life on the line as a result.

So Colin provoked. He started to throw the rest of his rocks furiously at the creature's head. He was using all his strength, I could see. He grunted with the release of each rock. The rocks hit the head and bounced and rolled into the water. When all the rocks were used up, we returned to staring at the un-moving island of fur and warts.

"It may take a little more than that to provoke it," I said.

"Shut up, Sailor," Colin shouted.

He got so mad he stamped his foot, not exactly the best way to express your anger on a raft. The back edge of the raft came part way out of the water while I was busy falling forward into the murky pond. Of course I hadn't thought to strip for action and I still had heavy clothing on, which made me flounder around harder. In my confusion I also had not inhaled before falling beneath the surface of the water. Feeling as if my lungs were about to burst, a physical discomfort that at least took precedence over my nausea, I whirled a half-circle underwater and came face to face with our monster.

Its eyes watched me, looked me over as if I might be some new kind of bait. I know it sounds odd to say it, especially considering my endangered state at the time, but the creature's eyes seemed sad to me. They seemed aware of my imminent death and sorry there was such futility in the existence of sentient creatures. Fright forced me to work my arms and legs frantically and furiously, and I broke surface, scraping the side of my face against the edge of the raft. Colin's hands were on my arms instantly, and he pulled me back onto the raft. When I could breathe again, and talk, he told me I had hardly been underwater two seconds. I insisted it must have been more time than that. I'd had time to assess a monster's psyche. I had stared into its eyes a whole minute at least. Now I ask myself how I could have possibly seen the creature's eyes so vividly in those thick murky waters, especially how could I have seen enough of them to make such conclusions about them.

Before we could decide what to do next, the creature made its own decision. It decided to stir. The island of its head rose slowly out of the water, revealing soon those eyes that had acknowledged my existence within the world of its pond. I know, I can be accused of superimposing my later sight of the eyes on the earlier event. That's logical, I can't argue it. But I'll always vividly remember seeing those eyes while I was in the water, and that's all I can say about it. When the monster's head had cleared the pond surface, it turned our way and examined us with the same cold detachment with which it had stared at Colin during its first appearance. Out the corner of my eye (I dared not turn my head to look), I sensed Colin raising his crossbow. The creature turned its head away, raised more of its massive gray body out of the water. Perhaps the body was not really as massive as it seemed at the time. Perhaps it merely looked massive in the small pond, against an ill-defined landscape. Perhaps it was only a medium-size creature.

Colin was about to shoot. I put my arm on his.

"Damn it," he said, "you'll deflect my aim."

"That's what I want to do. Don't kill it."

"Ah, but it's so enormous, what a prize!"

"Let it be. You want achievements, not prizes."

"There's little difference, little difference. Let me aim before it swamps the boat!"

Each movement of the large animal was sending out bigger waves that were setting the raft rocking precariously. I could see that Colin was determined to have his way, shoot the damned thing. I just wanted the whole adventure over and I'm afraid, in my cowardice, lost my sympathetic feelings toward the creature. I raised my own weapon, to have a second shot ready in case Colin's first went awry. He steadied himself, took aim again, then waited an unconscionably long time before firing. When he did, the sound of it was like a little whine, not the usual blast that I had expected. The arrow went straight to its mark and entered the head of the creature, who seemed not to notice but continued apparently to loll in the water, sending waves toward us almost playfully. Duty perhaps called for me to fire my shot then, but I couldn't. So long as the creature was not attacking us, I saw no reason to shoot. Colin had his second shot ready in record time. His arrow seemed to float into position and had hardly touched the notch before he pulled the trigger. The missile traveled in an arc and entered the front of the creature's neck, or the blob of flesh that passed for a neck, at a slight angle. Gray blood spurted forth, and still the creature didn't seem to notice any change in its condition. Again I held back my shot. Colin was perhaps too eager on his third shot, or perhaps he was, as he said later, really aiming for the monster's eye. As the arrow gouged and sliced the gray eyeball, the creature made its first sound, a low moan that had in it only the barest hint of pain, or even anger. Its head turned back toward us, in a move faster than I anticipated, and its good eye seemed to discover us for the first time, as if we had been too tiny for him to discern in the earlier times he'd looked our way. It stared at us. It seemed to me for a moment to question our presence in its waters. Colin's next shot, accompanied by his yelp of excitement or possibly panic, just missed its mark and sailed past the creature. Then, with a roar that sharply contrasted with its earlier more gentle moan, the creature started to move toward us. It seemed to hover over us, ready to destroy us.

So, unable to talk myself out of acting, I finally shot.

My arrow went into its neck above Colin's earlier gash, and continued upward, twisting and slicing its way into the neck. Whatever was left beneath that heavy skin that might have been vital, my arrow struck. The creature died abruptly and flopped forward into the water beside our raft. Its wake very nearly sucked us downward, and we were flung back toward shore.

The creature did not take Colin into its mouth and chew on him for a while before Colin's victory. The creature did not spew fire or shake its gray head impressively against the gray sky. The creature did not holler out a curse in our language calling down all the forces of wrath upon us, although if he had it would explain certain of our later fates. At least the creature did none of this back then. It did them later in Colin's versions, in which incidentally the killing shot was his and not mine, and the subsequent adaptations by dreamy historians.

The creature did sink immediately out of sight. Our boat did hit a particularly rocky bit of shore, flinging both Colin and me off its ill-made surface, against large boulders. The impact with rock knocked both of us out.

When we came to, I doubt either of us felt any exhilaration from the experience of having had an adventure.

There were times, when I heard the later versions of the incident, that I would momentarily wonder what really had happened, Colin's version of the event or mine. I wondered if the knock on my head had somehow caused me to lose my memory, especially those parts in which Colin or I acted with a particular heroism.

Before the incident it seemed as if we had just been wandering. I always thought Colin was merely looking for adventure. Maybe he was. Whenever I brought up the subject of Q Colony at that time, he found reasons not to seek it. After the incident, he announced we were going to find Q Colony now. It was as if the road to the colony led away from the pond. I always thought it odd he never told his father about the killing of the pond-creature.

I often wonder if Hannie would have told us her wonderful tales if she had known the uses Colin and I would make of them, the ways we would reinterpret history in the terms of childhood stories that had originated on a planet far across the universe from us. In a sense we imposed on a rather mythologically poor culture a secondhand mythology that, it turned out, was quite fitting for it. Colin was always willing to take one of our sublimely ordinary, even repellent, escapades and transform it into some sort of transcendentally bizarre and mysterious adventure.

The magical hordes, a favorite legend among our people now, were in reality a nomadic tribe of rather emaciated-looking travelers. They didn't attack us, we ambushed them. They had no real powers, only an unusual kind of shell-tent whose force-field barriers proved individually impenetrable and caused Colin to wait until they were on the move to attack them. They had no political significance, were not on the way to attack anyone, had no awesome leaders. I think of that event with sickness in my stomach, especially since I stood with Colin and Joline, and killed two of the tribesmen myself.

And what of all the other adventures, other lies, many of whose details were mine?

The Conquering of the Dream City—a relatively uninhabited village with a defective barrier. The citizens had merely kept the malfunction a secret. Nobody ever attacked anybody anymore, they thought. We attacked. The city seemed to crumble to dust at a touch. No citizen survived to give the lie to our rather attractive version in which the dream city appears shimmering upon the empty desert and the troops of a darkly beautiful queen, transformed from the real village mayor, an old crone, swoops down on our peaceful army. (By that time we had collected a few ragtag individuals Colin chose to call an army.)

The Battle with the Knight of the Red Beard—an especially Hannie-influenced tale. A farmer blocked Colin's path on a day when Colin was feeling quite irritable. They argued who should step aside. The farmer, who indeed did have a red beard, untrimmed and looking like bent pieces of rusty wire, moved to the side with a mock courtesy. Colin felt the move made him look bad in front of his army, who probably were not paying that much attention, who probably were grousing about their current lack of pillage profits. Colin let loose a string of insults even a mild-tempered farmer would have been hard put to ignore. Red Beard was hardly mild-tempered. He attacked Colin in a leap I'd not have thought possible for one of his size and girth. The fight itself was a good brawl. The army loved it. Soldiers gathered in a circle, cheered Colin on, made

bets among themselves. I was irritated with those who bet on
the farmer. The legend is quite correct in saying the farm-
er/knight had the upper hand for much of the fight. Colin kept
going, more because he was stubborn than able. The historical
version errs in the part where Colin picks up Red Beard, holds
him for a long moment over his head, then flings him at a
nearby tree. The part about Colin winning the fight is true
enough, except it leaves out the horror of it by having him
pierce Red Beard with a sword. Actually, he strangled the
farmer in front of all of us. The strangling went on for a long
time, much too long a time, before life finally went out of the
farmer's staring colorless eyes. To this day I don't understand
why nobody from our army has stepped forward with a truthful
version. The part which says Red Beard was honored by being
placed on a high bier and burned is also wrong. We left the
man's broken body behind on the road.

The Spell of the Enchanted Princess—this one's a bit too
sordid for an old man to think about in detail now. Suffice it
to say that Colin spent some time under her roof and in her
bedchamber, then exacted the penalties of the conqueror, taking
enough loot to satisfy our avaricious army. Years later I discovered that her people had developed their own tale from this
lurid and ludicrous escapade, one in which the clever princess
swindles the barbarian conqueror. And this without Hannie's
tales to guide them.

The Abduction by the Twin Magicians—well, they really
were twins, but the closest thing to magic they performed was
stealing into our camp, kidnapping Colin, and transporting him
back to one of their twin cities. One brother controlled a city
on the northeast side of the river; the other's was on the south-
west. The only reason they abducted our leader was that they
heard of our plundering travels and feared we would attack
their rather easily defensible cities. We had no intention of
attacking them. We knew when the odds were against us. They
believed we could pierce their barriers with our own brand of
magical swords. (Our embellishments, as they traveled ahead
of us, did have certain strategic advantages.) They held Colin
in a damp dungeon for several days before they remembered
they should ask for a ransom. Originally they had just intended

to separate the leader from his troops. The ransom was rather easy to supply. We had riches by then, and the brothers asked for too little. Over Colin's protests that we must revenge ourselves on the twin cities, Joline and I managed to convince our army to travel on and leave the cities alone. I think they realized our chances were slim anyway. The part of the story that has me disguising myself as a minstrel and singing our plans under Colin's jail window has no factual basis. Everyone who has ever heard me sing already doubts that part.

The Slaying of the Faceless Dragon—I don't know where this one originates, not from anything I was witness to certainly. I do find it a rather attractive tale and wish I had had some part in creating it. But, unfortunately, it was Colin's totally. I'm rather taken with the incident in which he, after slaying the dragon heroically, takes a cloth from his belt and wipes away the dragon's face to discover nothing underneath, just smooth skin. There's an uncharacteristic sadness to the way Colin mourns the faceless dragon that would have moved me had I been able to see the events that inspired the tale. I doubt Colin ever felt sad about such a victim. Outside of the pond-creature, most of the animal life we encountered wasn't particularly colorful or even threatening. I'm rather glad about that. I've always liked—liked, not loved—animals, and I'd hate to think that we'd gone around killing them off just to add some spice to Colin's dramatic restructurings of his life.

And there was the Rampaging Giant—he was tall and he did fret a bit. Or the Mesa of Horse-Headed Men—they were homely and they did stampede us. The Flying Pirates from the Moons—they did seem to swoop out of the sky at us, but it was from trees. Even though they had the advantage of surprise, they were easy prey for us. I don't know why they attacked us in the first place, and have never been able to find out who they were or where they came from.

So Hannie's tales, derived from her own history, designed to entertain two irritatingly restless youngsters, became twisted parodies through our successful lying. What uses imagination can be put to! If we had not allowed the actual events to filter through our imaginations, if we had reported the truth instead of glorious deeds amplified from sordid misadventures, Colin would not have captured the public's attention and could not have been the right person in the right place when the opportunity for violent revolution came. Amazing what stories can do.

Hannie came and sat beside me today. I couldn't see her, of course. I am not growing senile. I am fully aware that she is dead. I am talking about ghosts here. We don't have too many stories of ghosts among our people, a few here and there, for the nomadic tribes, for the peoples beyond the sea. Farmers have quite a collection of ghost tales. But, by and large, my knowledge of ghosts comes from Hannie. She told Colin and me of ghosts on Earth, how they roamed restlessly in old houses, castles, on ships, how they rode carriages and crawled out of water. So I know a lot about ghosts and could easily accept the knowledge that an Earth person could become a ghost on my planet. I am also aware that Hannie's visit could have occurred in my aging mind. I no longer care about such distinctions. Hannie was here. Real or not, ghost or not, she was here, that's all I know.

I sensed her settling easily down in a chair beside me. My caretaker had set that chair there, I don't know why. He usually sets out extra furniture when I am to have guests. Perhaps that also means guests from the other side. It seems possible to me that he knew what he was doing, that he expected Hannie even before I did.

Nevertheless I felt her beside me, smoothing out folds in her ghost-clothing with the palm of her ghost-hand. At first she didn't seem to want to talk to me. I felt that she was comfortable just being there, observing me. I could feel her gaze upon me, no matter where I looked. I considered going away, leaving my daily post in the garden. I have become so irritable I didn't want Hannie to see me in one of my moods. I fidgeted with the paper of my notebook; there are small creases in the corner of the page on which I now write. I tried to think of something to enter on the page, tried to remember what I had just written, what I had wanted to write next. All I could think of was that Hannie was sitting there, beside me. I saw nothing, felt no tangible physical sensation, received no message directly through my senses, but I did know she was there. She was there because I felt in my mind she was there, I heard her talk to me there. I require no other proof.

I'm glad to see you writing down your memories, your thoughts, Sailor.

"Ah, but they're so jumbled, Hannie. I can't even hew to a straight narrative line."

Don't fret yourself, that's your way. You rambled in your life, in the expression of your thoughts, in your shifting from one political position to another.

"What you say doesn't exactly raise my self-esteem, Hannie."

She laughed. The laughter was like a breeze without a source, the force of it just brushed my cheek.

I couldn't raise your self-esteem, Sailor, if I provided you a certificate from heaven guaranteeing your sainthood.

"But I can't be a saint in a religion originating on your home planet. I'm not a Christian, Hannie, and what I am I'm not allowed to talk about."

Not even to a ghost?

"Especially not a ghost. You might be a spy for competing afterlives."

There's no competition here, Sailor.

"Anyway, if you're a ghost, shouldn't you know all about religions and afterlives, no matter whose they are?"

Oh, I know. I was just teasing. All that stuff isn't really as important as we think it is. We're just given guidelines and a few legends, myths, and tales from which we mostly build irrelevant and usually too rigid structures.

"I always feel a little embarrassed by religious talk, Hannie."

That's because your culture treats its religion the way mine treats bathroom matters. Anyway, Sailor, I plan to have you with me when your time comes.

"Is that possible? I mean, with two religions and two afterlives?"

Of course. Anything is possible here. Bargains can be made. Our universe is based on the principle of the bargain. We bargain with each other, we bargain with our gods; it should be obvious that bargains take place here. There's nothing a deity likes more than a good bargain. In this case I profited on a bargain. That happens.

I could almost hear the sound of her voice, hear its softness, its comforting nuances. I glanced toward the chair, expecting to see her there, but all I saw was painted metal, corroded in places where bits of paint had been scraped away.

"I'd like to quit right now, Hannie, stop this writing, burn the notebook. I'd make a bonfire in the center of the garden and burn the various editions of my books at the same time, and then sit down here and, well, ease into the afterlife."

You want to die without pain, Sailor?

"Well, that does seem desirable."

I died that way.

"I know."

I guess it was easier. On the other hand, I found it a bit of a shock to wake up dead. I hadn't planned on it after all. Seemed to me it wasn't at all fair. When I think of all the people who know they're going to die months, days, minutes ahead and then have time to settle with their gods, it doesn't seem fair that some of us don't get that opportunity. What if I had hidden some egregious sin? I wouldn't have wanted to come here a sinner; they do things to sinners here.

"You couldn't sin, Hannie."

You'd be surprised, Sailor.

I felt her draw away from me, the way she had when a thought suddenly struck her, when her eyes became distant.

"Will you help me burn the book, Hannie?"

How could I do that?

"I don't know, stir up the wind, something."

Well, I might be able to do just that, but I'd rather not. You have to continue, it's your duty.

"I no longer have any duties, that ended long ago. I never liked the idea of duty, anyway."

Why not?

"Duty always meant doing something I didn't want to do, like obeying some foolish order of Colin's, or letting Joline tell me I had more important matters in my life than the courting of her."

Courting her wasn't exactly a duty, Sailor.

"I thought it was."

Go on with your writing, Sailor. It will be the only surviving record of your life.

"And Colin's?"

Colin's, too.

"But all the histories, all my records of our achievements . . ."

They will be lost.

"I can't believe that. They are too great, too awesome."

Conquering weak peoples and conducting futile tyrannies are hardly great and awesome achievements.

"But some of it was really quite impressive. Colin could be quite heroic when he set his mind to it."

I saw. Well, I saw some of it. And Colin reminds me of it in his rare visits to me.

"He's there, too, Colin?"

Oh, yes. There is probably no one here who thinks he's earned his place here more than Colin.

"You don't sound proud of the way he turned out."

Well, I am and I'm not, but please don't ask me for more information about him. He's here and he sulks a great deal, worrying about his mistakes, that's all you really need to know.

My heart was beating faster by that time. I thought for a moment I could be joining Hannie officially at any minute.

"And Joline?"

She's here, too. Why are you smiling?

"I'm thinking of my death. I want to see Joline again."

No need to rush your own passing just to see her, she'll wait.

"Does she want to see me again?"

I don't really know. She spends all her time discussing peculiar philosophies with Stoner. I wouldn't have thought either one had it in him or her.

"But she hated Stoner."

Perhaps she still does. That might explain the philosophic talk, too.

"And Dominique?"

She's not reached here yet.

"Wherever she is, she must be very old."

She doesn't look as old as you do now. Dominique has held up very well, Sailor.

The feel of Hannie's presence became fainter. It was something like a voice fading out.

"Will I die soon?" I asked.

I heard or felt no answer. She had left. I reached out and touched the surface of the metal chair. It was cold, cold metal on a warm day, colder than it could have been even if it had been standing in the shade.

I felt stronger after Hannie's visit. Perhaps what she said did come out of my own mind. Perhaps it's I who feels that Colin's achievements will not be remembered, and not an otherworldly visitor from my past. Although I would hate for Colin to be obliterated from our history, I wish I could have my versions of it eliminated. Ah, it's just an old man's weariness. I must just finish this notebook.

My caretaker just came to me. He looked drained, his face white, his eyes almost as pale as his skin.

"Would you like some tea?" he asked.

"No," I said.

"Are you sure you wouldn't like some tea?"

"I'm sure."

"You usually have some tea at this time of day."

"I no longer like tea. I haven't liked tea for some time."

"Is there something wrong with the way I prepare it for you?"

"Nothing at all. It is like all the other tea I have had in my long life. I have had enough tea for a lifetime. For two lifetimes."

"Would you like your bath now?"

"I will not bathe today."

"But you—"

"Not today."

"As you wish. Will you require anything?"

"Your absence."

"I would be quite pleased to fulfill that request without hesitation, sir."

I should have chastised him for his insolence, but I rather

enjoyed it. In fact, I have grown to consider his insolence his best trait.

I should put down again the tales of Colin's heroism, restore them to their proper place. If they are to be lost elsewhere, I should give at least an indication of his greatest deeds here. All that I wrote in my other works was not lies, only most of it. But I can't go over that ground again, not anymore. With my porous old man's memory I would probably only make new lies out of them. Perhaps his fame will live on. I have no reason to believe there was really a ghost of Hannie here.

I spent a great deal of time worrying that Colin would kill his father, so it came as quite a shock to me that it was Joline who actually made the attempt.

As usual I was late in arriving at the actual event. I came into the large shack that had once been Q Colony's main laboratory just in time to see Joline springing at Stoner, a knife in her hand pointed at his throat. Colin was reaching toward her, and his hand just missed her arm. Dominique was running forward around a thick and massive examination table. Stoner stood still. It appeared from where I stood in the doorway that he had at least a half-smile on his face, as if inviting Joline to dispose of him. I, too shocked to move further into the room, merely stood flat-footed in the doorway. My usual place in history: standing to the side, watching events unfold without the slightest understanding of what was happening. I became a historian after all because I called myself one and, except for the occasional overcritical dissent from colleagues, I was able to comfortably remain one all my life. You can accomplish a lot in life if you know how to name things, even if you are quite wrong. Dominique taught me that.

I had come from a long negotiating session with the small company of Q Colony rebels. At least they called themselves rebels. They were a few of the original Q Colony scientists and workers from the two hundred or so who had elected to remain on Kew after the mission was canceled. They weren't really dangerous rebels. Their attacks were little more than raids of childish vandalism. Some time before, they had come to the conclusion that the colony and mission had been in the hands of Stoner and Dominique for too long. They decided they wanted representation for the younger element in the group. Not that they were young people. The youngest of them was a woman in early middle age. Well, she had a child, but I never counted him as one of the rebels. If he'd kicked my shins or growled at me, I might have included him, but the few times I saw him he sat in a corner working on intricate math puzzles.

There had been a time, earlier, just before Colin and I arrived at Q Colony, when these rebels had been feared. They had taken to camping in the abandoned city, a point from which they made their little nuisance raids. Stoner felt for a while that a real revolution was at hand, but, as it turned out, the rebels had little stomach for rebellion. They just liked to dirty things up a bit, break a few less valuable items. The time that Joline and I fled from them and wound up trapped in the cave, I had felt real danger from these people and, in fact, had suspected them of causing the cave-in that shut us in. Later it was clear that unaided nature had done that job. The rebels had been nowhere near the cave and, in truth, had not even considered pursuing us. We were just as much of a nuisance to them as they were to us.

Finally, tired of the way the laconic revolution was dragging on, Dominique had asked me to negotiate with the rebels.

"You're so good at compromise," she said to me.

"You don't really want compromise," I replied, "you just want them out of the way."

"That's what compromise is for, isn't it?"

"I always thought it was for providing at least the minimum of allowable improved conditions."

"Well, we'll provide that, too, of course. We've always been able to provide that. I just don't want any one of them in a position of power. Not because I fear them, but because they can't handle it."

"How do you know?"

"I can't explain. It's based on an instinct that only leaders have. I have it, but I can't describe it."

"So you want me to swindle them into a state of passivity."

"No, Sailor, I'm not asking you to swindle them. Every point you'll go in with is a legitimate one. You're not a swindler. If anything, you're a walking tranquilizer."

"I'll do it. For you, I'll do it."

"Thanks, Sailor. How can I pay you back?"

"Never compromise with me."

"Agreed."

The task had been easy to fulfill. The rebels were ready to give in. They were tired of being away from the communal dining table. Revolutionaries are rarely good cooks, it seems. They not only agreed to the compromise, they thanked me for being the bright youngster who could deliver it so well.

I felt mixed emotions on my stroll back to the laboratory. On the one hand, I was quite delighted that I had performed my diplomatic role with such aplomb and efficiency. Perhaps I was really meant for the diplomatic life, I thought. Power, the kind of power wielded behind the scenes, the king-making kind of power, might just be my forte. Instead of living a life as a creative but anonymous baker, the life Colin had wrenched me away from, I could be a creative and anonymous power-monger. The idea thrilled me. On the other hand, I disliked the trickery required by such a role. Instead of being a simple and well-liked workman, I would become a deceptive politician. I wished I had not had to deceive the rebels, to bring them back to a rather lethargic fold. Still, I had not liked them enough to be more than minimally sympathetic.

I'm sure I passed through the laboratory door with a step as unsure as my thoughts.

Joline finished her lunge, burying the knife in Stoner's chest.

The knife went in smoothly, only a little spurting blood traveled up the blade and onto the handle. Dominique finished her run in time to catch the falling Stoner and kick out futilely at Joline. Colin grabbed Joline around her waist and roughly pulled her away, knocking her body quite hard against a thick wood table. Joline's eyes glazed over, her body untensed, and she leaned her head against Colin's shoulder in what looked almost like a happy young woman placing her head on her lover's shoulder. Colin put his arms around her, also in a lover's way, although most of his weight was being used to support Joline.

Dominique looked over her shoulder, saw me, shouted: "Sailor! Come quickly. We need you."

I rushed to her side, although I recognized immediately there was scant possibility my healing abilities would be of much use. With such a wound, healing generally can do no more than relieve some of the pain. Even the best healers cannot make a knife or gunshot wound disappear, and I was certainly not among the best.

"Get her out of here!" Dominique yelled to Colin, her voice near hysteria, as I leaned down to examine Stoner. Colin grabbed Joline's arm tightly, but she offered no resistance anyway. They left the laboratory.

I rubbed my thumb along my fingertips, stroking harder than usual to force my nails to change from gray to silver, to force the healing energies to surge through me. After opening Stoner's shirt, I placed the back of my left hand lightly against the entry wound, let his warm blood coat my skin, flow upward between my fingers. As I did this, Dominique assembled medicines and bindings, quickly began unrolling a long bandage. She handed me a wet cloth and I gently wiped away the blood accumulating around the knife cut. I could see that it was small; Joline's aim had been direct and steady. I also felt his heart beating strongly. I willed as much healing as I could to flow from my fingers, then sat back on my heels, sat silently while Dominique applied some sort of gray salve to the cut, then sealed it off with a piece of cloth. She wrapped the bandage around his chest gently, but quickly and efficiently, reaching under the unconscious Stoner with an uncharacteristic delicacy. When she was done, I placed my hand on the bandage, over the wound, and concentrated. I'm sure it all must have looked impressive but I knew, then and now, that my work had little to do with Stoner's survival. Joline had managed to aim the knife blade in a route that pierced no vital organs, and Stoner was too stubborn to die from anything else.

He died, in fact, in his sleep, much as Hannie had, but that happened a long time after his wounding by Joline, after she was dead and Colin was famous. The news came to us from a Q Colony scientist acting as messenger, and Colin received it indifferently. He said to me he could no longer recall what Stoner had looked like or why he had ever sought him out.

That was bravado, of course, a disguise to hide his disappointment that he could have such modest and somewhat repellent beginnings. Colin also tended, in his conversations, to denigrate the goodness and intelligence of Hannie, since she had after all lain with Stoner in order to conceive him. Great men should come from gods, Colin believed, or—failing that—from other great beings. To him his parenthood was like a scar running across a beautiful face. If I hinted that greatness in life has little to do with origins, he scoffed. In fact I rarely brought up such topics, since I rankled at Colin's reactions. After all, in my more despairing moods, I felt that he was indeed stupid, and I could not abide that thought. His stupidity would conclusively prove my stupidity. Since I had begun to believe that a meaning to our existence was essential, seeing myself as stupid would have been something of a setback.

I am a strikingly intelligent example of my people who has written highly praised books, great books, which are in fact lies. I am a clever man who has devoted himself to the rise, reign, and fall from power of a great man, who was in fact a selfish, vainglorious, and somewhat limited (if not actually stupid) opportunist who made the best of some rather peculiar and haphazard circumstances to achieve a questionable power. I am a reflective old man who has reached a tedious but honored retirement, which is in fact a disposal by a society that was weary of his timeworn platitudes and outmoded theories but couldn't, in all conscience, because of a newfound political and moral fastidiousness, get rid of him in the way most desirable to it, by taking him to a forest in chains and hacking him to pieces. Dominique once told me that some human beings believe that life, or reality as they're fond of calling it, is an illusion, that nothing is what they think it is. I have come a long way in life to realize for myself, if for nobody else, that illusion is the reality. I have devoted my life to making my illusions reality for others.

I just remembered that Colin received the Q Colony messenger in his quarters. After dismissing the man, he did not come out of his rooms for a long time. When I approached my secret entrance to his bedchamber, I found he had locked the door from the inside. He rarely locked that door, even when he had a woman there with him. He didn't seem to mind what I interrupted him doing. I don't know why I forgot all these details. Perhaps his sourness when he did emerge from his quarters has dominated my memories of the incident. When I tried to introduce the subject of Stoner, he merely said: "Stoner is dead. That's all of it, Sailor."

"Your *father* died. That's not all."

"Stoner is dead. That's all."

He spent the rest of the day tending to the most trivial business, business that in other times he couldn't be bothered with, business he usually left to me, saying I was more suited to it. The only other time after that I ever heard Colin mention his father's death was when he told a group of councilmen and women, most of whom were as drunk as he was, that his father had died when a gang of outlaws had chained him to a rock in the desert and allowed predatory birds and animals to devour him by degrees. He did not even remember the story in the morning. I doubt that any of the other politicians did either. Another time, in another besotted state, he told me Stoner did not exist for him anymore. I asked what had Stoner done. He told me to figure that out for myself.

I have slipped away from my subject again.

Dominique and I sat by Stoner for a long time. The only time she spoke was to wonder if he should be taken to his quarters and put to bed. I shrugged and said it might be better not to move him for a while. A few minutes later I looked up from the spot of floor I'd been staring at and found Dominique staring at me.

"It looks to me like he'll be all right. Don't you think so?"

"Yes. It's not a very damaging wound. Joline probably didn't intend it to be. I've seen her use a knife. She knows how. Why'd she do it?"

Dominique sighed. For humans the sigh can be a kind of political device, a way of putting off things they do not want to say.

"There was a scene," she finally said. "Stoner told Joline she shouldn't marry Colin. Not couldn't, he hasn't the backbone to stop anyone from doing anything anymore, but shouldn't. He explained our customs, our taboos regarding incest. I hadn't realized there were still taboos against incest, especially for someone with the morals of Stoner, but he jabbered on about it. It was especially cruel of him, since he knows he has no influence over Joline. She does what she wants, always has. She's inherited something from her mother, thank whatever god is responsible. But Stoner was just jabbering, jabbering to make her feel bad, to make her worry, force her to think that any offspring would be an idiot. I said it had more reason genetically to be an idiot because it would be inheriting Stoner's genes. He didn't like that. He went on anyway, attacking Joline, calling her terrible names, prodding at her. She said she didn't care, she loved Colin and—I'm sorry, Sailor, I'm being heartless. I started out being heartless on purpose, but I can't stand that sad look in your eyes. I'm hurting you, I'm sorry."

"It's all right. You have to tell me all now, anyway. I'm all right."

But I wasn't of course. I was suffering from hearing what I already knew. I had known for a long time that I could not win Joline. I had even suspected that she was steadily being drawn to Colin, after rather despising him at first. She needed to respond to the godlike in the person whom she loved. The only godlike skill I ever displayed was an ever-growing skill at treachery. As Dominique talked, I had some difficulty imagining the force of Stoner's jibes at Joline. As I've noted elsewhere, I came from a society where incest was neither frowned on, nor encouraged. Where it existed, it was accepted. Nor were there, as in humans, any evident genetic abnormalities caused by our inbreeding.

Even the pain I felt at Dominique's words was not harrowing or sad. I was ready. What it confirmed only caused a mild sadness in me, enough for the look she saw in my eyes. I loved both Joline and Colin; my sorrow for myself seemed trivial when compared to the ultimate joy I would present to them when I got out of my mood. I feel more pain at my loss of Joline now, as I write this account of it, than I did at the time. There is a life that I didn't have that I would have preferred to the one I lived. I suppose many of us have in them such nonexistent lives, such unachieved futures. We are even familiar with their aspects and dimensions, their heights and depths, their gains and losses.

My nostalgic desire for the life I missed with Joline is more pointed because I know now the futility of Joline's subsequent life, her sacrifice to Colin's fame, the stupidity of her quite spectacular heroism, Colin's apparent disregard for her memory. Colin usually ignored me when I mentioned her name. Like Stoner, she merely seemed to pass out of his life. If I had died before him, I might even have been expunged, in his versions of our adventures, from my dramatic roles in heroic exploits that never took place. I am sorry I was not around for Colin's last words. I had always expected that they would be as well planned as his tales of heroism, but it was reported to me by the witnesses that all he said was, "Mother, it hurts." Still, I feel a certain pleasure that the ghost of Hannie might have been beside him in his last moments, taking him to her with love and affection. He might have said more, might have uttered something planned, something to fit him well into history, but for the dying assassin who managed one more blow before falling across Colin's body.

"Anyway, Sailor," Dominique continued, her hand now caressing the back of my neck, "it makes no difference what Stoner said to her. Heaven knows his words and tone and sarcasm were no different from the hundreds of other times he's said mean things to her and to me over the years here. Do you know we stay here because *he* wants to? Joline and I could have taken the last supply ship out of here easily. He kept us here. The place suits him, he likes it. He came here on what was supposed to be a short tour of inspection, and the place became slow quicksand under his feet. Rare to find one's own suitable paradise, bleak and useless as it is, I suppose. For all I know, the real reason Joline tried to kill him was that she'd wanted to leave this place so much. Stoner really wasn't at his best today. He wasn't clever. His sarcasm was petty. He was really off his oats. I don't know, perhaps it was all a dispute over style. If his style had been better, so would hers, and then—forget it, Sailor. Have we hurt you enough?"

I could not answer for a long time. I merely watched Stoner's increasingly stronger breathing and wondered if I would have regretted observing him at that moment as a corpse instead.

When I finally did look at Dominique again, I was surprised

by the changes in her face. It was not just the softening of her detachment, but that there were so many differences. Her eyes were concerned, her mouth was trembling, even the lines of her face seemed to have shifted, the shape altered. Meeting her on a crowded street, I might not have recognized her.

"I don't understand," I said to her, "but don't try to explain it all to me."

She nodded, smiled, blinked a few times, rubbed at her eyes, said: "Fair enough, Sailor."

After a while we relaxed our vigil. Stoner seemed to be sleeping peacefully. There was no reason to move him from the floor. Dominique and I sat in a different part of the lab and drank some of the wine that I'd made up right after Colin and I had first arrived at Q Colony. I tried to tell her about my negotiations with the rebels. I couldn't get the words out straight and she didn't listen anyway. She told me that, whatever I had done, she was sure it was all right. I realize now that that was pretty much the same attitude that Colin would take later when I did some essential but drab diplomatic job for him.

"Do you love Joline?" I abruptly asked Dominique. It was the kind of question I never knew I could ask.

Dominique's eyes teared up a little and she looked away.

"I understand why you ask," she said, "and I'd hate you for asking it, but what the hell, it's you, Sailor, and I doubt you ever ask anything for a bad reason."

"Don't be so sure."

She hugged me suddenly. I didn't know why then, I don't know why now. Years of reflection do not seem to have improved my perception very much.

"I love Joline," Dominique said finally. "I know it doesn't seem that way to you. Or to her, although I think she knows it. There's a lot to be said for warmth and gushing and touching, I suppose, but they've never been part of my regular repertoire. But remember, Sailor, you weren't here when she was a child and hanging from my neck like a necklace of boulders. And all the rest, the growing up, the disappointments. For that matter, you'll never know the Joline who delighted in telling jokes, usually bad jokes she collected from the Q Colony personnel. Or the Joline who cried her eyes out the day she did reach out for love, from Stoner, and didn't receive it. I won't say what happened that day, so don't ask. I love Joline. I even love Stoner."

"I'm touched," Stoner said, without opening his eyes or indeed changing his position on the floor.

Dominique muttered something I couldn't hear, then said: "I don't know why I let you feed me your wine, Sailor. Look at the trouble it gets me into."

"I'm also impressed," Stoner said, "at your skillful between-the-lines portrayal of yourself as martyr, Dominique. Neatly done, I must say, though I doubt, my dear, you love me. That's an idea you've devised to bring you some comfort in your old age."

"Of course it is. I just wanted to keep Sailor in confusion. How do you feel, Stoner?"

He sat up. His rise was too sudden, causing a pain in his chest. He put his hand there, pressing so tightly the move brought him more pain. His first grimace was mere pain, then he remembered we were there, and so the second grimace announced his imminent death. No matter how much pain showed on his face, he still looked pleased with himself.

"Say that I died singing," he said.

"Sure," Dominique said. Her voice was surprisingly gentle.

"Better—say I died with a poem on my lips."

"If you like."

"You're so agreeable."

"I tend to be agreeable about agreeable topics."

"You'd like me dead, Dominique."

"Let's say I wouldn't wear black for long, Stoner."

"You don't have anything black in your wardrobe."

"That simplifies matters, doesn't it?"

He touched the bandage on his chest, touched it lightly, did one of his theatrical grimaces.

"I'm going to disinherit Joline for this," he said.

Dominique clearly didn't want to smile, but she did. "I'm sure she wanted this, all this," she said. "She'll be so disappointed."

Stoner didn't want to smile either, but he did.

"I suppose I'll have to be the one to scold her," he said,

"just like when she was a child."

"It would come hard for me."

"She'll probably just try to do it again."

"She always was persistent, even as a child."

I cannot explain it, then or now, but in spite of the flat, even irritated, sound of their voices, there was much affection in them. Then I noticed that Dominique held Stoner's hand. Stoner was squeezing her hand in return. I felt very much in the wrong place and I quietly backed my way out of the building.

"I'd like a drink or something," Stoner was saying. "For the pain."

"I'll see what I can do," Dominique said.

Outside, I had to look around for a while before I could find Colin and Joline. They were sitting against the wall of a Q Colony building. Her head was on his shoulder. She was asleep. Streaked dirt around her eyes showed she had been crying.

"She's all right now," Colin whispered.

"Yes. I can see that."

"We had quite a fight after . . . that."

He pointed in the general direction of the laboratory.

"Fight? About what?"

"She was repentant, quite repentant about what she'd done. I didn't like that. I was proud of her for doing it, and her repentance spoiled it for me."

"Colin . . ."

"I know, Sailor. I'm wrong. That's what you're here for. What you're always here for. To tell me when I'm wrong. I don't want to hear it now."

"Aren't you going to ask about Stoner?"

"No. He's a tough bastard. He's indestructible. He's all right."

"He's dead. He just died."

I don't know why I said it. Just to elicit a reaction, I suppose. But Colin didn't react. Maybe he shrugged, or maybe the movement of his shoulders was just to relax a strained muscle.

"No, he's okay," I said. "You're right, he's tough."

"I know."

"Wouldn't you have felt at all sorry?"

"I don't know. I might."

Joline stirred a bit on his shoulder but did not wake up.

"Let her sleep," Colin whispered.

I stood there, looking quite stupid I am sure.

"Go away, Sailor," Colin said.

"All right."

I started backing away.

"Sailor?"

"Yes?"

"I'm sorry."

"Sorry about what?"

"About you, about Joline, me."

"It's all right."

"No, it isn't."

"It really is all right."

"Damn it, Sailor, damn it. It can't always be all right. Go away, just go away. We don't want to see you for a long while."

I didn't like him including Joline in his wish for my exile, but I did leave. As I went past the laboratory, I could hear Dominique and Stoner laughing softly. I felt very much alone.

Although he depended on me for counsel, although he insisted on my presence beside him at important battles or ceremonial occasions, although he cried for me when he was in pain, although he embraced me when his pity for himself had submerged him, Colin was never quite the same to me after that. Nor was he the same *for* me. There was always an infinitesimal distance which I could no longer cross to get to him. A miniature bridge defended by the ablest warriors.

Joline, from then on, talked to me to the point of chattering. It was quite unpleasant at times. I never wanted to be with her. I could not be the lovestruck abandoned swain. I could not be pleasant just to make her feel better. I tried to be distant with her, display my own infinitesimal distance, build my own miniature bridge, but she never seemed to notice, just went on chattering.

• • •

Not long before he was killed, Colin bade me come to him. He had not sought counsel with me for some time, and I had thought I was out of favor. I told him right away I was surprised that he had called for me.

"I'd forgotten about you, Sailor. Your fault."

"Mine?"

"You stay out of the way. For a long time I would look for you, peek down corridors I passed to see if you were loitering in them, expect you to come up to me quietly during my walks in the gardens. But you stayed out of the way."

"I thought you preferred not to see me."

"See? Your fault, Sailor."

"Acknowledged. What did you want to see me about now?"

"I want you to join with me. Rule with me. You are the kingmaker, you should share the throne."

"Why would you want that, Colin? It would only confuse everyone. They would lose confidence in both of us. A dual reign would be disastrous."

"I accept your counsel on the matter. But I would still rather you would accept my offer of kingship. It's what I want, and I should have what I want. I want you with me at all times. I don't want to lose you to the evils of courtesy and the darkness of corridors. If I make you king along with me, you have to be with me. That's what I want."

"It can't be."

"Nevertheless it will be. You have to do what I ask. They have to accept what we do. There is no real problem. I need you here, Sailor. I love you. I have never really loved anyone else. I think of the life we have shared together, and I know it must have some meaning, some outward meaning, some declaration of how we have striven together, how we have succeeded. My achievements are yours as well, Sailor. It's necessary to me that you should receive the benefits also."

"You said yourself I can't make decisions."

"You won't have to. I'll make all the decisions."

"Then I won't really be king."

"He who has the honors of a king is the king, that's all there is to it. Forget your objections. Rule with me. I need you by me."

"All right, all right, all right."

"Go away before you see my tears."

A pleasant scene to ponder. The kind act. The reconciliation before sudden death. The kingly gesture. The offerings of friendship and love. Colin becoming what he should have been from the start. A very pleasant memory. It's too bad it did not happen. I imagined it so much that I almost thought it did happen. It has almost become a part of the real life of a senile old man. Perhaps it did happen and has only become dreamlike for me.

Before they retired and exiled me, I traveled back to Q Colony. There was no good reason for my trip. I had just felt myself drifting, felt the initial pulls of the drift that has beached me here in this dry, decaying estate. I don't know what I expected to find at Q Colony. I had already heard the place was in ruins. Perhaps I wanted a token, a little piece of something to remind me of someone, it didn't matter which something or which someone.

I traveled alone. I didn't want to have to explain to anybody the purposes of my trip.

Coming over a hill I saw the first shards of the former Q Colony buildings. Blackened, charred, they stood like knife points in the air. As I got closer I saw the more conventional wreckage, the charred pimpled boards tossed into piles. Walking around the old paths, I had difficulty remembering which old building had been which. I could not decide which of two buildings had been the one in which Joline had stabbed Stoner, could not even guess at which one had been headquarters. I crouched in several ruins, sorting through pieces of metal and wooden debris, trying to mine out something that would remind me of Colin or Dominique, of Joline, even of Stoner or myself. To be sure, I found things. I found small metal clasps that had once had scientific purpose; I found folders with cramped writing I couldn't read in them; I found plates, tubes, pipes, silverware, odds and ends from many phases of everyday life at Q Colony. I kept some of these, put them in a sack I carried. But nothing reminded me of anybody, there was no way to project anything specifically human onto the charred and bruised artifacts. Oh, of course I could imagine anyone I knew using a fork or clamping a metal brace onto a piece of equipment, but there was nothing to call up a specific memory of any of the people whose memories I needed to call up. What I got was a collection of human exhibits that a museum paid me a significant amount for. If anybody else had brought them in, the payment would have been less. I understand they have devoted a whole room to Q Colony, but I have never gone to see it.

I try to remember the last time I saw Colin. What were the last words he uttered to me? I think we were discussing a budget. Budgets were not part of my prescribed duties, but the two budget directors were both leftover uncles of the bride Colin took for a short time when the idea of heirs was on his mind. Although he exiled her, he kept the uncles around as if he had no memory of the nepotism that had brought them to him. The upshot was that I had to correct all the financial work of these woeful incompetents who didn't even know the proper vocabulary for their jobs. Come to think of it, lack of proper job vocabulary was fairly common on Colin's various staffs.

Colin acted the way he usually did when it came to budgets or any other of the everyday trivia of rule. He shuffled papers, made odd funny sounds inside his mouth, sought distractions, nodded off into a half-sleep, or did anything else that would hide the fact that he couldn't understand a word of what I was telling him in what I thought was an economical succinct fashion, one that I had developed in the panic of trying to find fewer and fewer words with which to express myself when doing any one of my various jobs or duties. When there was a problem, I presented it to him and he asked me what I thought should be done about it. After I had told him, he said something like "my thinking exactly, Sailor, go ahead with it," then sat back quite pleased with himself.

This last time, if it was indeed the last time, if the last time was not some other forgettable event, he was particularly impatient with my succinctness. I can remember rushing to my conclusions, and feeling a discomfort, a tightness in my upper chest, wondering if indeed I would talk myself into an early grave because of Colin's impatience. I know Colin will be the death of me, I said to myself, but I never suspected I'd die of budgetary discrepancies.

When the budget meeting was over and Colin had just barely adhered to the ritual of approving my conclusions as his own, he fell into a sullen silence. I was used to that. Since we were children, he had been afflicted with severe sullen silences almost on a monthly basis. I remember Colin in the first days I knew him, sitting atop a wall, his eyes sad, his mouth downcast, running a rather sharp knife along detailed routes upon his visible skin, sometimes testing the skin by pressing the point against it slowly and deliberately, a couple of times drawing tiny beads of blood which caused him momentarily to lose the sullen look. It was that same look I saw in him at that moment. He stared at his own skin as if he wanted to draw blood with the look alone.

Following my usual custom after ascertaining he was in a deep sulk, I started to quit the room as quietly as I could. When I was near the door he said something to me, and it's that something that I would like to write down exactly, but unfortunately my memory is failing me.

It was about the monster we killed at the pond, that much I do remember. He either said that we had had a fine day that day, one of our best days, or he said he often wondered just what did happen that day since he could no longer tell what aspects of the tale as he told it were embellishments developed over the years. I like to think he said the latter, but I suppose it was the former. To his death he probably thought it had been a fine day. Anyway, it was like him to brood over the good times.

They have taken my caretaker away. Perhaps for good.

I came upon him lying flat on the floor of the front corridor underneath a chipped gilt mirror. I had remembered I had not eaten in a while, that he had not prowled around me with his annoying offers of food, tea, or a good wash for some time, and I hollered for him to come to me in the garden. When he didn't come, I tried once more. Failing that, I assembled the pained and broken pieces of my body and managed to stand up and go into the house.

I soon found him. He had fallen in some kind of twisted way, his hip was thrust out unnaturally. He had the look of death about him, his face had gone whiter than ever.

I knelt beside his body and touched his face. It was warm and I sensed immediately that there was still life in him, not much but at least more than what some call the spark of life. My first impulse was to heal him, then I realized that I hadn't summoned the healing ability in some time, not for longer than some lifetimes. I put my hands to my forehead, remembered the severe pain I now experienced in the joints of my fingers and I wondered if ruined hands could possibly heal. Nevertheless, as I rubbed back and forth I could feel the familiar rush of healing energy. I could feel my hands begin to swell with it, feel my bones melting at the same time. With more effort than I thought I would have needed, I pulled my hands away from my forehead, and stared at my caretaker through my own transparent skin as my left hand began to wave over his body, searching for the area of most pain within him. I found it soon enough. It was near his heart, a large terrifying pain that made my own body heat up and weaken, that made my own pulse come irregularly, made me gasp for breath. Whatever was causing his death, it was in a blood vessel and it was large. I concentrated on it, placed my right hand beside my left, began to push gently against his chest, tried to shape the pain into a tangible form my mind could envision. The shape that came to me reminded me of nothing familiar, it was merely an irregular undefinable lump. At first I could do little against it. Instead it attacked me, drew energy out of me, weakened me, wanted to absorb me. In that part of my mind that was not involved in the healing, I noted to myself that, in my aged decrepit state, I could easily die from this attempt to heal. My caretaker's death and mine could coincide. We could meet in some eternity's waiting room, and he could continue to bore me there with his attentions, his requests, his conversation. I did not want that, not at all, so I concentrated even harder. Mentally I took the lump into my hands and, kneading carefully, made it smaller and smaller, tried to roll it into nothingness. I suppose I succeeded, for the healing worked. I reduced the size of the pain, brought my caretaker back to life.

I don't actually remember doing it. I blacked out, and woke up from unconsciousness with a young man shaking me by the shoulders. It did not occur to me until later that he was trying to ascertain whether or not I too lived.

They took him away after a doctor's examination. The doctor took me aside and told me I had done well, but that even with that the patient's prospects were not good. He said not to expect him back again for some time and offered to contact the committee to instruct it to send me another caretaker.

I have been sitting alone in the garden for hours, watching evening come on, and I know now I do not want another caretaker. Oh, I'm not being sentimental. I'm not eager to have the old one back either.

Although I do wish I could scold him for something just now.

I am somewhat nervous, as I expect the doctor to return at any moment to tell me my caretaker has died. I remember that, even as I knew the healing would be successful, I did not feel in him much life beyond the pain.

I had no chance to heal Joline. Her wounds were too severe, too deep, too involved with vital organs for healing to have much effect. I did ease some pain, did touch her even when the touch meant bloodying my hands or seeing the blood ooze out of her through my skin's transparency.

As I watched her, I knew I would never have the conversation with her I had been planning for some time, would not say the words that I had been sure would bring her to my arms, into my marital bed. I would never say to her that I knew she was disappointed with Colin, that her disappointment had been growing for some time, and that we both—she and I—were suffering distress from that. I had intended to corner her, to try to work out everything so that she would feel better toward Colin and myself, but still become mine. In my pathetically wishy-washy way I searched for the ideal time and place to talk with her, but the dimensional configurations never meshed for me, and then she was dying.

I lied about her death in the historical accounts, both in my contemporary dispatches and in my books about the uprising.

I lied partially at Colin's bidding, partially out of my own need to avoid the truth. I was again failing her, since she would rather I told the true story of her death. Perhaps I thought if I made a permanent record of her death, actually put down all the details, it would become so imprinted on my brain that I would never forget it. I needed so much to forget it. Of course I never forgot it anyway. I don't know why I thought I could. It doesn't matter, I suppose, or it does. Or perhaps it doesn't matter that it does.

During the uprising Joline did face the mob with great courage, I never lied about that. I did eliminate details, but I didn't lie. Naturally, I never wrote anything about her threat to kill Colin, a threat that came only hours before her own death, a threat that I could tell she meant. She had looked at me with eyes that almost asked me to help her in the attempt. I didn't want anyone to know that she might have been an assassin if time and Colin's continued tyrannic catastrophe had allowed it. Joline is better portrayed as Colin's best ally, the heroic woman who was martyr, fighter, wife and sister all in one. It was all a difficult set of lies for me to propagate, putting the words down was arduous, but Colin needed it. Colin needed it.

And, I must admit, it has become a rather attractive legend. One of my best.

I also wrote nothing of the prolonged ugliness of her death. I made it sound as if she had gone down fighting, dying a proper hero's death. I also avoided telling that it was one of her own warriors who turned on her and killed her.

I can still hear her stating firmly, in spite of the pain from her several wounds: "I will not die like this. I have things to do. I will not die. There are things I have to say, things he has to learn. Things you have to learn, Sailor. Sailor?"

"Yes, Joline?"

"Love me forever, Sailor."

"I will. But you'll be—"

"Just love me forever."

I would of course have loved her forever even if she hadn't asked me to. But, in the time since, I have continued to hear her voice saying it. Now, in my cynical and crotchety old age, in my wonderful heartless senility, I wonder if she really felt anything about me when she said it. Perhaps she wanted me to love her forever as my punishment in life, a complicated revenge upon me for offenses I was not aware of. I suppose that's a bitter old man's idea, but I can't help thinking it. I have been without her too long, for four or five times the length of time that I knew her. I can't make her legacy vanish now.

She screamed in pain, several times. A doctor came along and said she was not a good patient. He meant to imply that she needed to present a good example for the other patients, the lesser soldiers, the ones who had been wounded with her, but she cursed him and said that the pain was too much and she didn't want to die. She would have said more, but she had another spasm of severe pain and all she could do was scream. It was the kind of scream that tore walls apart. Everybody else's screams, including her later ones, seemed gentle after it.

Not long before the life went out of her, she said I should stop doing what Colin told me to, especially elevating second-rate escapades into legend.

"I love Colin as much as you do, Sailor, but we have to leave him be."

"No," I said. "He needs us."

"I am pleased that you included me in that. He needs you, if anyone. He doesn't need me. That's part of what I'm complaining about. I just want to be you, Sailor. I want to mean to Colin what you do."

"He's devoted to you, he—"

"Not really. I'm just one of the hangers-on, the disciples. But you, you, Sailor, you—"

She could not finish what she was saying. Later she said again: "Love me forever. I need for you to love me forever."

"I will."

Anything else she said was incoherent. She died in the midst of great pain.

Colin never came to her bedside. Later he attempted to excuse himself by saying he had been trapped in a skirmish during the uprising and could not come to Joline. He described his part of the fighting in some detail and was disappointed that I didn't seem interested in writing it all down. I never did write it down. Anywhere.

In the following days he guided me in the lies I told about her death. He kept saying we had a great opportunity to solidify our position by conveying Joline's martyrdom to the people. As usual I did his bidding. I can't really explain that, excuse myself in these futile scribblings in a notebook I never requested. There was always a part of me that was very like Colin. Calculating, lusting for power, even a behind-the-scenes power, ready to manipulate facts to advantage. I really did like some of that. I saw that the story of Joline, mistold but with certain basic facts correct, was inspiration to its readers. And, in a strange way that seemed to contradict my grief for Joline, I rather enjoyed seeing the effect of the tale as it was accepted by more and more readers, rather enjoyed the way it did, as Colin predicted, solidify our position.

And none of that, performed as cynically as it was, has interfered with my loving Joline forever.

There are so few clear pages left in this notebook. My writing has now become so small, it will take high-powered lenses to read it. I can't go on holding my pained arthritic fingers tightly on the pen in order to keep the handwriting microscopic. Perhaps I can get another notebook. Perhaps another caretaker will show up in my garden and hand me another notebook. At least that doctor has not returned with news about the condition of my old caretaker. Or maybe he came and told me, and I forgot it.

Hannie often said, after telling us one of her tales, that we create legends to do those things we can never do, to live in the imagination lives different from the lesser lives we lead. If she were here now, in ghost-form or otherwise, I could tell her that her view simply is not true. Our legends are our lies, and that's all they are. That's not fair, I suppose. I guess I can only say that my legends are my lies, and that's all they are.

If I can acquire another notebook, and I almost hope that I can, there is much more I can do, more I can write. I think I am ready now to counter the lies I have told in my books about Colin. I can do my historical duty, put down as much truth about Colin as I can remember, correct the tales of him I left behind, redo my life's work. Perhaps I can put down my own life, limit my new book to my own point of view—an autobiography. Yes, I'd like to do an autobiography. Every detail accurate up to my own death. In my autobiography I can't die, since of course I can't describe my own death. There is no way a reader can see my death. I'll go on writing now, fill out the rest of this notebook and many others. I have to. There is so much more to write down in them.

THREE

ALEZASE

I have to say right off that the document I am now transmitting to the Committee may not be authentic. I, frankly, do not know, nor do I care to muddle the issue with an opinion whose tentativeness would only undercut any value it could have. Many of my colleagues, more eager than I to give their names prominent file-status, have questioned the manuscript's authenticity. However, some of them may be quibbling because of their own self-interest. They are, after all, struggling along with hard-to-translate treatises on difficult subjects, while some of us are able to coast along on the plainer language of journals and diaries. I fully admit that the uncomplicated language and grammar of the Alezase Document was an easy task for me. I claim no more credit for translating it than the job deserves. Later I will be transmitting to the Committee a more complex and, if I may say so, important work on the geographical history of Kew, which I trust will help to secure my reputation much more than will this minor journal. Nevertheless, since I was as-

signed the translation of the work by our estimable commander, interrupting my main major study at a critical time, I do not wish to have my reputation soiled if the Alezase Document does turn out to be some sort of peurile hoax.

The Alezase Document was not a part of the find in the record-keeper's cave, but was rather brought to us by a Kew native who has taken a curious and jovial interest in our work. This native, an old decrepit wine merchant who has been supplying the team with an abundance of tasteless but potent native vintages, has already shown himself to be a whimsical, even impish, sort of fellow in his humor. I suspect he would not be above faking a manuscript if he thought he could give us a good runaround with it. Nevertheless, there are compelling reasons to view the manuscript as authentic. For one, it was written on Ellda paper, the kind that would have been used in Q Colony and on which the earlier-submitted Q Colony document, the Stoner Journal, was written, so it is likely that a survivor of the colony would have appropriated such paper, as the text of the manuscript clearly states. Further, it is doubtful that the old wine merchant would himself have known about the preservative properties of Ellda paper. I doubt that he would have stolen or discovered some, unless he of course is much craftier than he appears. Also, internal evidence, details about Dominique LaPointe, Henry Stoner, their daughter Joline, his son Colin, a Kew native called Sailor, all tend to correspond with some exactitude to the Stoner Journal and the Sailor Papers. These correspondences have, in fact, prompted our commander to urge me to finish the translation quickly and send it on without waiting for its authenticity to be reasonably established. We do want the Committee to credit our work here and are willing to take risks if they will facilitate the overall study that is being undertaken at headquarters. I trust that, if approached with a reliable amount of scepticism, Alezase's manuscript will help fill in gaps caused by previous material. As the old saying in our profession goes, every little phoneme helps.

The Steila village referred to in Alezase's manuscript
apparently still exists. The wine merchant supplied the
location, saying he found the manuscript under a bed
there, in a cottage that had been converted into a ware-
house for storage of their abundant wares. Some members of the current exploratory section of our team have
already visited the village, not to verify this manuscript
but merely in their travels. Another expedition there is
being mounted in order to see if other manuscripts were
left there by Alezase or by any of the others mentioned
in the manuscript. I have been told that the Steilas of
this village, an odd species of stunted-growth Kewians
for whom we had not had a descriptive name before, are
still living in quite the same way as were those described
in the manuscript. They still manufacture items with a
certain skill and evident craft. One of the members of
the archaeological team showed me some examples of
Steila goods. The pottery did not overly impress me,
although it did remind me of some stuff I had seen back
in an Earth museum. Mesopotamian stuff, I think. There
was a certain unevenness to the shapes of the pottery
items, and the designs etched in and painted onto them
were no doubt beautiful to Steilas and to other natives
of Kew. On the other hand, I was shown a piece of cloth
with an intricate design on it, thin lines all in various
shades of blue, that I thought was quite lovely.

I will supply no specific notes about my translation,
except to say that the lorwel referred to so briefly in
Alezase's narrative is a species of animal that still exists
on Kew. Its milk is, however, quite bitter and none of
the current team has been able to digest it. We have not
been able to use the milk as a baking or cooking ingre-
dient either. The animal itself is, as the manuscript indicates, quite ugly. It has horns that seem to come out
of the back of its head instead of from some normal horn-
bearing area. It is usually fat and has a pelt like little
needles sticking through its skin. A milker cannot lean
in close to it, as those who do that job on Earth often
do.

I feel I must comment on an unfortunate, potentially

harmful situation predicated by one of my colleagues. I hope the members of the Committee will realize, since I was once married to the woman, how difficult it is for me to make the following declarations. It has come to my attention that she, the translator of the Sailor Papers, referred to me in her message to the Committee. While I do not know exactly what statements she made, it was alleged to me that my competence was questioned by her, and perhaps my honesty. That was no surprise, really, since in the latter days of our relationship she took to accusing me of being shortsighted and narrow-minded. I understand she also made scurrilous observations about our life together. While I was willing to allow her opinion of me in private, I did not of course expect it to be shared with our superiors. Since she is an acknowledged self-confessed thief herself, I sincerely hope that the blatherings of a criminal will not be taken seriously by the Committee. Some of my colleagues believe that she has, to put it as delicately as possible, jettisoned the controls that should steer her. She certainly sulks around camp like a witch collecting grudges. At any rate, I want to say here that I cooperated with her to the best of my ability on the Sailor Papers and never wished to undermine or challenge her hegemony with them. I did discover the Sailor Papers but, as the Committee realizes, I have properly registered that fact and do not expect to be awarded any more promotional points than I deserve for the discovery. I hope I am not out of line in commenting on my colleague's comments about me, but I am the sort of individual who prefers that the records, all records, be set straight. To verify my position on the matter, I cite my long service to this project and to others, along with, if I may say, my efficient accumulation of promotional points.

One further observation: I wish to state my belief that the statue which our archaeological team recently unearthed, the words on whose base indicate that it is a monument to Dominique LaPointe, is probably authentic, at least if this and other manuscripts that refer to her are not hoaxes. The physical description of her corresponds to the features and proportions of the statue. I believe it should be shipped to the Museum of Exploration and Discovery, so that some tangible record of our earlier expedition to this planet may be represented there.

Dominique has instructed me to write about her. I don't know why she thinks I can do it. I've never written anything about her or anyone before. She's dying, so I have to do it.

She waited patiently while I dragged out the huge box of paper, the last of several boxes she had brought here with her. I remember seeing her come into the Steila village that morning, laboriously hauling that small cart, her body weary but refusing to fall. Later in the day, when she had announced she would stay with me at my cottage, the boxes of paper were the first items she unloaded from the cart. I helped her carry them into my home, wondering what anyone would want with all that paper, not realizing that one day we would have used up all but this last box. After the paper, we carried in her clothing and many sacks of odds and ends salvaged from the burned Q Colony. The last thing she carried in was an old-looking sword which was stained in several places. Many years passed before she told me that the sword was all she had left that had belonged to her daughter, Joline. Joline had been killed in battle while helping Colin, the son of her husband by another human named Hannie. I suspected the stains I first saw on the sword could have been blood, whether Joline's or some adversary's I couldn't guess. By that time the sword had been polished to a bright shine and hung in the study of my son, Valyset. It is still there.

Dominique has been watching me write this. She tried to sit up to watch but couldn't. She is weak. There is a circle of darkness around her eyes, but the eyes themselves are still clear and strong. They have always been clear and strong, all the time I've known her. As she stares at me from the edge of her pillow, I suddenly become very conscious that I do not always display the grace of movement for which I have often been praised.

She will talk now.

"I want my name on paper somewhere, Alezase. Some fraction of my life remembered by someone. Almost everyone who's known me is gone. You are left, Alezase. You and Valyset. Of everyone I've cared for, loved, you're the ones left. Unless Sailor is alive somewhere. Will you ask me about Sailor? Well, I'll tell you anyway. He tried to make love to me once. As a favor. I asked him. I was drunk. So was Sailor. We tried. Oh, did we try. Although it didn't work out the way I'd hoped (Sailor was quite unable to perform), I remember that lovemaking better than any other. Do you remember any particular times when you made love, Alezase? Any time when it was so much better for you that all other times fade in your memory? No, you don't have to answer that. I don't want to hear your answer. You'd probably tell me it was one of the times with Henry. Henry would certainly have said it was one of the times with you. I had to live out my life with him knowing that, if he could have gotten one more shot at you, he would have taken it. Easily, without a thought of me. He would have left me for you, did you realize that? You could have had him again at any time. You could have glided down from your hideaway here in the hills and taken him away, any time. He talked of you often, so often, too often. I begged him to please shut up about you. He called you the Oonaa woman, did you know that? Never knew your name. Never called you anything else, just used the offensive word. It never fazed him. He liked to use the word among your people, and did use it regularly. He saw how much they hated it, enjoyed using it all the more. Kind of hairpin he was. Henry was often an offensive man, even a devious and evil one. He died offensive, devious, and evil."

Dominique has not talked now for a long while. I've sat here poised, her pen in my hand, the pen from Q Colony, and earlier from her home planet, waiting to record her next words. She is just staring off into space. I thought for a while she was taking one of her frequent naps, but she's looked suspiciously toward me a couple of times. Now her eyes have closed, just now. She nodded off as I wrote this.

I hope that Dominique doesn't require this document to be elegant. I am only doing it because she asked. I am not fond of words. I rarely talk. To me words are tasks, each one an individual labor.

I am Alezase. Dominique came to my cottage after Henry Stoner, her husband, died. She said she had wandered for a long time, searching for me, tracking down clues to my whereabouts, before she ambled into the Steila village and found that its inhabitants could lead her to me. The first thing she told me was that Henry was dead. She expected me to be sorrowful. I had not even thought of him in years. She described Joline's death in some useless battle that Colin had conceived. Colin's reputation had even reached my hillside hut, but at that time I didn't tell Dominique that. Two of Henry's children were dead, she said, and she very much wanted to see what had happened to the third, to my son. At first I feared that she had come to kill Valyset, to finish off the last of Henry Stoner's offspring. I resolved not to tell her anything about Valysct. At that time I didn't even reveal his name to her, although she requested it often enough. Eventually I became convinced that she intended no foul play, that her motives were a mixture of kindness and curiosity.

She is awake again.

"Did you find the paper? Of course you did. I can even see it from here, with my slowly darkening vision. I won't survive to finish this, Alezase, so you'll have to. Don't look so frightened. You can do it. My God, you looked like I'd just planted a knife in your back. All you'll have to do is put down what you remember about me. Just a few notes. A record. I want some kind of record. A record is all . . .

"I'm sorry. Did I doze off there? For a minute I think. Can't get my thoughts together. Mind's sinking into a deep lake, settling to the bottom. Write something down, Alezase, while I think. Don't look so scared. Anything. Just anything. Write down what I look like."

I don't know what she wants. What does she look like? I don't know. She looks somewhat old. But not as old, she tells me, as a human should for her age. From what we have been able to figure out by comparing numbers and the slight difference between a year on her home planet and a year here on Kew, she is about a decade and a half older than I. In Kew years. She says my people don't grow old in the ways her people do, with wrinkles and disintegrating skin and loosening teeth and eye-growths. That seems to be true. I don't show my age in the way she does, nor do most of my people. We might not have noticed if the humans hadn't come here and demonstrated that to us.

Dominique is a tall woman. She is taller than most of us. Henry Stoner was almost as tall as she. I suppose that is why Valyset is so much taller than I. He is approximately the same height as Dominique.

But she wants me to describe her. How is it done? She has interesting shoulders. They come to points, and there are hollows just above her small breasts. The hollows have become more pronounced as she's grown old. Now that she is sick and dying, they are cavernous. I don't know what her sickness is. That does not matter, since she will not allow me, or anyone, to treat it. I don't have much healing ability but often, when she is asleep, I try to summon it. I put my hands on some part of her body and concentrate. Nothing is healed by the attempt, but she does tend to awaken more cheerfully.

She says she is ready to talk again.

"I dreamed of Joline. She should be alive now. She could take care of me, too. God, she could chatter on about one of the stupid ideas that could so easily grab her attention and devotion. I don't mean to cast aspersions on you, Alezase, but even you admit you don't talk about ideas. You don't talk about anything unless people, unless I tear the words out of you. Joline could talk. Pity you never saw her, met her. I liked watching her grow up, I really did. I didn't much like her grown up, but I liked everything before that. If she hadn't loved her father so much . . .

"She tried to kill Henry. I told you about that long ago. Just sprang at him with a knife when all he was looking for from her was a clever insult. Afterward, when he'd recovered from the wound, he always laughed about it. He seemed to like her all the better for wanting to kill him. Crazy man, a difficult man. I think he wanted to be killed in some violent way, wanted to die with drama. He didn't. I've told you about that. I'm tired for the moment, so write down what I told you about Henry's death, Alezase."

I can't remember what she told me. She talked of Henry often enough, but I really didn't want to hear about him. I stopped listening when she mentioned his name. I recall that she said he died normally. Of some illness. In a bed. Cursing every god he'd ever heard of in detail. Spitting out the words and causing a spatter of wet spots on his bedclothes. Telling Dominique that he'd loved her and loved me and even loved Hannie, the mother of Colin. I guess I heard more of what she said about his death than I'd thought.

When I left Henry the last time, came to this place in the hills, pregnant with Valyset, I never wanted to see him again and I did not. If I had never heard of him again, if Dominique had not come here to live with me, I'd never have thought of him again. No, that's not exactly true. Valyset did ask me about his father from time to time. I said I had formed the alliance with Henry out of a kind of thoughtful curiosity about our human visitors. Valyset had grown up and been married before he suddenly realized that what I meant by thoughtful curiosity was lust. There are, actually, no excuses I can make for my liaison with Henry. If Dominique is right, I could not have chosen worse among the men or women at Q Colony. But there was something about him then that excited me, a way in which his eyes had nothing to do with the rest of him.

Dominique told me to write about his death. I don't recall any more than I've already related. I'm sure he went through the actual moment awkwardly and indelicately, but that is about as much as I can remember of the long story Dominique told me more than once.

She's been staring at me for some time, probably thinking I am stretching the resources of my language to describe poetically the death of Henry Stoner.

"You're done? Good. I wish I could see what you've written, but my eyes won't focus right, especially for the scrawls of your language. . . .

"Joline loved Henry. In a way he loved her. He paid attention to her, which was about as much love as he could work up. For a long time he became interested in the geology of Kew, even though geology wasn't one of his fields. He took Joline on long treks collecting rocks. They dug holes, chipped away at representative stone on the buildings of the abandoned city. Joline was about, oh, eleven. He liked when she asked him questions about the rocks they found. He patiently explained how difficult it was to analyze specimens with the wrong equipment, how we'd never been awarded first-class stuff because headquarters considered us a second-class operation. They sent Henry here in the first place to prove we were a second-class operation. Anyway, Henry seemed delighted by Joline's enthusiasm about rocks. First thing he knew, she took to studying them more intensely, doing research, finding correlations that Henry hadn't noticed. Suddenly he was bored with rocks. I remember her holding out some kind of crystalline hunk and suggesting there were traces of an extremely valuable Kew ore in it. Henry grabbed the rock away from her, walked to the border of Q Colony, flung it into the fields beyond. I was ready to run to Joline, cuddle her in my arms or something. But she just stood there. Just stood there and calmly watched the rock fall into a bog or something. She showed no emotion. She knew the rules, the rules as laid down by H. Stoner. She knew...."

Dominique has fallen asleep again. Or she is feigning sleep. She is probably asleep. She is making those peculiar noises that, she says, humans are prone to make when they are sleeping and in the wrong position.

I left the cottage for a while. The night stars were bright. I sat on a rock and watched them. Down below me, on the lower hillside, the Steilas were dancing one of their intricate graceful dances. They had lit many fires. Dominique has said that their name, Steila, reminds her of an Earth word for stars. I felt pleased by the notion of stars above and below me.

When I had tired of the stars in the sky, I walked downhill toward the Steila village. I stood in the shadow of a tree and watched the Steila ceremony. Valyset sat by a Steila hut and observed the dance. He made quick notations in a notebook,

one of the many Dominique gave him long ago from her
Q Colony supplies. He has made them last a long time. Valyset
says the Steilas' dancing is one of their many modes of communication. There is organization and pattern to it, he told me.
I said I had always known that, but had never realized that
organization and pattern had anything to do with communication. He gave me a long lecture on the subject.

The firelight made Valyset's eyes seem a little mad. The
apparent madness was only a distortion of the bright blue colors
of intense interest in his eyes. As was usual when his eyes'
colors gained in intensity, his angular face, so like mine, appeared whiter in contrast. Often he tapped at his thin nose with
the Q Colony pen he was using for his notes. His shoulders,
permanently rounded from years of field and desk studies, were
dragged down further by the grasp of his youngest son's skinny
arms around them. When he had a note to write down, he held
the notebook awkwardly against the back of his son's legs.

Valyset's wife, Threnas, came out of the hut and took the
child off his hands. Sitting beside Valyset, she rocked the child
to sleep, and from time to time whispered her own observations
to her husband. They study the Steilas together. They have
done so for many years. I sometimes wonder whether the success of their marriage is based on mutual interest in the Steilas.
The Steilas regard Valyset as a leader, at least as much a leader
as they will accept in their leaderless society. They gather
around him rather easily and do their best to look like students
around a beloved teacher. Valyset knows they do this to please
him, and he is happy about it, because it does.

While Valyset basks in Steila glory, and works on his study
of the Steilas, Threnas gets more done within their community.
She suggests the laws, codifies the customs, presides at marriage and funeral ceremonies, gives advice that is ignored by
the Steilas who love hearing it more than acting upon it. Threnas
is, I believe, a little mad, or a touch loony. Even Dominique
has said that sometimes Threnas acts crazily. I have watched
the children of Valyset and Threnas, my grandchildren, for
signs of her malady. So far they seem quite sane, a trifle
impulsive but without Threnas's strange-eyed color shifts. I
am always uneasy around her, tense, a bit put off by her chat-

tering amiability. However, Valyset clearly loves her. He sees beauty and moral virtue when he looks at her. I suppose what he may see is himself reflected in her. Valyset is intelligent but not especially bright.

I watched them study the Steilas for a long time. The dance became frenetic and, in the manner of Steila dances, chastely sexual. When it had gentled to a finish, I returned home.

Dominique was still asleep. I think she is unconscious for the night. She will wake up somewhere in the middle of the night and, I expect, talk again. Or she will stare at the wall before dropping off to sleep again. I checked her face to make sure she was still alive. She was. The twitch of her mouth that always comes to her in sleep was there.

She would like me to write more about her, I suppose. Words seem to be holding down my hands, pressing them toward the paper, ready to crush my fingers against the paper. My fingers are the only part of my body that show my age. They are heavily veined, they remind me of the twisting rivers I can see from the peak of this little mountain. My skin is graying and looking odd. My fingers continue to hurt. But I write.

In her first days with me Dominique plagued me with questions. Why had I retreated to this cottage in the hills? Did I want no more out of life than to tend my gardens, feed my animals, watch over the Steilas? Where was my child? Was it male or female? Did I feel any regret over the man I had killed all those years ago, the human who had assaulted me without my invitation? (She said he probably deserved to die. I don't know that. I believe I misunderstood, judged him as one of my people instead of as a human, acted much too quickly. He, after all, did not know I didn't want him to touch me and that it was my right to choose who had that privilege. I was afraid of humans and compelled toward them. I was wrong. I chose to conceive by a human, by Henry, as a way of repayment for my taking away of a human life.) Did I still remember and feel sorrow for the death of my brother, who had been Dominique's lover? Did I still feel anything for Henry? Where was my child? Who or what are the Steilas? Is there anything at all that you could bring yourself to tell me, out of kindness, sympathy, or for old times' sake? Anything? Where was the child? I answered her sometimes. Sometimes even with the right answers. She suspected when I lied. "You will trust me," she said. I should have known that I would, should have perceived her tenacity, her willingness to sacrifice any dignity to ask a question. She said her curiosity had become dormant during her life with Henry and so she had a lot of it stored up.

All the while she pestered me with her repeated questions, she followed me around and learned my chores. Soon she was grabbing tools away from me, clipping away at flowers, pushing me away from the lorwel and milking it herself. "It's something like pulling on a cow's dugs back on earth, though this nightmarish-looking beast doesn't in any way look like a cow. We call cows contented. This ain't contented." I could not see what Dominique saw.

Her assumption of my chores left me with more time for my studies. I had begun to translate into my language Q Colony books and papers, those which Dominique had saved before personally setting the colony afire. I started instructing Dominique in the lore of my people. She took copious notes. "I'm writing a book about Kew and your people, Alezase, based on Q Colony research, my own observations, and what you're telling me. It'll be my passport back to one of the main colonies." Later she asked me to accompany her on this off-planet escape, but I of course refused. Eventually she lost interest in leaving Kew, but she did finish the book. Its manuscript sits in a corner of this room. Some of its pages have been ripped, others have turned odd pastelish colors.

After she had stolen most of my chores, she invented some of her own. I would walk into my home and find her on her hands and knees scrubbing floors, a task to which I had never been attracted. She scrubbed floors with tiny strokes, lingering over small floor areas. I started to tell her that such meticulous craftsmanship wasn't necessary, but she looked so pleased with herself that I praised her achievement instead.

The chores and the studies were not enough for her. She took to observing the Steilas, with an approach similar to what Valyset uses now, if somewhat less sensible. I used to follow her around the Steila village, very much enjoying the movement of Dominique among its inhabitants. It was a comical sight. She was so tall and they were so short. Most of the Steilas came up only to her knees, and only a few were much taller than that.

Dominique said she found the Steilas to be an attractive people, even though their heads resembled boxes and their bodies were frail. She was fascinated by the delicacy of their long fingers and the way the fingers tended to be constantly in motion. "The best part of their dancing is the way their fingers move," she told me, "sometimes like curtains in the wind, sometimes like a vibrating drill, sometimes in a kind of ripple that goes against all the laws of anatomy I know." When I suggested there are no laws to anatomy, she said was sure of that, now that she had seen the Steilas.

Once she made a few of the Steilas sit still for a physical examination. She spent a lot of time just holding their hands in front of her eyes, so close I could not see how she could possibly focus on them properly. "Their hands are perfect," she reported to me. "Seven fingers, many jointed, a thumb that works like ours. If I had the equipment here, I'd talk one of them into trading with me. Transplanting Steila hands onto my wrists. Impossible, I think, but I'd try. I'd love hands like theirs." Often she would sit in the middle of the Steila village and watch the Steilas go about their daily activities. She was delighted by all of it, even the dull stuff, the day-to-day routines. She smiled often. Occasionally she would clap and urge them to continue whatever performance they were concocting for her. At first she did not see that what they were doing was exactly that, a performance designed by the Steilas to satisfy what they saw as her expectations. Dominique merely saw them as lovable creatures, a view which apparently corresponded to a high number of myths from her own culture. I knew where she was wrong but saw no reason to tell her. I never corrected her on anything unless I was asked.

She finally asked. "They're too much like children in a playland," she said. "Yet they live well, they eat well, they wear clothes of good cloth, they seem well versed on cultural matters. Whatever I tell them of my own culture, history, literature, they pick up easily, absorb it. From what I've been able to interpret of their dialect, they handle abstract ideas easily. Nevertheless, when I come around, they act like happy-go-lucky kids. Why is that, Alezase?" I told her the Steilas were a private people. While extremely friendly to intruders, they tended to perform for them, alter their actual life to conform to their ideas of what the intruders wanted from them. Since Dominique had encountered them with a highly maternal set of attitudes, they became children, a community role which was particularly easy for them because of their small stature and squeezed-together features. Steilas are very patient, I told her, they would have continued to transform themselves into children whenever she was around, at least for as long as she maintained her maternal ways.

"What are Steilas really?" she asked. "What do they really do? What are they really like?" I replied that, since privacy was their habit, it would be wrong for me to tell her what I did realize about them. Later I submitted the same argument to Valyset when he asked me about the Steilas. He set about his own exhaustive study of the Steilas as a result of my stubbornness, as he called it. Dominique went on pestering me for explanations and, when I did not provide them, she cursed me for my prudence and delicacy of taste. "These damn Steilas might be your very own offspring, Alezase, the reflections of your own stubborn hold on your privacy." I smiled and said I doubted that, I couldn't have put up with her silly mothering for as long as the Steilas had.

The next day Dominique approached the Steilas differently. When they started acting childishly as before, she mocked them. Whatever childlike act they did, she imitated it with exaggeration and more than a touch of obvious insult. Steilas are extremely perceptive, and so it took very little time for them to perceive that she was tired of their current performances. Some of them accepted her exaggerations of their behavior and embellished them, acting in a theatrical mock-childish manner. Others took to dancing in a way which, despite their short legs and chunky bodies, quite resembled Dominique imitating a Steila. Many of the village residents chose to form a quiet audience, enjoying considerably the spectacle of Dominique and their neighbors working so hard at making fools of themselves. When Dominique saw the trap she had set for herself, she became enraged and stalked out of the camp, with a bunch of Steilas following her with a synchronized rendition of her long-strided fierce walk. I watched it all from one of my customary nooks, a large rock which overlooked the Steila village. I laughed often, delighting in the mixture of haughtiness and embarrassment in Dominique's face. On her next visits to the village she was cautious and distant. The Steilas perceived this also and allowed her the kind of privacy they liked for themselves.

It was just after the day of Dominique's humiliation that Valyset returned home. I almost panicked. I didn't want him home yet, not before I had decided whether or not I could chance Dominique meeting him. Valyset had been away for a long time, on a tour of several cities and villages, ferreting out scholars and consulting them about Kew history. He was part of an apparently worldwide impulse to renew interest in all aspects of our declined culture. He believed that the practice of history was in a particularly sad state and at that time was intent on organizing a network of scholars who would share their knowledge, information, and interpretations. Eventually, due to the labors of Valyset as well as others who thought like him, this project became successful. It at least salvaged a large quantity of information. History was the project of Valyset's youth, just as the Steilas are the work of his middle years. Dominique feels that Valyset's stubborn determination in whatever he chose to do was a perverted inheritance from his father. They chose radically different goals, she said, but their tenacity was similar. On the other hand, she said, smiling slyly, so is yours, Alezase.

She is awake now. Staring at me. Waiting for me to stop writing and look directly at her.

"You seemed so intent on what you're writing, Alezase. God, you were writing with such speed. Perhaps I should've had you write to me all the years I've lived here. On those pages you just wrote, there're probably more words than you've spoken to me since I've been here. Spoken voluntarily, that is, I don't count the words I get out of you with my prodding and questions.

"No, I'm not hungry and I couldn't get any food past the pain. I want to talk again. I was thinking about Henry. Most of the time he was rather a stiff proposition. You know, distant, ironic, witty in a clumsy way. But, after Joline was born, he went through a period of being quite foolish. He was happy, I suppose. Anyway, I don't know if I can believe my own memories. He actually performed little musical numbers for Joline's benefit. I don't mean just singing to her. He performed them. He'd dress up in whatever asinine clothes he could find and do a whole production for her. Singing loudly, it was like the vocalization of a stomach rumbling, that voice. And dancing, the dancing was the real clownish stuff. You grew to rather like the singing. But the dancing! He couldn't make a move without looking stupid. His arms weren't attached to his body anymore. Their movements had no correlation to the rest of him, at least. His legs were just as bad, stumbling along as if his feet had turned to concrete. But Joline loved it. One day she cried out, 'Daddy dance good,' and he cried. He really did, he cried. Not long, mind you, and just a few tears, a trickle down one side of his face, but real crying. It was her first sentence, you see. Daddy dance good.

"God, Henry was a joy to live with then. He even insulted me less, and I let him off the hook most of the time. I considered having another child, beat that. But then he changed again. I don't know what did it. He became more reserved, if you can imagine that, more quietly sarcastic than ever. It hurt Joline. She was just a baby really. She didn't understand. Neither did I. As years went by, he got worse. He became grizzled, unkempt, hairy. He'd never been particularly hairy before. I don't know why old age brought on all that hair. It was stiff and white, and bits of it grew in opposition to other bits, so it made him look scraggly and, if truth be known, rather awful. Pity you couldn't have seen him then, Alezase. I hate you for having only memories of Henry as a young man. Whenever you think of him, you can only picture him as virile, energetic, slightly gone to seed but only slightly, a fierce and efficient lover. You missed out on all the awful years. For months at a time there was no chance I could love him. But occasionally something would happen, like the time he and Joline got interested in geology or the time when he decided I was more beautiful than I'd ever been before (and this at a time when my face was collapsing in on itself). There'd be an interlude, a remission. He was quite receptive to interludes. He would become cheerful, loving, pleasant. But, over the years, he gradually grew meaner.

"He kept making Joline love him. Just when she was ready to give up on him altogether, he'd shift into one of his rare good moods and he'd amuse her or do something tender or credit her with being a worthwhile human being, something she didn't feel too often. And she'd fall for him all over again. She'd become the baby and it was as if he danced for her again. She knew after a while that his good moods wouldn't last long, but she welcomed them anyway. Rare as they were and short as they were, I think she liked their intensity. She didn't get much intensity out of us otherwise, either of us. Certainly none of the maternal affection I provided so steadily, if not intensely, made her particularly favor me. Henry was her favorite. Whatever mood he was in.

"That time she tried to kill him, she tried to get Colin to do it first. He couldn't. He loved Henry too, I suppose. Colin wasn't really a killer, not then. I find it difficult to accept the notion that he ever became a killer, for all the murderous exploits of his I've heard about. I suspect he did little killing himself, if any. He probably hired soldiers and assassins, maybe he made Sailor assign the dirty work. When Colin couldn't kill Henry, and she saw he couldn't, she made the attempt. I saw her try it. I think I told you about it already. No mind. She didn't really want to kill Henry, I suspect. She knew how to kill even then, Henry had taught her that, too. She knew where to plant a knife effectively. Or maybe she did mean it, maybe she just botched it. She never showed me or Henry any remorse. Came around a few days later, acted normally. She'd been off someplace with Colin. She joked with Henry. He loved it, slid into one of the last of his good moods. They both ignored me for days.

"Write about Henry, Alezase. About Henry and you. I have to sleep some more."

As she quickly eased off to sleep, I watched her closely. A

long time passed before I could see that she was indeed still breathing. She seemed so weak. Her voice had been weak. There was a weakness in her face that I'd never seen before. She won't last much longer. A little blood had come out of her ear, and I wiped it away with a cloth. She did not even stir.

She told me to write about Henry. I don't know why she expects me to do what she tells me. What can I write? He was a strange being to me. All the humans at that time were strange beings to me, and to my people. Even Dominique, who then and now worked so hard to make herself understood by us, by me, even she was a strange being.

Henry first caught my attention because he looked so healthy. The colony had been ravaged by a plague before he came, and the surviving colonists were pale and sickly. Dominique, the healthiest of the lot, had begun to show the strain of leadership and was herself a bit sallow. Therefore, Henry stood out from the others just because there were splashes of red in his face, an eagerness in his eyes. The eagerness, I suspect, was merely the human version of the desires I had begun to feel. I had no trouble forcing him to make love to me. There was no real force involved. Dominique told me recently that Q Colony biologists had not anticipated the possibility of fertility between humans and us. They were quite surprised when Henry and I proved them wrong. She said some of the scientists who arrived later rejected the possibility of it, especially since Valyset had never been seen by a colonist, not even Henry, although many of the humans observed the early stages of my pregnancy. Our people of course did not expect infertility between us and the humans. We were so much alike. We have always believed they *are* us, in spite of the minute physical differences. There had been a time when Kew was an advanced and powerful planet. Legend has it that we did send boats into space. Many scholars, however, dispute that and claim our ancient history is a reflection of our dreams and just as fantastically conceived.

I never made love with Henry again after I had caused the conception of Valyset. I did not want to. I had seen the despair in his eyes by then, eyes whose colors normally hid his emotions, eyes whose pretences were more varied than the emotional colors of the eyes of my people, of the Oonaas as he called them. Also, there had been battles and killing, and the death of my brother in one of the battles, and I was confused. Henry had been part of the killing, I knew, maybe one of its planners, yet he had seemed to be a peacemaker. He and Dominique had conspired together in some way I have never understood, in some human way whose messages could not be transmitted to us. Too many people were killed. My brother was dead. I had to leave. It never occurred to me, until Dominique told me later, that Henry would have wanted me to stay. It did not occur to me he might have wanted to see Valyset.

That is all I remember about Henry, or at least all I care to record in this manuscript.

Dominique remained asleep, so I walked down to the Steila village. Dawn had just come. The morning was cool and the air was pleasantly scented by smoke from Steila pottery ovens. The Steilas had been up and about for hours. Some were weaving, some were making bowls and vases, some were stitching together large swatches of cloth into decorative hangings, some were cooking and baking, some were forming metal into utensils. They were, in fact, engaged in all the useful activities that form the day-to-day lives of the Steilas. Their products were in great demand everywhere on Kew, but they were hard to procure since there were so few Steila villages, almost all of them located in remote areas. Besides, the Steilas did not much care for the hue and cry of commerce. They could not bargain, set prices, even imagine a value for their works. They could not see why anyone would want the things they made. They made them because they wanted to. Making things was their life. They enjoyed doing it, and they didn't mind storing away their handiwork until they found uses for it or for those rare moments when they could prompt themselves to sell some goods at prices below their worth. City people pay dearly for Steila-crafted merchandise. Still, traders and businessmen have ceased coming to Steila villages, claiming that the enterprise is uneconomical. They say that, in spite of the high return they receive on Steila items, the detours they have to take and the risk of leaving the village empty-handed (there are times when Steilas just will not respond to commercial pleadings) have made their trips too speculative.

Years ago Valyset set about trying to improve the Steilas' commercial situation. "If it's so difficult to get the Steila goods to the market," he told me, "perhaps then we should take the Steilas themselves to the market." I laughed, thinking he was joking. He became hurt, angry. The ghost of Henry Stoner materialized in his face momentarily as he expressed his determination to help both the Steilas and their economy with his brilliant idea. I was sorry for hurting his feelings, but I stood by my belief that Steila life should not be disturbed by us. He became petulant. I became condescending, a mother's right in such circumstances. I had forgotten how really young he was. At that time he had just grown tall, and his face had suddenly become older than his years. With these physical changes came an authority, an assumption of his presumed destiny as an adult. He declared he would try out his idea and immediately went among the Steilas to persuade them. He seemed genuinely surprised when at first no Steila showed interest in leaving the village to become rich in one of the cities. "I thought surely there would be some discontents among them," he said. I told him that, as far as I knew, as far as I could remember, a Steila never went anywhere. With renewed boldness he said he would convince at least one to come, even if he had to try abduction.

As it turned out, he was able to talk three Steilas into making the trip with him. They all left the village, drawing behind them wagons full of Steila creations. The trio of Steilas were a curious lot, each one in some way physically malformed. One's face had been scarred by a fire, pottery flames that caught the wrong draft and blew out at her when she was merely checking the progress of her artistry. Another had a deformed arm that twisted unnaturally away from his body. Nevertheless, he was an expert weaver, able to use his bad arm to make needle incisions into cloth with extreme delicacy. The third was the most normal of the group except that he was tall for a Steila. He was just a bit shorter than I, and severely emaciated. As he led the craftsmen trio down the road, Valyset smiled sheepishly back at me. I was afraid for him, but at the same time impressed by his overwhelming determination. I expected that his experiment would be successful.

He returned to us soon after. I saw the confusion on his face immediately. The goods they had brought to the city had fetched fine prices, mostly due to Valyset's cleverness. He had also been able to barter well for food supplies for the Steilas of the village, along with equipment they could use for their gifted works. However, he was sad. One of the Steilas, the tall one, had died soon after their arrival in the city. "I feel I killed him," Valyset said to me, and it took all my resources as a mother to soothe him, to make him realize he should not take on the responsibility for the Steila's death. Halfheartedly, he agreed with me, then went on about the job of apportioning the supplies he had brought back for the Steilas. Word came that another of the Steila travelers, the one with the scarred face, had also died in the city, where she had been hired by a merchant to manufacture her pottery. Not long after that, news of the third Steila's death arrived. Valyset pretended to respond sensibly to my attempt to assuage his guilt for initiating the project, but I think he still feels responsible for the three dead Steila artisans. He abandoned plans of establishing productive Steila settlements within the cities. We found out eventually that other such experiments which attempted to transplant Steilas to new places had also met with disaster. We have since concluded that a Steila removed from his community will simply die.

Going to his house I found Valyset, like the Steilas, up and about. He had been awake for hours, and so had Threnas. She was tending their fields in the valley below. I had once been the grower of food in those fields, and Dominique had taken the task from me, although sometimes we harvested together. Threnas took it over when it became too difficult for Dominique to make the trip to them every day. Valyset and Threnas have enlarged the cultivated land area so that reserves of food can be accumulated for emergencies. Fortunately, over the years, with sudden illnesses and minor disasters, their stored-away supplies have been used well, often saving lives.

I particularly enjoyed seeing Valyset when Threnas was not around. I've never been able to decide whether I like Threnas or not. I do find her a bizarre mother and a chatterer beyond belief. When she was not at home, Valyset and I could at least share quiet. He had been transcribing his notes from the night before. I told him to go on with it. He did.

I watched him work. I've always liked watching him work, watching him run his fingers over paper he's just written something on as if he can test the truth of his observation through touching the pen strokes. It seemed to me that he looked sadder today, a bit older. Although we may not show age as dramatically as our human friends, we do exhibit a discoloring here, a deepening of line there, a suggestion of gravity pulling at our entire body more and more as years go by. To avoid seeing the age in his face, I wandered about his study. For a scholar it is a rather neat area. He stacks his papers with their edges precisely aligned. His notes tend to be piled in numbered order.

Above his desk I saw the sword that Dominique had brought with her to the village, her daughter's sword. Although it's been on the wall above Valyset's desk for some time, I don't usually notice it. It is like all the other pictures and documents that adorn the walls of his study. Once you've examined them closely, they become a background blur that only occasionally comes individually into focus. The sword should have been more noticeable, though. It caught light easily and made the room seem brighter. Sometimes Valyset takes it with him to the forest and practices with it, pretending to be a swordsman, thrusting at bushes and tall grass. He does not know I have seen him playing his warrior games. He generally smiles broadly, pleased with himself, each time he defeats a bush or blade of grass. I suppose he spends much time cleaning the sword and sharpening it to a fine edge. He has worked with its handle too, replacing its lost gems with delicate smooth costume jewelry. He does not have the best sense of color and the effect is somewhat garish, but it is still a formidable-appearing weapon. I think Valyset enjoys its oddness in a scholar's study. On the rare occasions when he has welcomed an outside visitor into the room, I have noticed that he searches the visitor's eyes to see if the sword is the first thing they notice about the room.

When Valyset finally looked up from his work, rubbing his eyes with just the tips of his fingers before settling his attention upon me, I told him he looked gloomy. The remark made him smile. "Not gloomy really," he said, "just a little, oh, disoriented. I saw someone today I wasn't prepared to see again. Are you going to ask whom?" I told him I couldn't even guess. "I was out walking before dawn. Threnas doesn't allow me to start my work unless I get some exercise first. I skirted around the village and walked through the valley, toward the forest. I could even feel the hike doing me good and walked farther than I'd intended. I discovered some nomads camped just at the edge of the forest and watched them from the rim of a hill. They seemed to be a rather seedy-looking group, and I noticed a couple of knives in belts, a sword lying by a tent flap, but all in all they appeared to be harmless. Just peaceful nomads going about their business in the usual nomadic ways. I was about to come home when I saw a young man come out of one of the tents. At first I thought he might be a child, he was so short and his stride was so jaunty. Then I noticed something about him, a swing of the arms that seemed familiar. I stared at him for a long time, and even now I can't be certain since he was just a child when I last saw him, but, mother, I think it was Steffan. He looked like Steffan grown up."

Steffan. I had forgotten about Steffan. So much time has passed since he first materialized outside my door, his arms swinging in the manner Valyset had apparently recognized. A distinctive arm-swing that suggested confidence, even arrogance. He said he wanted to see Dominique. How he knew she was in the cottage, he never explained. Steffan was, after all, a youngster of about thirteen or fourteen then, although I might have guessed younger since he was so small for his age. His face was unattractive. He had heavy glowering lips that dominated his face and seemed to preordain cruelty. His nose was too flat. His eyes were so buried in his skull that you had to concentrate your gaze to see them. His request to see Dominique was spoken aggressively. We didn't realize at the time that he regarded his aggressiveness as an inherited duty.

Dominique emerged from the cottage. I remember that she was especially good-looking then. Her skin was weatherbeaten and dark with tan, her hair was a stark white which accented her skin's darkness and made her seem lovelier than any time before or later. I suppose I should record here that I have loved Dominique for some time and, despite the fact that we have made love only infrequently, I recall the details of our physical relationship precisely and with a sentiment that brings tears to my eyes when just writing about it coldly as I am doing now. I do not care, however, to present those details for other eyes to see, no matter how much accuracy Dominique might require for this manuscript.

Dominique confronted Steffan with a practiced sternness, the studied reaction she presented to anyone who intruded into her life, regardless of the intruder's age or size. Steffan responded with an arrogant smile. He looked much sillier than he could have suspected. In a speech that he must have practiced extensively, he announced that he was the son of Colin, a declaration that even took Dominique aback. For a while it made him the center of our attention, as we busied ourselves with questions of who he was and how he had shown up at our doorstep. He explained that he had been adopted into a family of traders with whom he traveled. He had uncovered Dominique's whereabouts by asking about her wherever he went, pinpointing the exact location through some chance remarks made by some other traders who had been disappointed in their attempted commerce with our Steila community. He then persuaded his own family of traders to make a try at obtaining Steila goods. He said, in an aside to us, that his family would probably fail since they weren't particularly good at their profession, but he didn't care since he had achieved his own objective. Dominique asked him what precisely his objective was. He said he had longed to meet the fabled Dominique LaPointe. "Fabled?" Dominique said, laughing. "Hardly fabled." Steffan smirked and replied, "Well, I heard about you from my mother before she died, and she made you sound formidable. She never met you, but apparently my father spoke of you often and in glowing terms." Dominique said she couldn't imagine Colin giving her any credit for anything. "At any rate," Steffan said, "to me you're fabled. You're a character in my mother's stories. And I'm not the only one who's heard of you. I've encountered others. Your reputation has spread far. You were Henry Stoner's wife and he was the father of Colin.

You were the leader of Q Colony, and were responsible for the initial communication between humans and Oonaas." Dominique flinched at Steffan's use of the word Oonaa, but held back her criticism. "You're a part of history," Steffan said. Dominique laughed sarcastically. "I'm not too crazy about being that kind of footnote," she said. "My connections to your history are too tenuous for me. I dearly hope that my part in it all will be soon forgotten." Steffan dismissed Dominique's statement as trivial misplaced modesty, then suddenly made the boast that we were going to hear many times in varying words during the few days he spent with us: "I plan to carry on in my father's tradition. I'll conquer even more than he did, become more famous than he."

Dominique had to labor a bit to extract Steffan's history from him. Although the task should not have been difficult when dealing with so talkative a subject, it proved harder than she'd expected because, despite his youth, he was as discursive as a bad philosopher. He was also reluctant to consider the obvious doubts about his parentage. His was a story easy to doubt. The way he told it, his mother, Follase, had been a servant of Colin's court. Eventually she became his favorite bed-sharer and was quite delighted when she discovered one day she was pregnant. She reported that fact to Colin with great enthusiasm. She figured that a ruler needed an heir, so she expected him to be delighted also. Instead, he banished her from the court, muttering something about not being responsible for the poison inside her womb. She left the capitol city and traveled to a small village, where she became a house-servant and gave birth to Steffan. Most of Steffan's memories of her were of her telling and retelling the history of his parentage. "Mother wanted me to be like him. She said I had a destiny, a great future." Follase had died when Steffan was seven. The orphan was not wanted by the family who had employed his mother, so he ran away and found a new family in the trader-nomads. "My father's death came too soon. Too much of what he gained is now lost. I'll not only avenge his death, but make his name greater by making mine supreme." His hearty bombastic declarations never failed to draw laughter from Dominique. She liked having him around. He amused her. Steffan, for his part, did not seem to mind her laughter. It was as if nothing, not even failure and death, could erode his confidence.

I told Dominique that first day that I did not believe Steffan's story, that either he had made it up or his mother had lied to him. She said that lying was possible but she felt he was telling the truth. Not only that, she believed he could be Colin's son. "He has the eyes," she said. I told her they were surely human eyes, lacking the emotional color changes of my people, but I felt it was just as possible he was the by-blow of any human with Follase. "No, Alezase, they're not just any human's eyes, they're Colin's eyes. Don't you see, they're Henry's eyes. Hidden a bit by the brow, yes, but Henry's and Colin's eyes. Joline's eyes." I said, a bit petulantly I suspect, that they were not Valyset's eyes, and she agreed.

Steffan strutted around our lives for a short time and then, when his trader family had indeed failed with the Steilas, he was gone. Unnerved by Steffan's too frequent resemblances to Henry Stoner, I was relieved and happy to see the boy go and hoped never to see him again. Now, if Valyset was right, Steffan was lurking at our borders, like a Colin readying for battle.

"He's still a small one," Valyset said. "But he's grown some, and his face has aged more than I'd've expected." Valyset had not liked Steffan. He had hardly spoken to the child years ago. At that time Threnas was nagging him about their not having children, and she seemed to take to Steffan as a substitute for her own nonexistent child. Valyset confided to me then that he was worried about a possible lack of fertility in himself or barrenness in Threnas. Because of the infertility and because of the scholar's distaste for the arrogant child-braggart, Valyset clearly resented Threnas's interest in Steffan. Very soon after Steffan's departure, Threnas announced her first pregnancy, and she has proved astonishingly fertile ever since.

"Why is he here now, Mother?" Valyset asked. I suggested that perhaps he was still a trader and that he had merely led another nomadic bunch here to deal with the stubborn Steilas. "Maybe. Maybe. But they didn't look like traders. They do have empty carts with them, though, the kind you hitch onto your shoulders and lug along yourself. Steila merchandise is mostly light, so I guess they could have bartering plans. But they're a pretty mean-looking and scraggly crew. They all looked like Steffan. Variations on him anyway." I told Valyset that he was probably exaggerating, that their cruel appearance might have been a trick of the predawn light, or his own predawn memories of Steffan. He smiled, said that was probably so.

He glanced at the sword on the wall and I didn't like the way his eyes expressed a longing to grab it and go off to practice, perhaps on Steffan. He caught my look and seemed a little embarrassed. He started fingering his papers, his usual signal that he wanted to get back to work. I had come just to see him, I did that every day, and I had seen him, so now I could leave. I said good-bye. Before I left the room, he asked after Dominique. I replied I didn't think she could live much longer. He nodded. A suggestion of tears in his eyes. "I'll come up, look in, later," he said. He didn't really have to say that, since he looked in every day, but I said that would be nice.

Just outside his dwelling I encountered Threnas, returning home from her tasks in the fields. She has an uncanny sense of when I'll drop in on Valyset. Even though I try to visit when she will be busy elsewhere, she generally manages to show up before I leave. As always I dug my heels into the ground, placed my hands in a position in which I could fidget unobserved, set my mouth into a smile that could not be felt beyond my lips, and listened to Threnas talk. I don't know now what she said to me. I merely know when to grunt, when to say something conversationally noncommittal, when to nod my head. She never looks at the pale colors of boredom in my eyes. She never wants to see that. She might realize they are the colors in the eyes of all her listeners. Threnas's eyes, on the other hand, are alive with color. They are dazzling. You can't help but notice her eyes anyway. Her features are so tiny, they are merely support for her eyes, that and the wild red-brown hair that sprouts from her head like the flowering ends of one of the strange hybrids she grows from a blending of human seeds left over from Dominique's Q Colony supplies with native seeds. Threnas is a small chubby woman, and I always leave her with my neck hurting from standing stiffly and staring down at her. I think this time she told me she'd seen signs someone was stealing from her garden. Later, after I returned home, it occurred to me that the theft might have something to do with Steffan's nomad-traders.

When I came into her room, I saw that Dominique was still asleep. I was alarmed. She usually wakes early, with a startled grunt. Examining her more closely, I saw perspiration streaming from her forehead. She perspired frequently, it had some connection to her illness. Touching her gently, so as not to wake her, I felt her face. Her skin was very cold. As always, I checked her body, careful not to move her too roughly. She had urinated extensively, and I gently removed her undergarment, wiped her with a damp cloth, and put a fresh undergarment on her. While I worked with her, her perspiration decreased. Her breathing became heavier but had a regular rhythm. Threnas had given me a flower from her garden, and I pinned it to Dominique's bedshirt.

She was all right.

After I had finished writing the above and nibbled on some fruit even though I was not particularly hungry, Valyset arrived. He was earlier than usual. I commented on that. He said he was worried about Dominique and could not concentrate on his work. He was losing faith in the study, he said, and that there would be no readers around who would interest themselves in a detailed description of Steila life. I suggested that, while that might be true, it did not matter. If he felt all those complex urges to do the study, then he should do it. "That's what I tell myself every night before I go to sleep," he said. He went to Dominique's side and, with his hands behind his back, studied her with the same intensity he devoted to his papers. It occurred to me, as it often does, that he will be devastated by Dominique's death, no matter how much preparation her long illness has given him.

On that day when Valyset returned from his trip, he found out soon about Dominique's presence in my quarters. The Steilas told him. He had always been close to the Steilas. With their skill at adapting to our needs, they had become perfect playmates for him as he grew up. And their treatment of him matured as he did. They were childish when he was a child, older when he was older. During his youth they showed an equal interest in his scholarly pursuits, and they encouraged him in them.

As soon as the Steilas told Valyset of the wild-acting Earth woman, he of course wanted to see her. And, as I have written, Dominique was anxious to see Valyset, too anxious I thought. My heart left my body and disintegrated as I watched them come together, he with his eyes brilliantly curious and his smile broad, she with a calm self-satisfaction just barely disguising her excitement. They began talking eagerly, chattering and laughing like old friends, exchanging information like familiar colleagues. An observer would have concluded they'd known each other for years.

"He looks something like Henry," Dominique said to me, when they were ready to allow me into their conversation. "Not enough to do him much damage, but just a small resemblance. Fortunately for him, he's mostly inherited your looks, Alezase. He's gorgeous." I had never thought of my son as gorgeous, and for a short time felt somewhat threatened by Dominique's approval, became even fearful of a romantic alliance between her and Valyset. I didn't like that idea at all, especially if I had to appear to endorse an entanglement between my son and the aged wife of his father. However, Dominique's and Valyset's interest in each other was more intellectual than passionate. Oh, I think he adored her, but as a goddess, an aunt, as a bizarre creature from another planet.

I was never able to judge Valyset's inclinations in romantic and sexual directions. Word came to me that he had trysts with young women, but he kept the women out of sight, perhaps out of politeness to me. When he decided to marry and presented me with his new bride, Threnas, I found myself even more puzzled by what romantic and sexual drives urged Valyset onward. Threnas was a practical choice and maybe he realized that. But that observation may be merely a mother's spite. Valyset loves Threnas rather slavishly, a mystery that I cannot penetrate.

Dominique and Valyset spent long hours talking over the subjects that were their specialties. She described the work of the Q Colony team. He set forth his ideas about Kew's history, about the Steila culture. They gave each other opinions, appropriated each other's opinions. They discussed anything at all at great length. They became friends. I don't think Valyset has ever had a better one. So, watching him now, looking down at her as if she were already dead, I could not hold back a few tears. They were, after all, the two people I loved, and they loved me. I can't stand the three of us all in the same room together anymore, it makes me too sad.

After he had maintained a brief vigil at Dominique's bedside, Valyset began striding around the room, talking as he always did of the trivial matters, of his life with Threnas, of their children, of his day-to-day activities, of the weather, of the pretty scenes up and down the hillside. He stopped talking suddenly and I realized he was standing over my manuscript and staring at it with a kind of hunger in his eyes. I knew what he would ask and, when he did, I told him that I was writing the manuscript for Dominique. "May I read it?" he asked, too much eagerness in his eyes for my taste. I said yes anyway. Since he had grown up, I had forgotten how to refuse him.

I couldn't think of anything to do while he pored voraciously over my pages. There were a million things to be done, but I couldn't think of one of them. Suddenly Valyset laughed. I felt anger and fear simultaneously, anger that he might be critical of anything in the manuscript, fear that his laughter was justified. Glancing up, he saw these emotions in my eyes and explained he had just read himself described as intelligent but not bright. I felt shame, why had I written that? "Don't be upset, mother," he said. "It's an apt description. It's what I am. I never thought you saw it, though. Never thought that." He went on reading.

When he had finished, he held the manuscript in his lap for a long time and did not speak. "I'm glad you're doing this," he finally said. I asked him why. "I suppose as a memorial to Dominique," he said, "and, for where you're willing to put down anything about yourself, as a record of Alezase. You've never written about yourself before, have you? Anywhere." I said that, except for my few translations of Q Colony material,

I had never written anything about anything. "Yes, I know," he said. "Why don't you ever report what you say in this?" I said I thought I did. "Well, in a way. Indirectly. I said this, I suggested that, I replied, I told her whatever. But you never directly report your words, never put down on these pages exactly what you said. You put down what we say, what Dominique says, what I say, even what Steffan said so long ago. But never what you say, never a direct quote from Alezase." I said I didn't care to report my words, especially my exact words. He was about to argue with me, but he saw in my eyes that I'd brook no argument from him on the matter, and so he just nodded. I asked him if he was angry about what I'd written about Threnas. "No. I know what you think about her. I'd put that subject aside long ago. You do well for me. She does well for me. Why should I care what you think about each other? I'd like for you to care for her more, but I see you can't. I see it even better now that I've read this. Threnas is, after all, not your greatest admirer either, Mother, although I suspect she likes you somewhat better than you like her." I had not considered the possibility of Threnas's dislike of me, didn't think she was capable of it. Nevertheless, I was hurt by the knowledge, and then confused and angry at myself since I had no right to expect her to like me. "Continue the writing," Valyset said. "If you allow me to read it when you are done, I'll be pleased. If you choose to keep it private, that is all right, too."

He left. Now that he has read some of this manuscript, I feel strange continuing it. Will it remain the private record which Dominique requested of me, or will I have Valyset in mind as its eventual reader, wondering what will he think of this, whether such a scholar would approve of that. Will I hold something back so that I won't hurt his feelings? I don't think I would have written that comment on his intelligence if I had thought he was going to see it. And I have already done Threnas enough damage with my spiteful comments on her. If I had known at the outset that writing this manuscript would bring me so much unanticipated trouble, I would have refused Dominique.

She is awake again, waiting for me to stop writing so that

she can speak and I record her words. So the manuscript has affected her behavior also. Normally, if she needed to say something, she would just start talking and not wait for a time when it can be written down. I think she plans her words ahead of time. Perhaps she structures what she says, thinks it all out beforehand.

"You're all fury, Alezase. Fury in your eyes, fury in your hand as you write. I've never seen your body so tense. Can you tell me why? No? Have it your way then. Steffan is somewhere near. I see I shocked you with that. He was here. While you were gone. I think he said he hid in a bush somewhere and watched you leave. I woke up to find him staring down at me. I couldn't read the expression on his face. It might have been arrogance, could even have been happiness to see me again, who can tell? You know Steffan. He said right off that he wanted to see me one more time before I died. I asked him how he had known I was going to die, who had told him. He said he hadn't known until he came into my room. He said death has already settled into my face, and it is only a matter of time. I told him he was right. I don't have much time at all.

"My throat is extremely sore, all down one side. It gets worse every day. I have to die soon. To please myself. Where was I? Steffan. I asked him what he was up to. Nothing, he said. I thought he was lying and told him so. 'You're lying,' I said. He seemed pleased I said it. I tried to sit up, with the intention of standing up, so that I could tower over him. I suspect he would hate looking up at me, but I could barely lift my head. 'You'd better not be planning any mischief,' I told him. He didn't respond to that. He stood over my bed for a long while. Sort of muttering just beneath his breath. I couldn't hear what he said. 'What are you saying?' I said. 'Whatever I've got's affecting my hearing. Stuff comes out of my ears and I pick it off the pillow. What are you saying, Steffan?' He didn't speak for a while. Just went on muttering. 'What is it, bastard?' I said, not even thinking of the fact that of course he is one. 'What are you saying?' He answered, 'Some prayers for you, old lady, some prayers.' Then he strode pompously out of the room. You're looking at me strangely, Alezase. Did

I dream it? I thought not. Tell me how you know. . . .

"I see. Maybe you should go meet with Steffan, you and Valyset. Try to ferret out what he's up to. Influence him against it, whatever it is. I don't think he's just traveling with nomads. There's something else. Whatever happened to his plans to be a world-conqueror? I'd like to know that, too. Like to know that before I die. Please find out for me, Alezase."

Dominique continued to pester me until she fell asleep again. I stopped writing down her words, which infuriated her. When she asked me to resume, I refused. She accused me of being stubborn, of being always stubborn. I said my fingers were aching from all the words. They couldn't work again for a while. She said I was lying, said I didn't want to continue writing just to spite her. I said I enjoy spiting her, but that had nothing to do with why I stopped writing. She gave up, her usual response to a spat with me, and fell asleep almost instantly.

I am not going to Steffan. I don't want to see him, talk to him. I don't want to find out what niggling little plot is inside his head these days. I haven't slept in a long time myself. I will nap now.

I am exhausted. I can hardly hold this pen in my fingers, this pen which originally came from Q Colony, with the marks of Dominique's teeth all over its end. I've got so much to write down, so much as happened. I must record it all before Dominique dies. Perhaps I can show it to her before she dies, read it to her.

I napped for only a short time. I dreamed of Steilas offering themselves as our food. My people never had dreams during sleep before the humans came. Dominique has said that she and her colleagues at Q Colony were never able to figure out just why or how the human presence on our planet has initiated our dreams and nightmares. She said it was a strange gift. I agreed, remembering the first time I had a dream. It was an innocuous dream, even a pleasant one, but I woke up ready to scream, sweat all over my body. When you've grown up not dreaming, any first dream is a nightmare. I still experience pleasant dreams as nightmares, and nightmares as something worse. I don't know why I dreamed of the Steilas. Maybe, in some spooky way, I was sensing what was occurring down in the Steila village.

Suddenly Threnas was shaking me awake. She was talking more rapidly than usual and I couldn't understand her. I thought for a moment I had just slipped abruptly into another dream. Her words seemed garbled to me. I don't even know how long she was talking before I came to full consciousness. I awoke in midsentence, it seemed. It was awhile before I could slow her down to a speed where I could comprehend her words. At first I thought she was merely being her usual self, lost in excitement over something minor, an incident that could be solved with a moment's thought or action. Then I detected the words blood, Valyset, all over the ground, behind his head. I sat up straight and began shaking Threnas by her shoulders. I forced her to express herself in logical sentences. She still talked quickly but at least I could understand her.

There had been an attack on the village, she said, a sudden attack. There was a lot of noise. She and Valyset heard it and rushed out of their cottage. The Steilas were running everywhere. Dust was being kicked up by them and their attackers. Valyset recognized what was happening immediately. "They're abducting Steilas," he shouted to Threnas and, running forward, disappeared into a dust cloud. Threnas followed, but lost him for a time. Seeing the attackers grabbing Steilas and stealing objects from storehouses to pile in carts, Threnas realized they must be the nomads Valyset had mentioned to her earlier. She tried to interfere with a couple of them, pulling at their arms and freeing at least one Steila, but they were able to push her to the ground. Rising, she saw a short man running toward her with a Steila vase under one arm and a long knife in his free hand. It looked to her as if he was going to lash out at her with the knife if she didn't get out of his way. It was a moment before she recognized the man as Steffan grown up. She hollered his name. He was clearly taken aback. Whether or not he recognized Threnas, she was not certain. But he did pull back from her and run away. He tripped over a rock and the vase crashed to the ground, breaking into many small sharp-pointed pieces.

The attack ended just as abruptly as it had begun, Threnas

said. She began searching for Valyset. A Steila leader helped her. He informed her that at least thirty members of their community had been kidnapped by this band. "What will you do?" she asked. He said there was nothing they could do. As she searched the village for Valyset, Threnas became frightened that perhaps he had been abducted, too, maybe as a hostage. Then she discovered him behind a hut at the edge of the village, unconscious, his clothes ripped in several places, blood in a pool around his head. When she ascertained he was still alive, she got some Steilas to help her carry Valyset back to their home. She started to tend him, but he came awake for a moment and told her to come get me. Leaving Steilas to finish bandaging Valyset up, Threnas rushed to my cottage.

For a moment I could not believe that all of what she said had happened. How could I have slept through a battle in the Steila village?

I told Threnas we must go to Valyset, help him. As we headed toward the doorway, Dominique stirred. "Don't let them get away with it," she said, "we mustn't let them get away with it." Going to her bedside, I told her to hush, we wouldn't, and to rest because I'd be back as soon as I could. She reached toward me, her arm trembling, and tried to say something, but I kissed her hand, held it momentarily against my cheek, said good-bye and left her room.

Running down the path to the village, Threnas stumbled and fell twice, and I helped her up each time. Tears were streaming out of her eyes now and she could not talk at all. She tried to form words, but they came out in little sobs and chokes.

There was a dusty acrid smell to the air within the village. Steilas wandered around, looking dazed, picking up shards of broken objects, shreds of ripped cloth, sweeping debris into piles. I saw, through the open door of one of the storehouses, that the usually neat Steila shelves were in disarray and many of their creations had been thrown to the floor.

We found Valyset bandaged and awake, sitting on the edge of his bed, looking quite alert and scarcely affected by the blow which had felled him. His oldest daughter sat beside him and gently stroked his arm, two of his boys sat on the floor and looked up at him, some admiration in their eyes. Threnas put the children under the charge of a Steila woman, who ushered them, all three of them protesting loudly, out of the room.

"We have to make plans, counterattack," Valyset said before he would let me ask him how he felt. When I did ask, he said it was just a minor wound, a trifling blood loss, and it didn't matter anyway. "They've taken more than thirty Steilas," he said. "Why?" Threnas asked. "I suspect they think they can take them and their wares to cities, sell them. Sell the Steilas as well as the goods." I said they couldn't do that, the Steilas would all die in the cities. "I am painfully in memory of that, Mother. I killed three in my time by taking them to a city. That's why I must get these Steilas back. I can't allow them to die! I can't!" He sounded like a disillusioned, dissatisfied child, and I wanted to comfort him, but instead I merely asked what could we possibly do. He said we had to pursue the attackers, rescue the Steilas, and return them to their homes. I asked him if he had worked out a plan that would accomplish all that. He said no, he hadn't. I did not know what to say. I wanted to bring back the Steilas, but I did not want Valyset to go up against a gang whose viciousness was already clear, a gang vicious enough to have Steffan as a member. I was too frightened of Valyset being killed.

Threnas was just as worried as I, but she expressed herself more dramatically. She threw herself onto Valyset's chest (he winced as she made contact) and begged him to forget plans and rescues, go to the authorities at the capital and make the government there force the nomads to give up the Steilas. "That takes too much time, Threnas," Valyset said. "By the time those fair-minded emotionless judges, with their precise views of law and morality, get the right machinery going, most of the Steilas'll be dead. No, it's up to us. And, if not up to us, up to me." I said we shouldn't endanger our lives, that we should go forward with caution. Threnas joined in my protest and, while I felt embarrassed by her support, I was not too embarrassed to interfere with it. "You can't do it," she cried. "We can't do it. There're too many of them. They're organized. We can't win against them."

"We've got to try," said Dominique. She was standing in

the doorway of Valyset's room, already dominating the room with her height, sending a long shadow into the room which ended at my feet. Her face was red with energy, flushed, a false picture of health. Her body was straight and her shoulders were thrown back, making the emaciation of the illness less obvious. She had managed to dress herself in fresh clothes, an outfit that had practically been her uniform back at Q Colony. A light brown shirt with what she called epaulets on the shoulders, a slightly darker pair of brown trousers that made her legs look longer than any other piece of clothing she ever wore. She had on boots that, in our closet, had never shown such a shine. She'd combed her hair neatly. I wondered how she could have had time to do that. She smiled and only I perhaps could see the tiny dried bits of blood on her front teeth. "We've got to try," she said. "Get up, Valyset. I got out of bed, you do it now. If we don't get on the move, those bastards'll be miles away before dark. Let's get to it, all right? Up, Valyset, c'mon." Valyset sprang up with a spryness I would not have thought possible with a bashed-in head. I went to Dominique, implored her to return to her room, to her bed. I told her she couldn't possibly go trekking through the countryside after bandits in her condition. "I don't feel the pain right now," she said. Threnas and I exchanged anxious glances. I turned to Valyset, tried to enlist his aid in getting Dominique back to bed, but he interrupted me to say he could see she was all right. He seemed unnaturally pleased, looking at Dominique's facade of health as if it were a miracle, perhaps indeed assuming that a miracle had taken place. "See, Alezase?" Dominique said quietly. "Your son is every bit as stubborn as you are." Valyset, ignoring her comment, told us we would get going now.

Before we left the cottage, Valyset went to his study. He returned with Joline's sword strapped in a scabbard to his belt. I was about to protest, but one angry look from him and I kept my silence. Some of the Steilas offered to come with us but, since they had no combative abilities, Dominique and Valyset agreed not to endanger their community further by taking them. Valyset and Threnas said good-bye to their children, who leaned out of the windows of their home.

As we walked through the village, I noticed that Dominique

walked as she had when I'd first seen her, back at Q Colony. Taking long strides, she covered ground quickly and gracefully. She had perhaps been a shade faster in the past but perhaps never so graceful. We crossed the border of the village without any hesitation or looking back.

We had no trouble picking up the trail. Our bandits had left plenty of signs indicating their escape route. There were more footprints and wagon wheel ruts than we needed. The trail went right through our carefully cultivated fields toward the forest beyond. Threnas muttered a series of rapid curses as she saw the damage to many of her crops.

We made, I am sure, a curious-looking quartet of avengers. Valyset kept up with Dominique's pace, stride for stride, while I stayed a little behind, watching bushes, trees, high stalks, and boulders for clues to possible ambush. Threnas stumbled along at the rear, her clumsy feet providing a steady argument for why she should have been left behind.

Catching up to Dominique, I asked her how she expected us to go up against armed thieves with no weapons. Pointing toward Joline's sword bouncing against the side of Valyset's leg, she said we had a weapon, and we had ourselves. Tentatively I offered the view that, fine as we were, we could possibly be destroyed by individuals less fine. She laughed, stopped walking long enough to hug me tightly for a second. Then she continued on. Her face was even more flushed than before. I couldn't be sure but I thought I saw her wipe sweat from her brow when she thought I wasn't looking.

We caught up with the bandits rather easily. Using the main path through the forest, they herded the abducted Steilas ahead of them. Four Steilas were hauling overfilled carts behind them, others were struggling along at a pace which, while something of an amble for the bandits, was too quick for the short legs of their prisoners. When a Steila stumbled or even fell, a bandit would pick him up and shove him quite roughly back into the uneven line. The cart-drawing Steilas were treated with equal severity. Once a pottery dish bounced out of a cart and broke. Steffan rushed up to the Steila pulling the cart and cuffed him a couple of blows around the neck. Another of the workhorse Steilas was beaten on the shoulders with a long stick by another of the bandits. When she saw that happen, Threnas almost ran onto the path after the bandit, but I held her back.

Overall, the caravan moved at a slow pace and it was easy for us to track it. As we made our way, crouching behind bushes, hiding behind trees, using the path whenever the caravan disappeared around a curve, Threnas kept muttering under her breath. It seemed that, even in a crisis, she could not stop talking. There seemed to be seven or eight slightly aspirated words combined with each breath she took. Valyset kept asking Dominique when we would do something. She said we'd have to wait until an opportunity presented itself. I noticed that, in the damp discomfort of the forest, she seemed paler and her stride seemed less certain. If we were going to do something, we had to do it soon, no matter what her talents at strategy seemed to dictate.

Finally the opportunity came. The caravan stopped to rest in a clearing that interrupted the pathway. I knew the clearing well. Dominique and I had often used to picnic there when we were both more hale and hearty. It was as far away from my home as I ever got in the time since I built my hillside cottage. While I watched the bandits alternately harass the exhausted Steilas and take swigs from bottles they had been carrying in backpacks, I could also see memories of Dominique and me in various areas of the clearing. Steffan strutted around the area, watching the Steilas closely and sometimes halfheartedly trying to get his cohorts to ease up on their drinking. He didn't seem to have much control over them. They gestured him away and took longer swigs.

Valyset looked toward Dominique, his eyes signaling a question he didn't have to put into words. "I think so," Dominique whispered. "They're relaxed. They think they're safe." I realized the sense of what she said. To them, Dominique was dying and Valyset had been left for dead. I doubt they anticipated much threat from Threnas or myself, the chatterbox and the invisible silent woman. My heart began to race. I could feel the uneven urgent beats inside my chest. There must be some reason why we don't have to do this, I thought. Some reason justifying the abandonment of thirty Steilas, letting them travel to cities where they would undoubtedly die. What were the lives of a few Steilas compared to the lives of Valyset and Dominique, the life of Threnas, even my life? Of course Dominique was going to die soon anyway, but I wanted the death I had planned for her, the passing of the spirit while I stood crying at her bedside. It seems to me even now that, if the deal had been offered to me, I would at least have considered the trading of the Steilas for Valyset, Dominique, and Threnas. Perhaps I would not have. Perhaps I would have realized that our urge to protect the people closest to us could interfere with our responsibility toward others. And perhaps one responsibility could outweigh the other. I don't know now. I didn't know then. Fortunately for the Steilas, I had no power to make decisions on their fate. Nevertheless, I felt downcast as I saw the eagerness for battle and revenge in my son's eyes.

"Valyset," Dominique said, "you sneak around to the other side of the clearing. I'll try a diversion, use your judgment when to attack. And don't try to kill anybody, except in defending yourself. These are thieves, not murderers. At least they don't realize they are murderers." Valyset nodded, but I suspected he didn't like the injunction against killing. He began moving sideways, away from us. I started to move after him, but Dominique grabbed me, held me back. Her grip on my arm was surprisingly strong. "I know, I know," she said, "you want to watch over him. We need you here, you and Threnas. When things get chaotic out there, I want you two to round up the Steilas and get them the hell away from here." I started to protest but she simply said that would be my job and to shut up before the bandits heard us bickering. It was probably sensible she said that, for I felt like screaming.

Before I was ready for anything to happen, Dominique walked into the clearing. She walked steadily, in long strides, determination obvious in the set of her face, the straightness of her body. She paid no attention to the other bandits, went instead straight to Steffan. He did not even notice her at first. Certainly his cohorts, intent on their drinking, didn't see her. When he did see her, Steffan reared backward, as if under surprise attack which was, in a way, true. Dominique waved her hands wildly to show she held no weapons, then yelled Steffan's name. This alerted the other bandits, but they merely sat watching, their bottles still in their hands. Even though she stood near Steffan, Dominique spoke loudly. "Is this what you've come to, Steffan? Small-time thuggery? What happened to the conquering of the world, the following of your father's footsteps? Eh?" One of the sitting bandits shouted, "Conquering the world?" and laughed. The others seemed equally amused. Steffan appeared beaten already. One could imagine him lying on the ground, his head bloodied, his sword flung away at his side, begging for a merciful death. "What of it, Steffan?" Dominique said. "What of your dreams?" Steffan stepped backward. "Are you dead?" he said in a pathetic voice. "Yes," she said quietly. "Now answer me." It was evident that Steffan was confused. "Go away, Dominique," he screamed. Dominique shook her head no. It was eerie, that shake of the head. It made her look as if she was already dead and a ghost. Whatever Dominique's intention, Steffan's reaction was that of the haunted. When she ordered him to answer her, he began babbling incoherently, gesturing wildly, pacing. What words I could discern seemed to be about money and ambition. I thought he might have said he needed the money to be obtained from the sale of the Steilas to finance his dreams, but I could not be sure. Dominique continued to stare at him. "Murderer," she said once. "Steilas die in cities." This statement made Steffan even more incoherent, and I could no longer even make out individual words. As he went on, he seemed to get angrier.

Steffan's babble was interrupted by a scream, the scream of Valyset as he ran into the clearing. He ran to the lead cart and, with a graceful swing, sliced through the harness that attached its Steila. Valyset's scream, in harmony with Dominique's silent eeriness, seemed to frighten the sitting bandits. Instead of moving, they remained rooted to their spots, staring at the two invaders as an audience. Valyset cut the harnesses of the other three workhorse Steilas, then he ran at the bandits, flourishing Joline's sword. He continued to scream. I wanted to strangle him. He was risking his life. Where had his common sense gone? Why was he doing Dominique's bidding so madly? Was this what had come from his clandestine battles with bushes and grass?

In the middle of the clearing Dominique disregarded Valyset

and held her gaze upon Steffan. Steffan was looking left and
right, unsure what to do, apparently incapable of directing his
men to action. The men, clearly bewildered, stumbled to their
feet, flipped away their bottles, and, grasping for weapons,
scattered out of the way of Valyset's histrionic charge. For the
first time I saw that one of the bandits had been wearing a
sword and, in a drunken series of misplaced grabs, was now
trying to extract it from its scabbard. Did Valyset know about
the sword? I thought, frightened. I wanted to run out from my
hiding place and pull Valyset back into the darkness with me.
As he ran past his adversaries, Valyset took a couple of dramatic
but ineffective swipes at them. He nearly tripped and fell on
one of the thrown-away bottles. Recovering quickly after some
uncertain steps, he turned to face his enemies, two of whom
had clumsily managed to draw out knives. One rushed at Valyset. Using the flat side of his sword blade, Valyset hit the
hand holding the knife in a solid bone-breaking blow. The man
dropped the knife and staggered away, his left hand clutching
the injured right one. The other knife-wielder, fascinated by
the blood dripping through his cohort's fingers, became cautious and began to circle Valyset while the remaining bandits
began assembling behind him. Ignoring the whole bunch, Valyset rushed past them toward the carts filled with Steila goods.
The force of his rush and an adept lift and push of his free
hand enabled him to topple the rear cart. He seemed amazed
that he had done it. Keeping his eyes on the bandits, who were
moving toward him, he started hacking with his sword at goods
in the other carts. Raising a large swatch of cloth with the point
of the sword, he flipped it at the face of one of his attackers.
As the bandit struggled to divest himself of the cloth, Valyset
ran his sword through the man's shoulder. Even Valyset seemed
surprised by the gush of blood that seemed to follow the path
of the withdrawing sword. The man collapsed to the ground,
holding the beautiful Steila cloth against his bleeding shoulder.
Valyset returned to the nearest cart and started hurling objects
from it toward his attackers. A vase which he threw at one
bandit forced the man to drop his knife in order to catch it. He
bobbled it, it slipped out of his grip and fell to the ground,
breaking into a number of large bright-colored shards.

The bandits' attention was now completely distracted. I knew that it was the time for Threnas and I to do our part in this crazed assault. Forcing my concentration away from my son's circumstances, I ran with Threnas into the clearing. We altered the Steilas, most of whom were calmly watching Valyset's performance, and in fact seemed to be quite entertained by it. Threnas and I signaled for the Steilas to follow us. They understood us immediately and obeyed. As the first of them passed me, I saw that there were cuts on their small squarish faces, and I cursed the bandits for their brutality. Threnas took charge of ushering the Steilas out of the clearing. I turned around and saw that Valyset was now atop one of the carts, kicking at the wares it held while staving off bandits with simple threatening feints of Joline's sword. Actually, the bandits had lost most of their interest in battle. In their greed they were attempting to salvage the merchandise that Valyset was hurling so recklessly at them. Their faces had the appearance of people watching their fortunes disappear. We, after all, had the advantage over them when it came to the Steila creations. They had at best only practical value to us, since we sought no profit from them.

My attention was diverted from Valyset's by Dominique's scream. Looking back toward the center of the clearing, I saw Steffan running away from Dominique toward Valyset's back. Dominique's scream was a warning. Mine blended with hers as I ran toward Valyset. There was a knife in Steffan's hand. Valyset was picking up a Steila vase to throw just as Steffan leaped toward him. Valyset turned and caught Steffan in the side of the head with the vase. Steffan fell forward, hitting his head on the side of the cart. The impact knocked him unconscious, and he lay sprawled on the ground beside the vehicle. Valyset jumped off the cart and stood over Steffan. He touched Steffan's neck with the point of Joline's sword. Steffan did not stir. Valyset raised the sword slightly. It looked to me as if he meant to behead Steffan. I yelled to him. He turned toward me and I saw that it was all right, he was all right, his eyes were calm. Whatever vengeful murderous instincts he might have felt had apparently vanished immediately. I felt tears of gratitude running down my cheeks. I grabbed his free hand

and together, Dominique keeping pace just behind us, we ran out of the clearing.

We caught up with Threnas and the Steilas a short distance from the clearing. They were gathered together in the middle of the path. Threnas was crouched over one of the Steilas, a female. A Steila male detached himself from the group and told us that one of the wounded bandits had ambushed them. Emerging from behind a tree, he had lunged at them, swiping at them with his knife. One Steila was superficially wounded, but the one presently on the ground had seen her chest opened in a wide slash with the bandit's second thrust. Threnas had attacked the bandit, twisting the knife out of his hand while biting the hand at the same time. Yelping, the bandit had retreated into the forest darkness. By the time we had reached the group, Threnas had applied her healing techniques and saved the fallen Steila's life. Valyset, picking the female up, ordered the rest of the Steilas to return to the village, an order they obeyed with alacrity. When the last one had disappeared down the forest path, Dominique sighed and fell against a tree. I rushed to her and asked if she was all right. She said of course she was but adventures did tend to wind her a bit at her age. The skin of her face had become splotchy and her eyes seemed to retreat from me. I knew she could not remain in the forest where the dampness would kill her before her illness did. I looked toward Valyset. He understood the message of my eyes and passed the wounded Steila to me to carry. Lifting Dominique from the ground, he carried her in his arms down the path. Threnas and I, with the wounded Steila, followed. I don't know how Valyset found his way, since he could not take his eyes off Dominique's paling face.

Dominique is in her bed again and looking every bit as sick as she did before the bandits' attack. Valyset was here for a while, sitting by her bedside, but Threnas had convinced him to return home for a fresh bandage to his head wound. He says he will return soon. Dominique is breathing regularly, though, and there is a kind of smile on her face. I must rest.

I woke to find Valyset sitting patiently beside my cot. I asked him if Dominique was all right and he said yes. The new dressing on his head made him look strange, otherworldly. Threnas had chosen some blue Steila cloth with an intricate silver-and-copper weaving in curlicues and waves on it. It looked to me almost like a crown.

"Steffan came to the village," he said quietly. "A brave action, I thought, since I might have killed him. I was tempted again, just the way I'd been when he lay helpless on the ground at my feet. But he was alone, carrying no weapon, and I decided I wanted him to just live out his useless life, because that might be worse." I suggested that perhaps he shouldn't be dismissed because of one failure. Valyset shrugged. "He looked quite pitiful, quite stupid. He said he was desperate, had been desperate for some time. He had remembered the Steilas, thought they would be easy prey. He said it was all a mistake, the whole misadventure. He apologized to me, said he was sorry. He said to apologize to you and Dominique. He would not have liked to be responsible for Steilas wasting away in the cities, he said. "I asked Valyset if he believed Steffan could be repentant. He shrugged again. "Maybe," he said, "but I let him go, and I have to say I enjoyed watching him go so dejectedly out of the village." Valyset stared at me for a long time, an odd smile on his face. "You're not going to tell me how foolish I was back in that clearing, are you, Mother? I can see you're not. You haven't told me what you think since I was a fairly young child. I don't know if you approve of me, of what I've done." I told him I approved. His eyes said he was not quite sure he believed me, but he nodded in agreement. "But do you think I was an absolute fool in the clearing?" I said he had got the job done and the Steilas were rescued. I said he'd done what Dominique had told him to. "But I was a fool, is that right?" I told him he'd been quite impressive, heroic. "But foolish. Foolish for risking my life, foolish for swinging a sword as if I knew what I was doing." I said yes, it was foolish, a little bit foolish, yes. He smiled. "I knew it," he said. "Hard to get words out of you, but worth the effort, Mother. You look tired, need your rest. I'll leave you alone for a while. I know you won't get to sleep if I'm hanging around here. I'll come back soon, check the both of you out."

He left but I couldn't get back to sleep. After inspecting

Dominique to see if there was anything to be done for her, I worked at cleaning the floor of her room. I was about halfway done with the chore when she began to speak to me. "We did all right," she said. I was about to criticize her for risking her life, but I realized that she wouldn't be any easier to talk to on the subject than Valyset had been. There was no point to it. Anyway, they both had the edge in any argument since the venture had been successful.

Dominique almost regained her old energy as she reminisced about the events of the day. Since she seemed so well, I asked her if she wanted to continue the manuscript, if she had anything more she wanted to dictate to me. At first she did not seem to remember that she had instructed me to write it for her, then she said, "No, no, I don't think so. I don't seem to have much memory left anyhow. God, I'm so wet all over I think I sweated out my memory drop by drop. No, stay over there, Alezase. I don't want you to tend to me just now. Did we accomplish much, in the writing I mean?" I showed her the pile of papers I had already written. She was impressed. "Read it to me, Alezase," she said. I told her she might not like some of what I had written about her. She said she probably wouldn't, but go on and read it anyway.

The reading was quite an ordeal for me. I kept glancing at her face for signs of approval or disapproval as I read aloud in a shaky voice, sometimes stuttering my words. Each time I came to references to her impending death, my voice, without my controlling it, dropped to a whisper. Once she told me to speak up, death is not a hard word to say. When I came to the sentences about the occasional physical love we had shared over the years, she made me stop reading and she kissed me before letting me continue. For almost all the reading she smiled gently, pleasantly. Her face was relaxed, her body limp. When I had reached the end of what I'd written until then, her smile widened. She said groggily, "Thank you, Alezase, I like it fine," and then she went almost immediately to sleep.

My weariness has returned. The floor will have to wait. I will sleep, also.

• • •

While I slept, Dominique died. Valyset woke me to tell me. He had returned to check us both. He said he sat in silence between us for a long while before he could stop his tears and collect himself enough to waken me.

I went to her bedside. A thin tracing of blood ran from the side of her mouth to her jawline, where it mysteriously seemed to disappear. She still had the smile on her face that she'd had when she fell asleep. I smiled myself, even as I cried.

As the Steilas, under Threnas's tutelage, prepared Dominique's body for the burning, I wrote this. I will keep this manuscript. She wanted her name recorded somewhere, that was what she originally told me. It will be here until these papers are destroyed or disintegrate with age.

We burned her body, according to the usual cremation customs, on a platform the Steilas constructed just outside their village, next to the fields which Dominique and I used to work, and which Threnas now cultivates so lovingly. Dominique could get almost childishly excited during the harvest of any fruit or vegetable.

Threnas performed the final ritual. Atop the platform, each of us touching Dominique's hand, Valyset and I said the final prayers, including two I had learned from Dominique's own religion, a religion she tended to disavow except when it was useful to her. Valyset placed Joline's sword beside the body. That was his idea. Whatever remains of it after the burning will be buried with Dominique's ashes.

We descended from the platform and, as was my right, I set it afire. Dominique's body too quickly became a shadow within the flames as the fire spread much too fast. Valyset collapsed with tears and, speaking softly and slowly, Threnas led him away from the bier. Their children followed. I stayed there until the flames completely hid Dominique's corpse. "Good-bye then, love," I said before turning my back on the fire and returning here to write this last entry in this manuscript.